The Wacky Waffle Whacker

JOANN KEDER

"Do the right thing. It will gratify some people
and astonish the rest."
-Mark Twain

For Mr. Kenner
Thank you for believing in me

Characters

Honeypie Chiffon Sweetwater: owner of the Honeypie Diner, formerly her grandmother's restaurant
Dexter Jenkins: Honeypie's fourteen-year-old son who hates everything
Tildie Bunce: Dexter's best friend
Frankie Flapjack: new chef at the diner
Mayor Thunder McCloud: Misty Cove Mayor

CeCe Scone: High school part-time help at the diner

Delores Tootwhistle: the band director's wife

Gwen Folds: coroner and owner of The Final Fold Dry Cleaners

Eliza Tumblewood: former resident of Misty Cove

Chapter One

A STICKY SITUATION

"You haven't heard anything about Misty Cove? I mean… online chatter can be so mean and downright wrong."

Honeypie Chiffon Sweetwater's normally olive-skinned face turned the shade of rhubarb pie.

"No, ma'am. I don't believe in reading news online or otherwise," said the dark-haired chef, as she leaned back against the booth while stretching her legs until they touched Honeypie's.

"I grew up in a small town in Colorado where the folks ran a diner. We didn't much care for outsiders or news from the rest of the world. It was a nice place, as long as you weren't hankering for a fluffy omelet."

Frances Flapjack, the seventh person Honeypie—or H.P., as she liked to be called—had interviewed for the position of head chef, was definitely the chattiest. Only Blue, the guy who smoked weed during their interview, came close to Frances in qualifications.

On top of that, Edna—her grandmother's friend and the longest-serving employee at Honeypie Diner—threatened to quit if H.P. didn't hire someone by the end of the day. "I'm leaving for good this time. Mom's been after me to go on the Fluffy's First Float Cruise down the Columbia River. Cat cruises are all the rage now, and Fuzz Aldrin is finally litter box trained."

Every time Edna told a story about her cats, they had different names. She didn't want to ask Edna how many she actually had, nor did she want that picture in her mind.

"The folks—well, MY folks, I should say—were more interested in making artisan sandwiches than breakfast," Frances continued. "Peanut butter, bacon, and honey on sourdough is a breakfast, NOT a lunch!"

Honeypie glanced out the window of the Honeypie Diner, where kids walking home from school were whacking each other over the head with their backpacks. Although she knew enough about brain damage to be concerned for their well being, she wished she could join them outside. Hiring new staff wasn't exactly her forte.

Edna Snarlwood, the first employee hired by her grandmother decades ago, urged her to add a part-timer to their staff so they could take time off when needed. Although she disagreed at first, H.P. soon realized the advantages of flexible hours for things like doctor's appointments.

Interviewing potential staff hadn't gone well. The

mother of two who wanted to bring her toddlers with her, the retiree who admitted she didn't much like people, and the man who was "just curious" about what this diner looked like left her feeling defeated.

CeCe Scone breezed through the door like the first sunshine of summer. A petite high school junior, she was blonde, bubbly, and decidedly sane. "I can use this as a work study, Ms. Sweetwater," she offered with an enthusiasm that filtered through every dark crevice in the diner, bringing sunshine with it. "I can leave school at one p.m. two days a week. Would that work for you?"

It took enormous self-control not to jump across the table and hug this girl. "It would work for me, yes. There's something so familiar about you. Do you come in with your friends after school?"

CeCe giggled with a light, airy sound like that of a tiny spring bird.

"Oh no, I don't eat after school. Mom's rules. It's how she's maintained her perfect figure! In fact, she's the reason I look so familiar. You two went to high school together!"

H.P.'s mind raced. Was this going to require finding an old yearbook and reminiscing about her awful high school years?

"My mom's name is Logan. In high school, she was Logan Berry, but for her marketing business, she uses the hyphenated Berry-Scone. She said you two used to gossip together in the bathroom between classes."

If by "gossip" her mother meant giving H.P.

swirlies in the toilet, then yes, they technically had words in the bathroom. "I see. How is your mother these days?"

"She's just FABULOUS. She does the marketing for Bliss Spa—have you been there? My dad says she looks exactly like she did in high school. We wear the same size!"

There was that giggle again. Where at first it sounded charming, now it reminded H.P. of the girls who thrived on her torture. If only she had other options. H.P. took a long, slow breath. "Okay, when can you start?"

When it came to hiring a new chef, she couldn't expect good fortune to strike twice.

Chapter Two

For almost a month, the position of head cook, or "chef," which, in these parts, was just a fancy word for someone who knew how to sauté vegetables, remained open.

"...I believe life is short, and we should all find what we're good at and leave the other stuff behind. That's why I refuse to make lunch."

"Huh?"

That comment snapped H.P. out of her stupor. "What do you mean, 'you refuse to make lunch?' I'm not asking you to eat it, just make a turkey-and-cranberry sandwich when someone orders one."

Frances shook her head decisively. "No, ma'am." Frances was built like a long-haul trucker, wearing a sleeveless, flannel tank top, revealing muscular arms covered in colorful tattoos. "I believe I wrote that at the bottom of my application." She reached across the table to show H.P., exposing a colorful tattoo featuring pancakes, eggs, and bacon.

"Oh, right, I see it now. It sounded more like a joke, I guess." H.P. laughed nervously.

"I'm firm on that one. Breakfast only."

Now that her interest was piqued, H.P. studied Frances, tattoos and all: baking tools like whisks, spatulas, and mixing bowls. She even wore a gold pancake medallion necklace.

"May I ask why? The ingredients are very similar—toast and sandwich bread are the same thing, and—"

"Got my reasons. It's not up for discussion."

H.P. took a deep breath and released it slowly. Edna's threats and lack of desirable applicants were still fresh in her mind. She saw no other option. "Okay then. Let's... let's talk salary."

"Oh, you're hiring me?" Her deep voice rose an octave. "Just like that? I thought there'd be a second interview with your employees and whatnot."

Frances used one finger to slide her bright red, square glasses up the bridge of her nose as she leaned forward. Her hands curled into tanned fists, and she knocked lightly on the table.

"The 'whatnot' is that we're desperate for a new chef, after our last chef left unexpectedly. We need someone yesterday." H.P. felt a trickle of sweat roll down her back. It wasn't so easy being on this side of the interview table. When she applied for countless sous chef jobs in San Francisco, it was always fun to critique those interviewing her, especially if she wasn't hired. Now she understood and offered a mental apology to the gods of the interviews for her misbehavior.

"I sold The Sunnyside after the folks passed, and boy, I made a full stack with butter on the side. Bought myself a home-on-wheels and set off for parts unknown."

Frances smiled, giving H.P. a glimpse of the large gap between her two front teeth. It added to her charm.

"I like to travel around and see this big, beautiful country," Frances continued. "All I ask by way of salary is enough to keep gas in my RV and food in the bowl for Sir Stackworth, my pup."

Edna Snarlwood, who was waiting on the mayor at the opposite end of the narrow room, pointed two fingers at H.P. and then back at herself. Hearing from across a busy diner was one of Edna's most irritating qualities. And she had many. She mouthed, "Do it or I walk."

H.P. slid a folded paper across the table. It was going to be her final offer, but because Frances was the only applicant, she put all her cards on the table.

Frances opened the paper and looked up in shock. "Well, I'll be a frosted chocolate donut, that's a third more than I was gonna ask for!"

Shoot. She could have held out.

H.P. half-stood and leaned over the shiny tabletop, offering her hand. "You're hired, Miss..."

"Just call me Frankie." She shook H.P.'s hand so vigorously that H.P.'s teeth chattered.

"Awesome. I just need to get your paperwork from the back, Frankie. Please excuse me for a moment."

As she exited the booth, Frankie stood and rapped her knuckles on the table once more.

Please, please don't let her reconsider. "Was there something else?"

"No, ma'am. Just... thank you!" Frankie saluted her with a precision that would have made any general proud.

"Ms. Sweetwater?" An airy giggle. "Is it okay if I leave a little early today?"

"Yeah, I guess, CeCe. We're not that busy. I'll see you next week!" H.P.'s second weakness as a boss was the inability to say no.

As soon as she'd reached the kitchen, H.P. glanced around. The temporary chef who was leaving town the next day was humming to himself. Luckily, he used earbuds after the breakfast rush, so it took Herculean efforts to get his attention. She opened the door to the walk-in cooler and stepped inside. "Gram Gram?" she whispered. "You come here this minute! I have a bone to pick with you!"

The sweet scent of her grandmother's signature honey pie filled the cooler first, followed by an ethereal blue light. Slowly, the light filled with the image of her grandmother, her twin. Gram Gram's gray hair, curled up tightly on top of her head for so many years, moved around her face in waves. It was just how H.P. imagined a mermaid would look in real life. The otherwise cool refrigerator filled with a love and warmth she could never describe later.

"What's wrong, Hun Bun?"

"You specifically told me to hire the next person who came through the door." H.P. paced back and forth, narrowly missing a box of carrots on the floor.

"And I stand by that, my darling. She IS the chef you've been waiting for." Gram Gram's eyes widened as her figure descended closer to her granddaughter. "You won't regret hiring Frances, I guarantee it."

"I've trusted you ever since you left me the diner in your will. Every day you give me solid advice on something diner-related. But this woman is a nut. No, she's one egg short of an omelet. She just told me she won't make any of the lunch items on the menu!"

Gram Gram "sat" beside her and crossed her shapely legs. She insisted on wearing short skirts in the afterlife, since she had the freedom to do so. "If I had a dime for every time you complained that your temporary chefs couldn't make your sandwich creations..."

"You've got a point there. But I'm not so sure she'll be of much help if she finishes her day before it's barely begun."

"Granddaughter, you can't afford to be picky. You need help, even if the menu lacks a good grilled cheese. I've never let you down, have I? Frances is the right choice."

A brisk knock on the cooler door startled them both. "Ma'am? You'd better come out here."

It had to be serious if it had gotten the attention of the interim chef.

H.P. opened the door slowly. "What's the problem?"

The chef pointed to the front of the diner, where people were panicking. Rushing to the front of the house, she found Frankie straddling Principal Nunsense from Boog R. Noseinair High School. His arms were pinned behind him as he flailed about on the floor. "I'm not the enemy! Please release me, madam!"

"Frankie! Let him go! He's a respected member of our community!" H.P. was horrified. How was she going to hire this woman now? The last thing she needed was a lawsuit.

"It's all right, Ms. Sweetwater!" Principal Nunsense said in a muffled voice. Frankie let go of him and stood, offering him a hand up.

As he stood and shook his arms to regain the feeling in them, H.P. noticed he was not wearing his usual gray suit with a peach dress shirt. Instead, he wore spandex shorts and a sweaty t-shirt that read, "Bandz Blast, Ballz Bounce." It was last year's t-shirt for the yearly Misty Cove band and basketball festival.

"The man came in here yelling about murder. Frankie Flapjack doesn't take those words lightly. I brought him to the ground until the facts could be ascertained."

H.P. stared at them both, wide-eyed.

"You were... okay with that, Principal Nunsense?"

"Quite. I appreciate someone who puts safety first." He smoothed his gray hair and glanced at Frankie with adoration. "The way you took me down was, well, it was art in motion. You'd do well as a self-defense instructor at my gym."

"What is this about a murder, Principal Nunsense?" H.P. asked.

"After my workout, I decided to jog home. I was rounding the corner of Giggler's Gulch when I caught something out of the corner of my eye. Just horrible..." Tears filled his eyes.

Mayor McCloud approached them with a somber look. "Let's not get ahead of ourselves." He turned around to face the room filled with anxious patrons. "I need everybody to stay calm."

"Right, Mayor McCloud." A young man standing beside Table Two frowned. "How is anyone supposed to remain calm when Misty Cove is dealing with a serial killer?"

Chapter Three

FLAT AS A...

"Ballz and Bandz Day is his thing, not mine, Gram Gram."

A yearly festival that brought high school bands from up and down the Washington Coast as well as three-on-three basketball players, also generated a much-needed boost to the local economy. All the high school kids were tasked with raising funds in the most creative way possible. Dexter Jenkins, H.P.'s fourteen-year-old son, volunteered to go door to door asking for donations.

"That doesn't sound like you, Hun Bun. You just got done telling me about a SECOND murder in Misty Cove. I'd think you were a little more careful, what with Barry D'live's death and now some gal. Surely you'll at least keep him away from the Noseinair mansion? Remember how you refused to let me even drive by that street? If I had a penny for every extra gallon of gas I spent taking the scenic route to your dance class…"

A chill rushed down H.P.'s spine. She'd never told Gram Gram the truth about that awful day, and now wasn't the time.

"Do you have any intel on who died and how they were killed? Mayor McCloud assured us there's nothing to worry about, and the person Principal Nunsense found probably died of a heart attack." H.P. sniffed. "We've heard next to nothing about Barry D'live's death."

H.P. seated herself on an overturned bucket inside the large walk-in cooler. Although Gram Gram had given her the secret location of her comfortable folding chair, (behind the water heater), H.P. didn't want to risk questions from Frankie, who was learning the ropes from Ted or Jed. She couldn't remember the name of her most recent temp. He never spoke and only listed his first name on his application.

"No, darling, I'm sorry. I have a better chance of finding the dearly departed than the nearly living. The departed constantly get hung up during admitting, since celebrities always volunteer for the welcoming ceremony. Starstruck is what—wait a minute—I recognize that face! I'm over here, doll!" Gram Gram hollered and waved, seemingly at the giant fan over the door of the walk-in. "H.P., can you hang on a minute?"

"Sure, Gram Gram. I've got nothing but time." She meant it as a slight, but her grandmother didn't seem to notice. After the mayor refused to confirm another murder to the group of concerned patrons, they exited the diner in rapid succession. No one wanted to be caught alone on the streets.

Although the mayor was probably competent, he certainly wasn't handling this situation with the openness and assuredness it required. Glancing down at her watch, H.P. realized it was much later than she thought.

"I've got to run, Gram!" H.P. hollered, thinking about the absurdity of calling to her dead grandmother as though she were out in the yard, pulling weeds. "Dex will be home from school, and if I'm not there to make him something nutritious, he'll slather peanut butter on frozen pizza and call it dinner."

Just as she was about to stand, she felt a lightness in the air and smelled Gram Gram's scent—a combination of baking pies and vanilla.

"Well, THAT certainly took longer than expected!" She touched her shimmering silver hair absently.

"So? Don't keep me in suspense. Who was it?"

"Just my old favorite water exerciser, that's who." Gram's eyes twinkled.

"I have absolutely no idea who that would be, and quite frankly, have no memory of you doing water exercise. Can you cut to the chase?" H.P. was running short on time and patience.

"Pearlie Gates. You remember her, don't you? She had a grandchild in your grade. Never could get the two of you to see eye to eye."

H.P. thought hard. "Doesn't ring a bell." Gram Gram was forever trying to connect her with people in Misty Cove with whom she had no connection. It was just one of the few bad qualities she attributed to the woman who raised her.

"What happened this time? Did she trip over the extension cord for the heating pad and crash into the television set?"

Last week, Gram told her the story of a man who lost his balance while trying to break the world record for the most bologna sandwiches consumed while standing on one's head. "He choked to death, Hun Bun. Now he has to go through eternity upside down with bread hanging out of his mouth."

The deaths reported by her grandmother could be funny. A little.

"I feel like you're making fun of me, Hun Bun. Pearlie was murdered in her home."

"What? Like, just now? Like, Principal Nunsense just reported her death? Like—"

"You know I don't respond when you speak 'like' a simpleton," Gram Gram snapped. She'd been very firm with all her grandchildren regarding language, especially the ones who worked in the diner. "No short-cuts," she would say.

"Yes, ma'am. You're right. But Pearlie, was she the victim of our serial killer?"

"Could be. The poor thing has a dent in her skull the size of a dinner plate, but it's an odd shape. I think it might be a cartoon character. Maybe she stuck her head through a television set?"

"That's not how television works. Is this another one of your crazy stories about deaths, Gram?"

"No, darling. I saw it with my own eyes. Pearlie also complained of a headache, but those pass after a few days."

H.P. swallowed hard. "Could this dent have come from a waffle maker instead of a television?"

Gram Gram's eyes crinkled, and she began to laugh. The sound of her laughter, an unexpected, high-pitched giggle, was one of the things H.P. missed the most.

"Yes, now that you mention it, a waffle maker makes more sense than a television. Pearlie only watched her stories, and she usually fell asleep when they came on. She mentioned in passing that there was a strawberry waffle with strawberry-flavored whipped cream left next to her."

Just like Barry D'live, only his waffle was chocolate chip. "Can you ask her about her killer? Did she have any enemies? Or can she just tell me herself? It would sure save time."

"If you're trying to get my gobble, I'm not going to let you!" Gram Gram crossed her arms and stuck her chin in the air the same way H.P. had the many times she had been disciplined.

"No, I'm not trying to get your... goat. I'm looking for solid information to give the police is all."

"She didn't have any enemies. Folks of our generation don't play those kinds of games."

H.P. worked to keep her face stoic. Could there possibly be more than one murderer?

"She'd just arrived home after water aerobics," Gram Gram continued, "when she felt something hit her in the back of the head. Next thing she knows, she's following Guide E. Presley to the check-in area." Gram rolled her eyes. "He's such a flirt, that one."

"I'm sure she remembers something! Please, can she speak with me for five minutes? That's an eye blink in your time, isn't it?"

"Sorry, Hun Bun. Pearlie chose the direct route to the afterlife. No lolly-goobering around with the livings or with us ghosts. That bus leaves so fast, I've seen folks hanging on for dear death if they weren't lucky enough to grab a seat."

For a moment, H.P. wondered why her Gram Gram hadn't done the same, but she pushed the idea from her mind. She'd come to relish these times in the walk-in, just the two of them.

"First, it was Barry D'live, and now Pearlie Gates. Gwen says there was a similar death in Oregon. The woman was a member of the Misty Cove gym, Fit Happens, but so far, there are no connections that we can find between the murders."

"Doesn't ring a bell. The only time I remember you all being quiet was when I asked for all fifty state capitols." H.P. chose to ignore that slight.

"The killer left a waffle calling card when Barry

D'live was killed. There was a chocolate chip with fluffy whipped cream plated next to his body."

"Why didn't I think to make a chocolate chip waffle? It sure makes sense. I bet it looked delicious!"

"Gram!" H.P. was horrified. "It was sitting beside a dead body! There's nothing appetizing about that!"

Gram Gram sniffed, her sign for "I'm insulted but I don't want to argue."

"I wonder if Pearlie had the same experience," H.P. said.

"I don't know what to tell you, darling. I don't know a waffle calling card from a jelly journal. Maybe Gwennie has some thoughts?"

Gwen Folds, the town coroner who also owned The Final Fold Dry Cleaners, was H.P.'s only current friend. Well, not counting Abe Bunce, the handsome attorney she positively-absolutely-never-ever would date.

Gwen had already seen Gram Gram's ghost, which made conversations with her so much easier.

"Good plan. I've got to check on my boy and then I'll see what she knows." H.P. rose and placed her hands on her hips. "Thank you for being here. I don't know why you chose this for your afterlife, but I'm grateful you did."

A shimmering light framed Gram Gram's celestial body, changing colors with her mood. With H.P.'s kind words, the light turned a fresh summer peach. "Be careful out there, granddaughter," she warned. "If it really IS a serial killer, you don't know how he chooses his victims."

"Ms. Sweetwater?" the sweet-as-a-double-frosted-cinnamon-roll voice of CeCe Scone said, alerting H.P. to the fact they were no longer alone. The door opened slowly and H.P. jumped up from her bucket, nearly bumping her head on the middle shelf.

"Don't come in, CeCe, I'd hate for you to slip on the...mayonnaise I spilled. I'll be out in a minute!"

"Okay! I was just going to ask if I could leave a little early again today. I'm getting my lip pierced."

After blowing her grandmother a kiss goodbye, H.P. opened the door without looking back. She always felt an emptiness the moment her grandmother disappeared.

"Can't you do that on Saturday? You're not working then."

CeCe shook her head, causing tufts of hair located outside of her ponytail to fall into her face. "I'm not a legal adult yet, so my mom has to be there, and this is the only day she has off."

H.P. struggled to remember where, exactly, CeCe's mother worked, if at all. *Shame on you, H.P. This isn't the big city, where people routinely make up excuses to leave work.* "Okay, fine. But please, can we not make a habit of this?"

"I promise." CeCe lowered her eyes and batted her lashes, a skill girls like her used to get whatever they wanted. The shiny sports car in the parking lot was evidence of that.

"I need to run a quick errand but I'll be back soon."

When H.P. opened the door to the cleaners, hot steam assaulted her. The amount of people crowded inside the small lobby only increased her discomfort. "Number ninety-eight?" Gwen's gravelly voice called.

H.P. chuckled to herself as she thought about Gwen's explanation for the numbers. "You start high so that people think they've really made progress. I tear off at least thirty numbers before I start my day."

H.P. found a pocket of cooler air to stand in and pulled out her phone. "Dexie? I'm going to be a little late. I have to close tonight by myself. Can you defrost the lasagna?"

"I hate lasagna!"

It wouldn't have mattered if she said they were having pepperoni pizza, double-stacked and slathered in extra cheese.

"Oh, I'm sorry. I meant the gallon of Triple Chocolate Guilt in the back of the freezer. The stuff that gives you cavities and more pimples on your face." The other end of the line was silent.

"Dex?"

"What?!" he snapped. "Does it matter to you that we haven't eaten out once this month? All of my friends get to go somewhere good, like for wings or tacos? And I'm stuck—"

"You meant to say grounded. You're grounded because, instead of changing poor Cinnamon Biscuit

Maker's litter box, you've been hoarding her poo bags in your bathroom. Poor kitty."

For the life of her, H.P. couldn't figure out why the boy thought it was so difficult to walk out to the trash bin. He walked further when he came over to the diner for fries.

"GOODBYE, MOTHER." He didn't wait for her response.

Raising a teenager wasn't getting any easier. In fact, his mood seemed to grow in direct correlation to the smell of his feet. Like a rank cheese she'd eaten in college on a dare.

"Hey, friendie!"

H.P. hadn't noticed the other customers leaving and was surprised to find her compact and sturdy friend by her side. Gwen Folds sported a short mushroom hairdo, predominantly silver with streaks of her original ebony hue. A thick, mustard-colored sweater swallowed her small frame and large, tortoise-shell-framed glasses sat low on her nose.

Glancing around the lobby to make sure they were indeed alone, H.P. whispered, "Gram Gram thought you might have information on the killer. You heard there was another murder?"

Gwen motioned for H.P. to follow her. They walked past long rows of clothing representing every walk of Misty Cove life. Bridesmaid dresses cleaned of food stains, suit jackets with after-dinner drink spills gone, and police uniforms, freshly pressed, all hung on rotating racks. They passed an entire long rack of band uniforms too. The Fighting Tissues band jacket was a sleek, tailored, pastel blue with white piping, creating a sophisticated silhouette.

The back of each jacket featured a tissue box with muscular arms blowing a nose and an embroidered design of a tissue box, the musical notes emanating from the tissue. The gold buttons down the front were shaped like miniature tissue boxes, adding a whimsical touch. Completing the ensemble was a distinctive shako hat in pastel blue, adorned with a plume that cleverly mimicked the look of tissues fluttering in the wind. The front of the hat bore the school's emblem encircled by a golden tissue box, proudly declaring the band's identity.

H.P. paused as the hurtful memories came flooding back. "Pleeease, Gram Gram! I won't ask for anything for my birthday or Christmas. I just want to play the clarinet. The band director says we can rent the instrument and it will only cost ten dollars for the whole semester!"

She'd worked on Gram Gram for months. Each time, her grandmother remained firm. "Yes, the instrument rental is cheap, but it's just like any other school activity."

Gram refused to look at her as she mopped the diner floor and only acknowledged her presence when she whacked one of H.P.'s legs. H.P. scooched further back on the counter, promising herself she wouldn't upset Gram Gram again. "What do you mean, Gram

Gram? It's a class. There's nothing else you'd have to pay for."

Gram Gram stopped and stood, leaning one arm on her mop. She pushed a strand of her then-caramel hair out of her eyes—Pretty Gal Dye #48 skillfully applied by twelve-year-old H.P.

"Yes, I know it's a class. But it also includes band trips and uniform cleanings. After that, you'll require lessons because, well, you aren't going to be satisfied being the worst in the room, are you?" Her words sounded exactly like something Gram Gram's friend Edna would say.

"Honeypie, those band kids all come from fancy homes. It's a shame they don't tell you ahead of time that it will break the bank."

It hit a lonely teenager hard, which was why she stole a clarinet from Notely Instruments and started attending band class anyway. She got away with it too, until Logan Berry came into the diner.

"I don't mean to gossip, but my mother heard that your granddaughter is a thief."

Gram told this story over and over, each time making it more dramatic. "The entire town knew about your thievery, Honey. You made me look foolish to my clients, as well as committing a crime."

H.P. spent most of her freshman year picking up garbage along the highway as penance. And, worse yet, it reinforced what she knew deep down: she was cursed.

She was forced to watch wistfully as the band

members, including Logan, with her fancy gold flute, slapped each other's hands in the hall between classes, exchanging phrases that only those on the band trip understood. Not only did they have a secret code, they also sat together during all assemblies, forming an impenetrable wall around themselves.

"Are you coming?" She was grateful that Gwen didn't hearken back to that time in Misty Cove. Their friendship was about two adults sharing similar likes and dislikes, not reliving high school.

Gwen led her through endless racks until finally stopping in front of an open door. She walked inside her office, inviting H.P. in. Even though they'd been friends for several months, this was the first time H.P. was allowed to join Gwen in her inner sanctum.

"I'd almost forgotten about Ballz and Bandz. I'm glad the band is going to look their best." She knew Gwen hardly charged anything when it came to supporting local activities. She also knew Gwen grew embarrassed when H.P. tried to give her kudos.

"This is my third year sponsoring the three-on-three basketball tournament and marching band festival. I get to be one of the judges!"

The walls of Gwen's office were painted green with colorful birds sitting on branches and palm fronds decorating the sides. To her left, H.P. noticed a water fountain bubbling. The sound of birds chirping filled the air.

"Gwen, this is—"

"Amazing? Stupendous? I'll also accept unique."

Gwen sat at her desk, using her hands to pull her as close to her computer monitor as possible. H.P. noticed that Gwen's feet didn't reach the floor, something she found curious. With as much detail as had gone into this office, why didn't she find a chair more suitable for her stature?

"I was called to the last murder scene. Let me find it... I think her name was Shirley?"

"Pearlie." Gwen used one hand to spin around in her chair. "How did you know that? Details haven't been released to the public yet."

H.P. took a deep breath and started formulating a valid response until she remembered who she was speaking to. "Gram Gram. They were in the same water aerobics class."

"Then she should be able to tell you what happened, right?" Gwen pushed her glasses up the bridge of her nose and smiled. "My mom was sure it had something to do with Pearlie always stealing the extra cookies after church socials. Apparently, Pearlie was known to bring huge bags with her when she volunteered for kitchen duty, just so she could empty the plates into her purse."

H.P. shook her head. "Okay, so she had a sugar addiction, and maybe a habit of taking things that didn't belong to her. That isn't a motive for murder."

"I want to show you something." Gwen hummed the Fighting Tissues school song as she searched her files. "There it is. You're not the squeamish type, are you?"

H.P. felt a little insulted by that question. "I've trussed an entire hog. There's nothing that will make me—"

As Gwen pulled up the first photo, H.P.'s knees buckled. Pride made her lean against the desk, and she hoped Gwen didn't notice.

"That... poor... woman."

"Not as gruesome as some, but it certainly wins the award for most unusual. If you'll notice here," Gwen pointed to the bottom of the screen, where Pearlie's head lay in a pool of blood. "She was struck on the back of the head with a waffle maker at least three times. But that's not even the strangest part."

Taking a deep breath as she gripped the desk, H.P. squinted, trying to believe what her eyes were telling her. "The killer... branded her?" It was just like Gram Gram said.

"Used the same waffle maker to kill her as he did to leave his mark. Far as I can tell, it's a cartoon character."

H.P. studied the scene again, this time without emotions overwhelming her. Pearlie still held her gym bag in one hand and her car keys in the other. She didn't have time to defend herself, poor woman. Sitting on the garage floor, beside an outdoor vacuum, was a plate containing a strawberry waffle with strawberry whipped cream on top.

"Pearlie is the second person who's died with the same injuries, at least in our community. Down in Oregon, I was called to the home of a..." She clicked quickly to another screen. This one had the words "Confidential Report" written at the top. "Sunnie Daze. She was whacked while weeding her wisteria flowers."

Gwen clicked to a cheery garden where a spandex-clad woman lay, face down between rows of bright purple blooms. In one gloved hand, she held a weeding tool and, in the other, a long black cord.

H.P. leaned in once again, squinting. "She's holding the cord of the waffle maker! How was she able to do that when the killer hit her from behind?"

Gwen turned to face H.P. "It's entirely possible that she heard the killer approaching and a scuffle ensued. Here, look at this."

She zoomed in to the dirt.

"What am I supposed to see? It looks like a normal garden."

Gwen's index finger traced the layers of dirt. "The ground is moved every which way, like there was a scuffle."

"Couldn't that just be from Sunnie moving around?"

Gwen's shoulders slumped. "Why didn't I think of that? Yes, it could. Stupid, Gwen! Stupid, Gwen!"

H.P. grabbed her friend's face. "Stop! I just meant that was a possibility. Poor Sunnie. Did she have any Misty Cove connections?"

Gwen's posture changed, but her expression didn't. She smiled adoringly at H.P. One thing about H.P.'s best friend, she never stayed in a funk for long.

"Sunnie had a gym membership here in Misty Cove. A place called Fit Happens."

"That's an intriguing connection. I suppose the team of Folds and Sweetwater should leave that to the police, though."

Despite the fact they'd solved Gram Gram's murder, H.P. knew it didn't make them professionals. Sleuthing made her feel alive, like nothing else, but she was ashamed to admit it, even to Gwen.

"There's one more thing that I know you aren't gonna like, bestie."

"Gwen? Spit it out. You know you can tell me—"

"Sunnie had a phone number in her pocket, belonging to a Maddysin Noseinair."

"Noseinair? My high school nemesis? Ugh! Why does that woman keep showing up in my life?"

Maddysin Noseinair was the head Glitter in the Glitterati, a group of bullies who enjoyed torturing whoever got in their way. H.P. always found her way on their radar, no matter how hard she tried to avoid them. It made her high school years miserable.

"The police chief has been tight-lipped to the point that I don't believe he's investigating. I've never seen anything like it before. Not that I'm saying you have to help me, but Ballz and Bandz is coming up soon and I'd hate for the killer to make an appearance." Gwen tilted her chin and used her soulful brown eyes to bore a hole right through H.P.'s resolve.

H.P. sighed. "I suppose I can talk to Maddysin and ask her what she knows about Sunnie. I've been avoiding her since my DNA test came back showing we're related. How could that be? We're nothing alike."

Had she known this in high school, maybe things would have been different.

"One more thing I wanted to point out," Gwen said, oblivious to H.P.'s inner turmoil. "First, her waffle, a banana split with bananas, strawberries, chocolate, and whipped cream on top, is completely clean."

"Meaning?"

"Meaning it was placed there after Sunnie died. Meaning the killer had time to heat up the waffle iron, or a different one with the same imprint. Meaning the killer also knew he had time to stage the scene without interruption."

"She was outside, in her yard. How would the killer know that no one else would show up?"

"That's the real question, isn't it?" Gwen grinned like a child enjoying their last bite of cake.

"Do you have pictures of the other victims?"

Gwen clicked the keys of her computer and brought up one more gruesome photo. It was a man this time, lying in the middle of a paved pathway. "Who is this?"

"Barry D'live. He was the groundskeeper at Cease & Desist Acres Cemetery and also the first cousin of our faithful mayor."

"What was Barry doing prior to his death? Jogging? He's wearing exercise clothing," H.P. said as she pointed to his shorts and short-sleeved shirt. "Gram said Pearlie Gates had just returned from her water aerobics class. We've got to figure out why gym members are being targeted!"

"All we know for sure about the day he died was that Barry D'Live had a call from his mother that morning. She says she wanted to make sure he was eating his fiber."

H.P. folded one arm over the other. "I can't believe the mayor hasn't demanded a thorough investigation. Barry was his cousin."

"I will tell you this: Our killer is taking his time, meticulously planning his next kill. He knows exactly how much time he has to commit the murder, stage the scene, make a waffle, and leave. That's pretty bold."

"Another investigation?" H.P. asked, already knowing the answer.

Gwen grinned. "We're just two crazy-good-looking-friends who love a good mystery."

Chapter Four

THE GLITTERATI

H.P.'s father was known around town for his active social life. He left town abruptly and under mysterious circumstances, without so much as a goodbye hug for his only child.

After it became obvious he wasn't going to return, one of her recurring fantasies was that he had more children after leaving her. In her mind, they were beautiful, kind, successful children whose adoration for their mystery sister was only eclipsed by their willingness to comfort the parentless child.

She'd given the results to Gwen, thinking it would soften the blow to hear their names from her best friend. Instead, Gwen explained that she and her high school arch enemy, Maddysin Noseinair, were second cousins.

"How can that be, Gwennie? Wouldn't Gram Gram have known?"

Gwen had lots of suggestions but no concrete

answers. So far, she'd kept the information between herself, Gwen, and, just recently, Dex. But knowing how much she loved to spring something unexpected on her arch enemy, H.P. decided it was best to tell her now. Although the information hadn't reached Maddysin's ears yet, Dex was so enthusiastic about finding a new set of relatives that he begged H.P. to help him gather more information.

"There's an old mansion on the outskirts of Misty Cove that was a museum of local history for years. It's a shame it isn't there any longer," Five Meal Gary, an affable man who ate at the diner five times each and every week said. "And rumor has it, the place is haunted. Not surprised, given its first owners."

"Who was that, Gary?"

"Only the Tumblewood family, that's who," he said, sticking his tongue in his cheek with an air of importance. When H.P. didn't answer, he continued. "Charles and Eliza, to be exact. He ran the Tumble-wood Tincture Apothecary until Eliza murdered him."

"I never knew the story, but for generations, we kids dared each other to spend the night there. There were all sorts of crazy stories about a murderess still haunting the place. I didn't realize the home was still standing! It's been condemned for years," H.P. remembered. "No one is allowed onsite."

She thought back to one frightening night when she and her friend Juniper were trapped inside. Peeling, flowered wallpaper and the strong yeasty smell of mold gave it an eerie feel.

"I need your help."

H.P. had spun around, unsettled to find no one there.

"You're the only one who can hear me! Please, Miss!"

Although H.P. had considered herself brave, encountering a real ghost was beyond the scope of her heroism. She and Juniper had tugged on the door until, miraculously, it opened.

Gary wiped the remnants of his eggs Benedict from his chin. "Maybe your son can find information online. You know how kids are. They can find everything and anything."

For Dexter Jenkins to find something more interesting than video games took a Herculean effort. That, or a fat wad of cash.

"I'm going to speak with Maddysin about your genealogy project. You and Tildie see what you can find in the library about our other relatives. Isn't it cool that one of them still has a home in the area? I bet the historical area has some good information?"

Dex nodded but his eyes never left the screen.

Today, as she brushed her teeth, H.P.'s mind wandered. What if she and Maddysin really were more alike than she thought? Did Honeypie Chiffon Sweetwater have a twisted side buried so deep that only a like-minded relative could unearth it?

Although Maddysin liked to brag the school was named after her family because of their prominence in the community, it had more to do with the shiny band instruments and football uniforms donated in memory of her grandfather, Boog R. Noseinair.

Any connection to high school made H.P. cringe. The Glitterati were easy to spot coming down the hallways because they all wore the same four-inch heels, shoes banned by the principal for their lasting effects on the shiny tile floors. Even he was afraid of them, or at least their influential parents. Not once were they reprimanded for breaking school rules.

Kids scattered when they heard their heeled steps come down the hallway, none wanting to be their next target. In hushed voices, the students talked about the teachers who shut their doors when they saw the girls coming. Make no mistake, it wasn't that they were ignoring them; they, too, were afraid of leaving school late one day and finding their car covered in heel scratches.

One homecoming, H.P. and a friend had decided to skip the festivities and raid her friend's father's liquor cabinet instead. Glassy-eyed and floating on an alcohol-induced high, they meandered without a care until they found themselves down the center of Cheddar Way, the street containing medium-sized mansions in Misty Cove.

The girls were enjoying Juniper's family recipe blueberry whiskey a little too much when Juniper pointed out Maddysin's fancy red sports scar. Should they enact their revenge? H.P.'s enthusiastic head nod sparked a decision that would affect the rest of her life.

With Juniper posted as lookout, H.P. let the air

out of a tire. As she was doing so, she happened to look inside the car, where a cashmere sweater and two books of poetry sat out in the open, practically begging to be stolen.

H.P. tested the door handle as she listened patiently to the hiss of air rushing out of the tire. Unlocked! She grabbed the sweater first and pressed it to her cheek. It was the softest fabric she'd ever felt—a softness apparently reserved for snooty people who didn't deserve it.

Next, she opened one book of poetry. H.P. knew Maddysin barely did her homework, let alone read something that would bore her to tears. On the floorboard was a half-eaten bag of French fries and several packets of ketchup. On impulse, H.P. tore them open and spread them equally on the book and sweater.

The clacking of heels alerted H.P. that a) they'd been discovered by the Glitterati, and b) Juniper had left her post, later to admit she'd wandered into a nearby yard to throw up.

For the rest of the school year, Logan had whispered in Maddysin's ear any time the girls walked by. That in and of itself was enough psychological warfare. But Logan and Maddysin exacted their revenge by kidnapping and blindfolding the girls one day after school before throwing them in the back of Mr. Berry's large truck.

H.P. felt a tug on her legs until she landed on the ground. "Ouch!"

"You'll be fine. Get up. You've got a date."

Without a clue where they might be, the girls trudged helplessly in front of their captors until they heard the squeak of an old door.

There was one final shove over the threshold before their blindfolds were removed. The room was dark and smelled of decay. "Where are we?" H.P. whispered.

"Rumor has it, you two losers need a date for prom. Nobody in the living world would take you," Logan barked.

"Being the kind and loving souls we are," Maddysin began, her eyes trained on her friend, "we found your perfect matches."

"What do you mean?" H.P. asked, although deep down she already knew.

"There are plenty of ghosts here in the Tumble-wood mansion. Only a few of them are capable of murder."

The two bullies giggled uneasily before turning around to leave.

"Wait!" Juniper called. "What do you want? I'll give you all the money in my bank account as long as you don't leave us here!"

Juniper had exactly $23.46.

Maddysin and Logan had glanced at each other before locking the girls in.

Juniper got pregnant by a senior boy and dropped out to get married.

H.P. never saw her again.

H.P. glanced up from the sink as she finished brushing her teeth.

The sound of the marching band, the award-winning Fighting Tissues playing the school song, "Wave 'Em High! High! High!" snapped her out of this rather ugly memory.

She swiped a dash of coral lipstick across her lips and dropped the tube into her pocket. H.P. was not only a grownup, but a grownup with a superpower—her conversations with her grandmother.

"Take that, Glitterati!" she sniffed. Although she lived in Gram Gram's home right next door to the diner, she grabbed a tissue and waited by the street for the band to march by. It was tradition that everyone within earshot of the band waved tissues as they marched past. She felt the same excitement she did in high school when she heard the bass drum rounding the corner.

The tall, white plumes on sky blue hats moved in unison as the school song blared from their instruments. As they got closer, she began to hum along:

In Misty Cove, where fog hugs tight and local stars shine bright, there's a school that stands, both proud and true, Boog R. Noseinair, we sing to you. From classrooms to the courts, the Tissues triumph without a snort. Our rivals mock, but they'll soon see, the strength of two-ply unity! Sneeze-em out. Sneeze-em out. Goooo team!

She tucked the tissue in her pocket and continued into the diner. It warmed her heart to see guests crowded around the windows as they, too, supported the band.

That evening, as they shared an everything-but-the-kitchen sink sandwich, she decided to question Dex about the current climate in Boog R. Noseinair High. "I was just wondering…" She paused as ketchup mixed with mayo dribbled down her chin. She pointed to the paper towel roll at the mercy of her blissfully unaware son. Their monthly make-a-sandwich-out-of-what's-in-the-fridge night always required more paper products than food.

Dex pretended not to notice her distress, one of his latest ways to irritate his mother. After she'd suffered an appropriate amount of discomfort, he handed the roll to his mother, grinning.

"Funny. Real funny." She smirked. Despite his often-moody behavior, they still had these moments together.

"What did you want to know, Mom? How my side tastes with barbecue chips? It's awesome. Like, one of the best we've ever created."

"That's cool, son. Real cool. What I was wondering was… well, you remember back in San Francisco, when the rich kids were picking on the kids who didn't have money for fancy sneakers?"

Dex took another enormous bite and nodded as the sound of his crunching filled the air. "Yeah," he said through a mouthful of turkey, ham, three types of cheese, two types of pickles, and other things H.P. couldn't remember.

"They were awful. That one kid, shoot. What was his name?"

"Edgar."

"Yeah, that's him. Dude that already had his own sports cars in the garage at age twelve. He followed some kid all the way home, throwing garbage at him the whole way."

The school board suspended Edgar for a grand total of one day. That's what private school got the rich kids: a ticket to bully any kid they wanted.

"I was wondering if there were kids who acted like that at your school."

"No. Tildie says this school is the chillest one she's ever attended."

Dex paused to lick his fingers, likely the only cleaning they would receive before his late-night shower. "Oh, wait! There IS a group of mean girls. The Glitterati." He rolled his eyes. "If they wanted a scary rep, they should have named themselves the Angry Angels or something." He chuckled at the thought.

H.P.'s stomach tightened, and she was fairly certain it wasn't related to her dinner. "Do you know anyone in that group of girls?"

"Yeah, I sure do. That girl you just hired—CeCe Scone."

Chapter Five

DRUMS AND PROCLAMATIONS

Edna Snarlwood appeared, carrying two steaming plates of scrambled eggs, toast, and bacon. "It's about time you decided to grace us with your presence."

Not one to be a slave to fashion, Edna's gray hair hung limply around her face with a large brown barrette yanking a section backward. In addition, Edna wore black, large-framed round glasses that made her appear menacing. Every single part of her body sagged in protest of her frosty personality. A smile never crossed her surly face in all the time H.P. had known her, at least, not a smile intended for her.

As H.P. removed her coat, Edna thrust a paper in front of her.

"What's this?" she asked.

"You've got two perfectly good eyes, and if I remember correctly, enough of an education to read." H.P. glanced at the page, typed in large print. She felt Edna behind her. "It's a proclamation from the mayor," Edna answered herself. "In all my years, I've never seen such a thing!"

"Yes, that's what I gathered, from the reading bit." Her eyes scanned the page.

"It's an emergency order," Edna continued. "The mayor's issued an emergency order-slash-proclamation that no waffles are to be served in any restaurant in Misty Cove until the killer is caught."

Ignoring her inclination to yell at Edna to back up, and a further inclination to remind Edna she'd expected H.P. to read the information herself, she exclaimed, "What? That's madness! How is that going to keep us safe from this killer? And can he actually enforce it?"

Edna shrugged noncommittally. "Guess it has something to do with using a waffle maker as a deadly weapon."

"The next thing you're going to tell me is that they're going door to door, collecting waffle makers."

Five Meal Gary cleared his throat. "That's what I heard is next. Have to pay for the Ballz and Bandz festival somehow. The kids will go around to every neighborhood, asking for their waffle makers."

"Harrumph! He's not taking mine! Without the promise of Waffle Wednesday, Mother would never clean the house!"

"I'm sure it's all rumor, Edna. That, or Gary is pulling your leg."

Edna's arms rose above her head before she brought them down with such force that H.P.

jumped. "You need to read the Misty Minds Talk Time page, H.P. Not only does the killer flatten his victims with the aforementioned appliance, but he also leaves a waffle calling card. You'd also know that each time he leaves a waffle, it's a different flavor." Edna smacked her lips with the satisfaction that she was in-the-know.

"Edna? You gonna wait 'til my eggs has grown into chickens?" Five Meal Gary asked impatiently. She frowned, or at least it seemed like something her face wanted to do had it not been in that position permanently. Edna reached into her pocket and pulled out a crumpled piece of paper, flipping it on the counter before retrieving Gary's food.

"What's this? I don't want to read about your personal business, Edna. Dex found the seedy novel your mother left on my doorstep and I didn't appreciate—" She stopped herself before she wasted more words on a lost cause. Instead, H.P. unfolded the paper and read:

> ***By proclamation of Mayor McCloud:***
> ***No waffle makers will be sold within the city limits of Misty Cove for the foreseeable future. Online waffle maker orders will be held at the Post Office until the killer is apprehended. If we all work together, we'll catch this heinous felon before we lose any more precious Misty Cove citizens.***
> ***Mayor Thunder McCloud***

"Seems like overkill to me," H.P. said under her breath. In her few dealings with the mayor, he appeared to be two eggs short of a Benedict. During the businessmen and women's breakfast, in which he'd forgotten what he wanted to say in his speech, he resorted to reciting the weather forecast for the next month. "Monday, rainy and windy. Tuesday, rainy and windy. Wednesday, a chance of sun, also rainy and windy."

"Your new chef's quick as lightning, that is, as long as I don't ask for a sandwich," Edna growled.

She'd been waiting for the opportune time to tell Edna about Frankie's "no lunch" rule. "Yeah, about that... Frankie insisted that she doesn't make lunch. I figured I'd take her place in the kitchen from two until closing. I miss cheffing anyway." H.P.'s apologetic smile did nothing to appease Edna, but just as the old grump opened her mouth to disagree, a customer hit the bell on the counter repeatedly.

First time anyone had used the bell. She wasn't even sure it was functional. Pushing her co-worker aside, H.P. moved to the counter, happy for the diversion.

"How can I help you?"

"Delores Tootwhistle!"

Was that an announcement, or did this woman expect H.P. to know her identity? Delores's appearance was a confusion of style and substance. Her straight gray hair was pulled away from her plain-looking back and held with a saxophone barrette. Possessing the soul-sucking glare of a grouchy librarian, she also wore a "Smile! Nobody else can toot your horn!" t-shirt. Tight Spandex shorts partially covered her legs, revealing impressive muscular appendages.

"My husband, Terrence, is the band director. I'm sure you already knew that."

"I heard them practicing today! They sound phenomenal!" H.P. replied enthusiastically.

"Why wouldn't they?"

It wasn't the response H.P. expected, but she'd learned in her years of restaurant work never to underestimate the oddity of the average customer. "That's not what I meant. I was just—"

"I'm short on time today, but we're doing a fundraiser to pay for the stadium rental so the band can perform their halftime routine during Ballz and Bandz Day."

"I'm happy to donate to the cause. I didn't realize the band had to fund the whole thing by themselves."

Dolores knitted her brows together and pursed her large, dry lips, an expression that reminded H.P. of the time she'd been caught by the school nurse after successfully hiding for most of the school year. "I'm not letting go of you, Miss Sweetwater, not until we're in my office and you're standing on my scale. Miss Berry very kindly told me you were hiding in the science lab closet."

"MIZ Sweetwater, since you're new in town, I'm willing to entertain the notion that you haven't educated yourself on the state of the arts in our state."

H.P. shook her head. "No, sorry. The diner keeps me very busy."

"Not me," Edna boasted. "I read Misty Minds Talk Time every morning. Nothing gets past me."

"Ignore her," H.P. said in a low voice. "What is the state of the arts, and why can't they use the stadium?"

Delores stared at H.P. like she was not just new to Misty Cove but new to the world at large. "You don't know? The school recently lost the funding of the Boog R. Noseinair Charitable Foundation. That accounted for half of their annual budget."

Something else to add to a growing list of discussion items with Maddysin. "Until future funding can be negotiated with the family, all unnecessary activities have been discontinued. That includes important classes, like Sarcasm as a Second Language, P.E. for Gamers: Finger Flexibility and Thumb Stamina, and Language Arts."

"You didn't mention the football field," H.P. replied.

"I'm getting to that!" Delores snapped. "In order to raise funds, the football stadium is sponsored each month. Jiminy Biscuit Corporation bought this month and refused to host the event unless we paid them double their costs."

"That's outrageous!" H.P. gasped. "They're trying to shake down a bunch of high school kids!"

"If they pulled out, there would be no stadium at all. It's the way of the world, Ms. Sweetwater."

Receiving no acknowledgment, Dolores continued, "We've added more fundraisers this year to help with the loss of funds. Blow Your Horn and Toot Your Tissues Gala is next weekend. We've asked the students to think of more suggestions for other fundraisers."

"I'm happy to donate gift certificates. Would five be enough?"

Dolores seemed taken aback. "That's fine." She didn't budge.

"Was there something else, Mrs. Tootwhistle?"

"I've... I've been told there's a serial killer on the loose, and that he's using waffle makers as his weapon of choice. Have you heard anything from your patrons? I'd hate for something like this to ruin our annual event."

H.P. tensed as she waited for Edna and Five Meal Gary to weigh in. When they didn't, she replied, "Don't you worry about a thing, Mrs. Tootwhistle. I'm sure the killer will be found long before Ballz and Bandz."

"Couldn't help but overhear," added an unfamiliar, deep voice from behind her.

H.P.'s head whipped around. Frankie wore a blue-and-gray plaid lumberjack shirt, rolled up to her elbows. Her tattoos were clearly visible. In San Francisco, where H.P. worked before inheriting the diner from her grandmother, no one thought twice about tattoos; in fact, many customers admired them. But here, in Misty Cove, it was a smaller collection of understanding souls, and H.P. still wasn't sure how they'd react.

She motioned for Frankie to pull her sleeves down, but Frankie wasn't paying attention. "I played the bass saxophone in high school," she mused. "There's nothing like the experience you get from making music together. I'd like to make a personal donation, if that's all right." Frankie pulled out a roll of cash from her pocket and peeled off two one-hundred-dollar bills, offering them to Dolores.

"Why, certainly! What a generous donation, Miss..."

"Just Frankie, ma'am. Glad to help the youngsters of Misty Cove."

None of your business, Sweetwater. None of your business.

"I'll have those gift cards ready for you in a day or so. You can stop by and pick them up?"

As if forced from her daydream, Delores returned to her surly demeanor. "Oh, good heavens! I don't pick up anything! One of the band kids will stop by to get them. I'm off to the gym."

Chapter Six

THE SEEDY SYRUP UNDERBELLY

Dexter handed over Sir Stackworth's leash. Frankie, as had become her habit, reached into her pocket for her ever-present wad of cash.

"No!" H.P. protested. "He doesn't need to be paid." She ruffled her son's curly brown mop lovingly, only to have her hand slapped away.

"Mom! Stop!" he protested. "She can pay me if she wants to! It's not like I get an allowance!"

Swallowing her ever-present desire to please, she turned to Frankie. "Dex needs to learn that kindness doesn't have a fee." He gave her his patented I-hate-you glare before exiting through the double kitchen doors. Even though neither one of them made any effort to remedy the situation, H.P. felt proud she'd at least voiced her objections.

"No junk!" H.P. called after him. She squatted down to pug level to pet his bubble-shaped head as Sir

Stackworth wagged his curly-tailed behind with gusto. When he flopped down on Frankie's shoes for his morning nap, H.P. stood and rubbed the back of her neck, hating these types of conversations.

"Frankie, you don't have to give me an answer if it's too personal, but you've been flashing wads of cash around. Even though Misty Cove is relatively safe, well, other than the two murders recently, I'm concerned you might be susceptible to being robbed."

"Didn't hear a question in there, ma'am." Frankie's expression remained serious.

"Right. I was wondering... where did all that money come from?"

"You're right to be suspicious of me, boss lady. I told you about selling my folks' diner, right? Well, I had a little side business too. I used some of my stash to buy an RV and me and my little guy hit the open road. We don't stay anywhere too long."

She wanted to believe Frankie. But something about that story seemed off. "I'm the last person to judge you, Frankie. I've made my share of mistakes. Dexter's father was a biggie." She paused, hoping Frankie would find that funny.

"Right! Funny!" Frankie's voice belied a fake cheeriness.

"If you need to get clean, I know of a good place outside of Charming, Oregon. It's not too far away and they have a sterling reputation." Her insides tightened as she thought about finding a new chef. Again.

"No, Ms. Sweetwater. I'm not on dope. I found a black market for syrup. I can move 300,000 gallons a month when I'm firing on all four burners."

H.P.'s mouth dropped open. "Did you say… syrup? Why would there be a black market for that?"

Frankie's face reddened and she balled up her fists as though she were going to lash out. H.P. took a preemptive step backwards.

"Nobody wants that artificial junk anymore. But most places don't want to shell out the big bucks for the good stuff. My roommate back in Colorado came from Canada, where her parents owned a maple farm. When she discovered the need in the States, she saw an untapped market. Just so happened my dad was laid up after heart surgery and the family and the diner were about to go under. Otherwise, I wouldn't have agreed."

"You're scaring me, Frankie. What are you involved in?" More than anything, she wanted to hug this poor, lost soul.

"My unnamed roommate smuggled syrup over the Canadian border, and I used my trucking connections to find customers across the country. We made enough money selling Sticky Fingers Syrup for me to pay off the creditors and cover my dad's hospital stay. Everything was going great. That is, until we felt the wrath of Big Syrup."

"Big Syrup?"

Frankie nodded. "They found out about us somehow and threatened to shut us down. Even more frightening was their plan to burn down every restaurant we'd supplied."

"That's unsettling. What did you do?"

"Things got a little soggy, ma'am. I told her about the threats I'd received from Big Syrup. She was cagey about it, said she wasn't concerned."

Frankie's chest heaved. "Imagine my surprise when this gal wanted a bigger cut! Her reasoning was that she put her folks in danger. I get it, but I was hauling product across the country without asking for one penny's worth of gas. The next week, when I went to pick up orders, she was gone. There was a note on the last box of product that said she was threatened by some group called the Breakfast Mafia and she needed to disappear."

Frankie placed her hands on her hips. "I packed my truck and Sir Stackworth and we hightailed it out of Colorado. I didn't know how much this Breakfast Mafia knew about me, and I didn't want to give them a reason to search for me, so I sold my rig and used the money to buy an RV. Sure has been nice seeing the country without a schedule."

H.P., although sympathetic, was having a hard time buying this story. It sounded ridiculous.

"I thought I was safe, until the day I was slinging hash in Idaho and the BM showed up."

"The BM?"

"Breakfast Mafia. Sorry. Their logo is a plate of waffles with a dollop of butter and those two letters pressed into the waffle."

"Frankie, if you don't mind my saying, it doesn't seem like you'd need to work here if you were flush with sticky money." She was positive Frankie was pulling her leg, but she was a good sport and decided to play along. "You were working in Idaho when the Big Omelet showed up?"

Frankie's eyes narrowed into slits. "Boss lady, this may seem like a big joke to you, but when I tell you what happened next, you'll understand the seriousness of the situation."

"Sorry." H.P. drew the corners of her mouth in tight. "Please continue."

"I was doing my thing, putting out lunch orders, when a man and woman came in and ordered two grilled ham and cheeses on rye. Next thing I know, there's screams coming from the front of the house. I peeked through the small window where I set plates for pick up. It was carnage, boss lady. Every lunch order in the place was covered in..." Her voice wavered. "I just can't talk about it. You understand why I can't bring myself to make lunch anymore."

H.P. nodded sympathetically, although she had no idea why something besides a ham sandwich would cause her to relive that horrible day. This whole experience sounded like a movie H.P. slept through and had to ask Dex what happened the next day.

"I can understand why you'd be afraid, Frankie. It concerns me that you'd put my customers in danger. How can you be certain they won't show up here, even though you've sworn off lunches?"

"I don't wanna spend all my days on the run. I'm hoping to build up a nice little nest egg so that I can take my pup and move—" She stopped abruptly. "Prolly better you don't know where. Just in case they show up looking for me."

Chapter Seven

PEACHIE KEEN

"Mom, pleeease?"

Dexter was hellbent on making her life uncomfortable this morning. Not that his methods were any different than, say, last Tuesday. In between trying to track down the serial killer and keep her business running, her son adamantly insisted on connecting with his new relations.

Up until now, she'd resisted telling him why Maddysin and a potential relationship with her was so toxic.

"Dexie, do you remember when you were in fourth grade? It was your worst year of school, all because Chad Tellingham constantly picked on you."

Dexter's face became blotchy as he relived his discomfort. "He followed me everywhere. I couldn't even go to the bathroom. I had to hold it all day, just in case he was waiting for me in a stall."

H.P.'s heart hurt, even though both Chad and

those experiences were hundreds of miles away. She'd gone to the school many times trying to convince the administration to hold Chad accountable for his actions. When Dexter reached the end of his school year without any relief, H.P. found a private school with a strict no-bullying policy. She worked two jobs and sometimes picked up private catering to afford it.

"Well, that's what high school was like for me. Maddysin Noseinair and her followers ran our school. Even the teachers were afraid of her group of monsters. I lost count of how many times she flushed my head in the toilet."

There was a lull in their conversation, and the only sound was water dripping from the kitchen faucet.

"I get it, Mom."

"Thank you, baby." H.P. opened her arms and reached for her boy. Instead of dissolving into his mother's embrace, Dexter pulled a surprise move.

"It's okay if you don't want to be a part of my new connection, but I want to see where this goes. Don't worry, I won't bring your name up. You shouldn't have to relive any of that."

That was of little comfort. H.P. bit her lip. She wasn't sure whether she wanted to cry in pride or pain. Either way, she'd sit in the bathroom for a good boo-hoo fest later. "Can I make a suggestion?"

Dexter shrugged. "I guess."

"Go to the city library. I know they have a section on genealogy. Find out everything you can and take

Tildie with you. When you're armed with the truth, you can win any battle."

"But you won't win the war!" they said in unison.

Dexter grinned. It was a line from his seventh-grade musical, "Tanks for the Memories." He played the lead character, Colonel Darrin Y-salute, a gruff general with a secret life in the theater.

When H.P. was certain her brave boy had left for school, she walked over to the diner. Frankie was busy prepping for the day, chopping meats and vegetables. Even though she refused to prepare anything of the lunch variety, she always prepped everything for H.P. As H.P. entered, Frankie glanced up, a quick smile passing over her face.

Today, she wore a matching apron and scarf, both colorfully decorated with egg dishes. "Hiya, boss lady."

"Morning, Frankie."

"I was worried you might fire me after our chat yesterday." She wiped her hands on her apron and handed H.P. a small bowl of fresh fruit. "Not trying to bribe you or anything."

"If I felt like I'd done everything right in my life, then I'd have just cause. But that day isn't today." She took the dish and set it on the counter. "I'll eat this later, after I do some inventory in the walk-in."

"You keep a tighter rein on that inventory than any chef I've ever known. Are you afraid the mice might carry some of it away during the night?"

"Something like that." H.P. walked to the cooler and

placed her hand on the handle before pausing and turning around. "All I ask is that you let me know the INSTANT you think the BM have found you. The INSTANT."

Frankie saluted her. "Already planned on it."

Stepping inside the cooler, she closed the door behind her. "Gram Gram?" she hissed. "I forgot my sweater, so let's make this quick!"

The sweet, fragrant scent of Honeypie's signature honey and cream pie filled the air. H.P. never tired of the smell.

"Hun Bun, I like that gal, but she's a liability."

"You were the one who told me to hire her!" H.P. protested. She hated herself for snapping at Gram Gram. This gift of extra time with her grandmother, even if it had to take place inside the walk-in cooler, was something she would treasure for however long it lasted.

"I'm sorry, Gram Gram. You didn't know."

And why didn't she? Gram Gram acted like she knew something wonderful about Frankie the minute she walked through the door. "We've got to find this killer before the city's tourism grinds to a halt. I suspect that a murderer on the loose is more of a priority than some made-up mafia. The police don't seem to be in any hurry. Do you know why?"

"You're assuming that my position gives me a bird's eye view of the entire universe? I can't leave the walk-in without losing two weeks' worth of ethereal energy."

"Then how did you know about my conversation with Frankie?"

"Can't leave," Gram Gram began, thunking her head, "but this thing can understand conversations within a five-block radius."

Although H.P. was curious just how that worked, given the fact that Gram Gram still had vision problems in death, she decided to table the discussion for another day. "Dex thinks he wants to meet with Maddysin, now that he knows they're related. Can you believe it? She'll tear my little boy into bite-sized pieces and spit him on the ground!"

"Don't underestimate the boy. You've raised him well." She smiled and waved her arms back and forth until she created a glittering, gold light that swirled up from the ground like a tornadic wind. When she was fully immersed, H.P. felt the warmth and security she'd craved since Gram Gram's death.

She closed her eyes and drank it in, wishing it could last forever. Even now, her grandmother knew how to comfort her. When the cloud slowly dissipated, Gram Gram lowered herself to H.P.'s eye level. "That was wonderful, Gram! I feel renewed!"

"Let's discuss Maddysin. How can I help?"

"Do you know how we're related? The FindYour-Peeps test said we shared great-great-grandparents. Those things can be completely wrong, though. I read—"

"It was my grandpappy. He was a scamp," Gram Gram replied flippantly.

"You... knew?"

Gram nodded. "At that time, Misty Cove was a rowdy, lawless place. The lumber industry was booming, as were the bars and brothels that followed. Grandpappy was a frequent visitor of both."

"Are you telling me that Maddysin's great-great-grandmother was a prostitute?" H.P. felt giddy.

"That's what Mother always said, but we never knew for sure. I suspected he'd fathered children with the 'other woman' because my mother told stories about his Saturday afternoon disappearances. She was forever starting and stopping this story until I begged for the truth. That's when she sat us both down, my sister Peachie and me, and told us the whole story. She ended by showing us a photograph of his out-of-wedlock child."

H.P. raised a brow. "Really?"

"I didn't ever tell my kids or grands. It was so far back in family history that it didn't seem necessary." Gram whirled around her like a gentle tornado of warmth and love before landing on a shelf, between an industrial-sized container of sour cream and another of dill pickles.

"Though Peachie and I had a happy life, she dissolved into tears when she saw the photo, so Mother never brought it out again. Children don't concern themselves with matters like that."

"Oh, Gram. I'm so sorry. That realization must've crushed you. How old were you?"

Gram Gram touched H.P.'s cheek. It wasn't like

the touch of a living, breathing being, but it still contained memories of her grandmother and her love.

"Oh, I'm thinking I was twelve."

"Whaat? You said you didn't understand when you were a child!"

"I didn't. This story didn't make a lick of sense until I was grown and, even then, my brain struggled with it. Mother and her sister went ice skating at Soggypants Pond every Saturday. One cold morning, they had the bright idea to sneak into the caretaker's barn to warm up. That's where they found them."

"Were they—"

"Yes, my dear. Sugar Noseinair and Grandpappy were snuggled up in the corner on a fresh pile of hay."

H.P. gasped. "And how did he explain that to your grandmother?"

"He was nothing if not brilliant. He bribed Mother and her sister into thinking it was an elaborate game. From then on, they went directly to the barn before skating. 'Oh, you've found me again, you clever girls! Take this dime to the candy store! But don't tell your mother, or our game will end!'"

"Who could blame them for keeping the secret? They were just kids. How long did that go on?"

"My recollection is that it went on until Sugar's death. But as they grew, Mother and her sister had less interest in the candy store." Gram Gram shook her head, lost in another time. "Your grandfather never understood why I became amorous around his brother's cow barn."

"I'll do my best to erase that image from my mind, Gram." H.P. shuddered at the thought. "And I still haven't heard why you'd think that was Maddysin's great-grandmother."

"Sugar gave birth to a child who looked identical to Grandpappy, all except for her gray eyes. When I was grown, I searched for more information and all I found was a news article on the Tumblewood family and their apothecary. That's what they called a pharmacy in those days. When Charles Tumblewood and Eliza Noseinair married, it was common knowledge, her parentage, you know. Eliza would be great-great-grand-mother to both you and Maddysin."

A sudden knocking on the door to the walk-in startled them both. "Ms. Sweetwater? You're needed out front. Sounds urgent."

H.P. looked at Gram Gram apologetically.

"I know, Hun Bun. We'll chitter batter tomorrow, my darling!"

As she scurried to the front of the diner, the phone began buzzing in her pocket. "Dex? Is everything all right?"

"Why? Because you think I'm going to get snuffed by the serial killer?" His young voice wavered between upper and lower registers, but even that didn't make his delivery humorous.

"We don't know who the killer is targeting, son. So, yes, I am concerned for your safety. Where are you? I'm making dinner tonight, so don't be late. It's pork chops with green beans. Your favorite."

"Don't bother. Tildie's dad's making Chinese. He said he'd drive me home after."

She paused to consider whether he needed reminding that he had to ask her permission before making dinner arrangements. Knowing he had a place and a friendship that made him feel safe, away from the Glitterati, was comforting.

"Okay. Home by eight, all right?"

"Yuppo."

Chapter Eight

A SUSPICIOUS WIND-Y

"I'll be right over, Gwennie!"

H.P. hung up and glanced around the half-empty diner.

"Don't worry, Ms. Sweetwater. I can handle closing up." CeCe, fresh from her lip piercing, was sweeping the floor after four toddlers enjoyed smashing cookies into a virtual sandbox.

"That's much appreciated. How did the piercing work out? Is it painful?"

She absently touched her face. "I love it! My mom said if I helped her, she'd sign the release. She almost passed out during the process!"

"Such a shame," H.P. replied with a glint in her eye.

"It was a reward. I—did some stuff—and it was her way of rewarding me."

"Oh, CeCe? I'm curious about something. Are you in any clubs or groups at school?"

CeCe paused and leaned against a booth. "You mean, other than the ones I wrote on my application?"

There had been many. So many that CeCe stapled an extra page to the back of the application. "I guess I said that wrong. I was wondering if you and your friends have a... name."

CeCe smiled in recognition. "Ohh. You mean the Glitterati! Yeah, that's me and my friends. We do charitable things in the community. We opened membership to include guys, so my boyfriend Timber joined too. He's our muscle." She giggled before quickly covering her mouth with delicate hands.

"Uh-huh."

Not even when she was a wide-eyed culinary student, easily duped into giving away her best knives to an evil chef, would she believe that story. H.P. grinned in the most sickeningly sweet way she could muster. "That's wonderful! How incredibly kind of you and your friends to leave others better than you found them. I'm sure that extends to your classmates too. Always polite and friendly?"

CeCe's face turned blotchy, her perfect skin suddenly uneven, making her appear at least twenty. She bit her lip before releasing it quickly. H.P. delighted in her momentary pain, even though she knew it was ten shades of wrong.

"Umm, yeah, something like that."

"Good! Great! I've offered to volunteer my time at the high school soon, so I'm sure I'll run into you and your Glitterati doing good deeds for others!"

H.P. had a definite spring to her step as she walked two blocks to The Final Fold. She found Gwen in an unusually empty shop, tapping her fingers on the counter.

"What's the big news?" she asked.

"Not a 'Hello, Gwen?'" Her voice belied a hurt. "I thought we'd become a little closer than that."

"Sorry. Hello, Gwen! I've not seen you for at least twenty-four hours, so your life must have completely changed!"

Gwen smirked at H.P. "I came here to give you early inside information. Nobody else in town knows yet. But if you're not interested—"

H.P. grabbed Gwen's small arm wrapped in a fuzzy, mustard-colored sweater, to ensure she didn't leave. "I'm interested." She moved closer to Gwen, whispering in her ear, "Who was it this time?"

"Windy."

H.P. released her grip. "Did you call me over here to give me the forecast? Because I've got a million more questions for Gram Gram about Eliza Tumblewood."

"You are such a goof." Gwen giggled her sweet little girl giggle. For all her education, Gwen Folds was still a child on the inside. "It's Mayor McCloud's wife. You don't know her?"

"What? That's awful!"

Although she'd only met the perennially upbeat woman twice, both times as she power-walked past the diner and called out, "I've got to try your pies some-time! I've heard they're divine!" H.P.'s heart sank knowing she'd fallen victim to the serial killer. "Can you give me more information?"

"They were green. Obviously."

H.P. was puzzled for a second. "Ohh, right. You're talking about the waffle. Why were they green? And no, I was talking about where she died, et cetera."

"The waffles were green because they were made from a recipe on Windy's website, using her protein greens. And Windy was whacked in her gazebo, where she was about to host a party for the people who'd lost one hundred pounds using her program."

Gwen pulled her phone from the pocket of her yellow-and-black plaid skirt with one hand and used the other to lift her glasses to the bottom bifocals. "The caterer set up at noon, hummus sandwiches, fruit and coffee. He left to get the cooler for the lemon water and was gone no more than an hour."

"Does it really take an hour to get lemon water?" H.P. asked with skepticism.

"No, he forgot his jacket at home, and his neighbor came over to complain that his garbage can was always in the middle of the street, and then—"

"Okay, okay. I get it. He was gone and the killer had ample time to kill Windy, make a waffle, and stage the scene. How is it that this killer always has plenty of time to set up every detail? What if one of Windy's guests showed up? Or her husband?"

Gwen used one short leg to springboard onto the stool seat before placing both elbows on the counter. "Well, if I were to guess, I'd say the killer stalked her for weeks, possibly months. Just like the rest of our victims, he knew when she'd be alone."

"And the green waffle?"

"Made with her own shake mix. I found a waffle recipe on her website for waffles, ironically. The killer must've known about it. On top—not on top of Windy, but the waffle—was a fluffy coconut whipped cream."

"The killer must've been one of Windy's customers," H.P. replied.

Edna, who was enjoying a rare day off, stormed into the dry cleaner. Her face was covered in a shade of makeup that was too dark, creating an orange ring. She'd applied a dark lipstick haphazardly, making the outline of her mouth appear somewhat frightening.

She marched up to the two women and slammed a waffle maker down on the counter with such fury, it caused the dry cleaning receipts to scatter.

"I take one day off and you leave the kid in charge? I don't trust that one. Not at all."

H.P. took a deep breath and let it out slowly before replying. "On your days off, I'm well within my rights as the owner of Honeypie Diner to staff MY diner as I see fit. And why are you toting around your waffle maker?"

"I'm on my way to the city dump. The mayor's given us a free dump day to dispose of these murder weapons. I stopped by the diner to get rid of yours, but I guess you already did."

"What? Why would I do that?" H.P. caught

Gwen's eye and understood Gwen to feel the same way. "There is no reason to start throwing our appliances away. I'm sure the authorities will figure this out soon."

"While Mother and I were at our water aerobics class this afternoon, Patti Crabby told us all about another murder today, though she wasn't at liberty to tell us who got the whacking. Patti's son-in-law works for the police department, and he says the mayor has requested help from other police departments up and down the Washington and Oregon coast. Patti says we should get rid of our waffle makers now, before they're confiscated."

"You don't need to worry, Edna. Our waffle maker hasn't been used in the commission of a crime. I have no idea why it wouldn't be on the shelf. I'll check into it tomorrow."

"It was Windy McCloud, the mayor's wife." Gwen blurted it out like she was ordering a burger. It was the least professional thing H.P. had observed in a town full of far-too-casual encounters, and the most shocking thing she'd witnessed all day.

Edna emitted a series of low-pitched gasps, like the sound a lawnmower made when it was having trouble starting.

"Windy? Who would want to end her life? The woman was on the school board and never stopped moving!"

"We were just discussing that, Edna. It's such a tragedy. Did you know her well?"

Edna was uncharacteristically silent.

"Edna?"

"I was thinking!" she retorted. "She was part of my bowling league until she started her diet business. Windy's Slim-Down Cyclone took up all her time and changed her personality."

"What do you mean by that, Edna?" H.P. knew full good and well what she meant, but something about Edna's obvious discomfort made her want to delve deeper.

"Not in the habit of stuttering, gal. Windy lost over one hundred pounds by facing fifteen high-powered fans while she exercised. She came out with her own line of clothing for the women in her class to wear, lightweight and wind resistant. Next, she invented a fancy shake mix for after those gals had blown themselves to the wall."

Edna paused here. "No one in town was happier to see her succeed than Misty Cove Power and Gas."

"Do you know of any enemies she might have?" H.P. asked. "Or even someone who may have disagreed with her dieting methods?"

Edna placed an index finger on her lips and tapped them as she thought. "Well, I ran into her one time at the grocery store and she did mention she was meeting some people from the gym. She made it sound like they were tasked with solving the world's problems." Edna grunted, her form of laughter. "Doubt the government would turn to an exercise nut for answers."

"Who was she meeting? Men? Women?"

Edna squinted, as she did when she was working up to an insult. "What's got you wound up today, girl? Not getting enough granola? Gals our age don't do the plumbing any favors when we're low on fiber."

"I'm NOT your age, Edna." She opened her mouth to volley an insult back, but Gwen squeezed her forearm.

"H.P. is concerned, that's all, Edna. Did Windy give you any indication of the topics they were discussing?"

Edna squinted. "You gals don't have one good pair of ears between you. I already told you; I have no idea. Windy said they always met for lunch at Scone and Stone Masonry. They've got a taco bar for employees, and Windy said it was a good out-of-the-way place."

Chapter Nine

FOOD, FUNERALS, AND FOLLY

"You've got a keeper here, H.P." Mayor McCloud motioned toward CeCe Scone as he shoveled another bite into his mouth. H.P. had witnessed lots of people eat their feelings, but none ever did it cheerfully.

Until today.

"I agree. I'll admit, I was skeptical at first." She considered how the mayor having his wife's reception here seemed wrong, given her unwillingness to eat at the diner. "I'm glad everything worked out!"

Not only did it seem odd that he agreed to the location, but Mayor McCloud also did it with joy. H.P. reminded herself that everyone grieved differently. When Gram Gram died, she and Dex couldn't afford the trip to Washington to go to the funeral. She'd pretended it didn't bother her for months.

"I tried talking him out of it," Duncan Sappy from Sappy Endings Funeral Home growled. "He was adamant." Duncan was the only person dressed in dark funeral colors and stood as though acting as a bouncer, close to the front door.

"The mayor asked that Frankie whip up something special," Edna whispered in her ear. "The mayor's gonna love this!"

"Wait! Nobody told me anything!" Before H.P. could put a stop to it, Frankie presented a plate to the mayor. "I wasn't sure it was appropriate, but Edna insisted the best way to honor your wife would be a delicious—"

H.P. gasped in horror. The plate contained four mini-green waffles with an odd-looking whipped topping and berries on top, exactly the same waffles that were placed beside Windy McCloud's body after her murder.

In her mind, H.P. pictured herself moving like a ninja. Instead, she lurched forward, hoping to intercept the plate before Frankie sat it down. She narrowly missed the edge of the counter and landed on a pile of French fries drenched in ketchup. As she wiped the ketchup from the backside of her uniform, she heard the mayor chewing with his mouth open.

"Chef Frankie, this is about the best darn thing I've tasted, and you know there's been more 'n a few delicious dishes in this gullet. Kinda familiar too. Have you made this before?" He wiped his fingers on his napkin, seemingly oblivious to the macabre connection to his wife's death.

H.P. swallowed hard. "We haven't actually made a

green waffle before, Mayor. We've been limiting our waffles since your ban."

"I know the rumor is we've confiscated all the waffle irons in town, but that simply isn't true. I only released that proclamation to show I'm serious about law and order. This needs to stay on the menu, H.P. Call it Thunder's Delight." He patted his stomach and chuckled as though he didn't have a care in the world.

"It was my idea, Mayor," Edna boasted. "Now you can think happy thoughts while you're eating waffles."

This was like another horror movie H.P. slept through, where the description said everyone acted as if the killer hadn't killed anyone.

"Can I get you more coffee?" CeCe asked cheerily. She'd somehow found a black uniform that matched the décor of the diner while at the same time being appropriate for the occasion.

"I wouldn't say no," the mayor replied. "You're a real credit to the youth of this community. Tell your mother I said so."

She filled his mug and patted his back in a familiar way that made H.P. uncomfortable. "As long as you won't tell my folks you saw me out past curfew last weekend." CeCe turned to place the coffee pot back on the burner, oblivious to the storm brewing.

His face became taut as he glared at her.

"Why don't I have Frankie make some waffles to take home with you?" H.P. said nervously.

The mayor burst out laughing. "Just joshing ya, CeCe. I know you're a good kid. You and your whole group of gals." The mayor made a finger gun and shot it at the teen.

There was a twinkle in his eye H.P. hadn't seen before. The man was having the time of his life.

"Mayor, Edna tells me you're bringing in extra help from Seattle to find the killer. Is that true?"

He took a large gulp of his latté and squinted. "Edna told you that? Police business and my office have a leak, apparently. Don't you worry about a thing, Ms. Sweetwater." He patted H.P.'s hand. "We'll have this case wrapped up before the tourist season begins. I guarantee it."

Her insides felt like pure mud as she thought about Windy power-walking by the diner. She deserved better. Much better. Maybe H.P. needed some quiet time in the office.

"Everything okay out there, boss?" Frankie asked as she walked through the kitchen. Frankie was hard at work washing dishes. H.P. told her numerous times that they had a dishwasher for a reason, but Frankie insisted that they wouldn't get clean enough if she didn't do a pre-wash.

"I'm getting a very weird vibe from Mayor McCloud today. It's almost as if he's relieved his wife is gone."

Frankie paused, wiping her hands on her pancake-patterned apron. "He is." She took H.P. by the arm and guided her into the office before closing the door behind her.

"What? How can you say that, Frankie?"

"Sir Stackworth and I attend weekly poker games with the mayor. He and Windy have been on the outs ever since she admitted to having an affair. Windy was sleeping at her sister's house and rarely spent time in the home she shared with the mayor."

A coldness coursed through H.P.'s veins. "So, he DID have a reason to want her gone. She must've come home to confront him and he—"

"You're twisting my words into a gooey cinnamon roll, Ms. Sweetwater. They weren't getting along, but he wasn't there when she died. She had some kind of luncheon set up. I know because she'd originally asked me to cater but changed her mind at the last minute."

H.P. studied Frankie for any signs of deceit. When she found none, she continued. "Did she invite you to come to her Cyclone classes?"

"Multi-level marketing is too risky for a gal who doesn't want her name passed around. Besides, I'm a vagabond. Sir Stackworth and I don't like any extra baggage."

"Where's my toast? You two letting the bread rise before you cook it?"

"In a minute, Edna!" H.P. replied. "Oh, I almost forgot. Do we need to talk to the mayor about this BM that might be coming this way? So we're all safe?"

"No! You can't!" she snapped, startling H.P.

"I mean, it's best to give him time to grieve, boss lady."

H.P. shrugged it off. Everyone was acting weird today. Funerals did that to people.

By the time she returned home, H.P. was ready to prop her feet up with some leftovers and a nice bottle of Sassy Lasses Marveline Merlot. Cinnamon Biscuit Maker would put on her best "I haven't eaten in months" face before admitting defeat and curling up on her lap. The perfect evening.

What she found when she opened her front door shocked her to her core.

Chapter Ten

THE UNEXPECTED

"Mad?"

"What are YOU doing here?"

Maddysin Noseinair, her high school nemesis, spa owner under the name "Bliss," and all-around unlikable human was seated on H.P.'s couch, petting HER sweet black-and-white cat, Cinnamon Biscuit Maker. H.P. could hear loud traitorous purrs coming from the cat as she slipped her shoes off. One more slight.

"Your son invited me." She stood, forcing their beloved family pet to slide off her lap and onto the floor. As Maddysin brushed cat hair from her expensive slacks, Cinnie trotted over to H.P., acting as though she hadn't just ripped out the heart of her favorite human and buried it in her litter box. Maddysin strode over to H.P. and stood, uncomfortably close, beside her. It wasn't as though H.P.'d missed their obvious height difference in the 999 times she'd done it before.

Maddysin wiped the corners of her mouth, removing excess blood red lipstick, or perhaps it was actual blood. "We've been having a LOVELY conversation. It's really a shame you missed out."

H.P. glanced at her son, whose expression was a mix of shame and excitement. It was the excitement part that ate at her the most. Just as she was about to give them both the dressing down they deserved, Tildie appeared, carrying a tray of bite-sized cakes.

"Oh! Ms. Sweetwater! Thanks for letting us use your living room to trace Dexter's ancestry. Here!"

She shoved the tray in front of H.P. as a very loud gurgle of betrayal emerged from H.P.'s unhelpful stomach. "Sure. Thanks, Tildie." H.P. took a bite and closed her eyes. "Mm. Are these your secret recipe vanilla coconut cakes?"

"Yes, ma'am. Dexter said they're his favorite."

There was no fighting them. Two earnest kids and one she-devil were competitors far out of her league today. H.P. opened her eyes. "Okay. Tell me what you've found."

Ignoring Maddysin's complete disregard for personal space, as well as the crime-against-smells perfume she designed (a scent with the strong, smoky undertones of a nutmeg factory explosion), H.P. flopped down on the one remaining chair.

"Mom, Tildie and I found out that Eliza Tumblewood is my three-times-great-grandmother. And guess what? She's Maddysin's great-great grandmother! Isn't that cool?"

Maddysin grinned. There was lipstick on one of her big horse teeth. H.P. could hang onto that thought and maybe, just maybe, her head wouldn't explode in the middle of the night. In all likelihood, Dex would just step over her remains anyway—in the same manner as he did his clean clothes.

"Dexter told me you've known about this for some time. I suppose you thought I was too busy for family business, given the opening of my air freshener factory and running my spa." Using her dinosaur-length neck to lower her pea-sized head to H.P.'s level, she whispered, "If you tell ANYONE else about this, I will end you."

H.P.'s cheeks felt hot, not as much from the threat as it was from an aversion to using curse words in front of Dex.

Stretching up to her full height, Maddysin batted lashes confiscated from a live animal and brought out her best syrupy voice. "Dexter, you and your darling girlfriend are a delight, but I must run. Don't forget to call Mother's secretary for an appointment. She'd love to share family history with you."

Maddysin glanced at H.P., perhaps gauging her reaction. *Did she know about the last time H.P. and Gram Gram visited?*

"Oh, I did want to ask you about something, Mad. I'm sure your broom needs a few minutes to warm up anyway."

"Moth-er!" Dex protested, using the voice she'd taught him by example.

Maddysin scrunched her face in disgust. It was a herculean feat, given the fact it was stretched tighter than the drum head used by the Fighting Tissues.

"Well? Get on with it!" she snapped.

H.P. leaned back and brought her fingertips together. "Sunnie Daze had your phone number in her pocket when she died. How do you know her?"

Maddysin's eyes darted from one face to the next, and H.P. wondered if she was formulating an escape plan.

"Hardly at all. We went to the same gym and she accosted me one day about meeting her for coffee, so I gave her my number." Maddysin sighed. "Are you satisfied, or are you so bored with your own life that you need to hear more?"

H.P. took a moment to relish this predicament. Maddysin was in the Sweetwater home, squirming like a garden worm. The day couldn't have ended better. The euphoria lasted only a moment, though, before she remembered this was an investigation, not her fantasy.

"So...you weren't at her home? In her garden? Poor, poor Sunnie was—"

"Mom! Stop it!" Dexter's face turned a bright red normally reserved for either Hal's Gonna Die Hot Sauce or his mother showing up at school unannounced. "Ms. Noseinair," he began in his most formal voice, "I'm sorry about my mom. She gets weird after a long day. Can I see you out?" He stood, just as she'd taught him, and walked Maddysin to the door.

They chatted amiably for a few minutes as H.P.'s blood boiled. When the evil witch finally sped off in her red sports car, the air became noticeably lighter. Dexter took his time before rejoining her and Tildie, choosing instead to straighten the shoes on the shoe rack and the rug in front of the door. Stalling was one of his more transparent traits.

"Mom, before you yell at me and ground me and stuff, let me explain."

H.P. took a deep breath. One thing she'd promised herself she would never do is lecture her son in front of his friends. It was one of Gram Gram's few faults—reprimanding her grandchildren about anything from toilet paper usage to bad grades in front of company.

"Ms. Sweetwater, we have a family history project at school, and I encouraged Dexter to research his roots. At first, he was going to research his father's side, but—"

"I called Granny Jenkins," he blurted. H.P. had always despised that name, as it made her think of a grizzled woman sitting on her porch with a gun in her lap. As it turned out, the description fit Sheralyn Jenkins to a tee.

"Dex, whatever she said, it's no reflection on you."

Eliot Jenkins' mother saw her grandson a grand total of twice. Once in the hospital and once when he was three. Sheralyn had been filling up her expensive car with gas at the same time H.P. put exactly ten dollars and not a penny more in her beat-up hatchback. They exchanged nods and Sheralyn bent down to peek through the window, where Dex was playing with his favorite toy, a blue plastic lid. "Looks like you," she had said without emotion.

"I know, Mom. Grandma said she didn't remember me and didn't have time to help me." Dex and Tildie shook their heads in unison.

Good. They were in lockstep about this, and Dex wouldn't have to bear her rejection alone.

"Ms. Sweetwater, she even had the nerve to tell Dexter that he should find a volunteer grandmother at his school, as they were more the warm and fuzzy type."

"Well, that sounds about right." H.P. sighed. "I understand why you didn't want to use your dad's ancestry. That makes sense. But you know, I have a whole goggle of cousins too."

She clapped her hand over her mouth. That was one of Gram Gram's nonsensical words that she'd used just yesterday. It didn't belong in conversations with the living.

"Yeah. I s'pose."

Dex lowered his head and H.P. instantly felt a pang of guilt. "It's okay that you called her, kiddo. My beef with Mad... dah-son... is mine alone. What did she say?"

Tildie rubbed Dexter's back sympathetically. "Ms. Noseinair told us about your shared relative, Eliza Tumblewood. We discovered she was imprisoned. For murder."

"What?" She thought back to Five Meal Gary's

boastful words. She hated it when he was right. "Gram Gram never said a word!"

"How would she know? We just came across this information!"

It was H.P.'s turn for the crimson face. "Right. I don't know what I'm saying. Maddysin told you about this murder?"

Tildie nodded. "She even gave us this."

Chapter Eleven

A DARK LEGACY

H.P. took a fragile, yellowed newspaper article from Tildie's hand and read:

Notorious Murderer Eliza Tumblewood Hanged Today for the Traitorous Death of Her Husband

Misty Cove Gazette, July 15, 1820
In an unprecedented event that has shaken the tranquil town of Misty Cove to its core, Eliza Tumblewood, a woman of thirty-two years, has been found guilty of a crime most foul and has met her grim fate at the gallows this past Thursday morning. The case, which has captured the attention and horror of our community, involves the tragic demise of her husband, Charles Tumblewood, a well-respected merchant known throughout the county.

A Crime Unveiled
The dreadful tale began on a stormy night in April

when Charles Tumblewood was discovered lifeless in his study, a victim of poisoning. The local constabulary were quick to respond, and an investigation ensued, revealing a web of deceit that pointed unmistakably to one Eliza Tumblewood. Known in society circles for her charm and wit, Eliza's transformation from a dutiful wife to a calculated murderess has left many in disbelief.

H.P. glanced up at the two teens. They were waiting for some kind of reaction. "Oh!" she remarked with a false cheeriness to her voice. "How interesting!"

"Mom," Dex huffed, "you've got to read the whole thing."

She brought the article to the kitchen table, where she could sit and give her tired feet a break.

The Evidence Overwhelming

Evidence presented at the trial painted a damning picture: a wife who scorned her duties as mother and instead retired to a hidden enclave to concoct poisons from herbs she found. Her discontent over her husband's success as apothecary at Tumblewood Tinctures was detailed in her diary, as was the exact ingredients of her deadly potion found in a vial after Charles Tumblewood's death. In addition to pages in her diary detailing her discontent with her marital bonds, damning testimony from servants who spoke of her growing animosity towards her spouse made at least one juror gasp in horror. Mrs. Tumblewood, it would seem, relished the idea of enjoying her husband's considerable fortune free from the shackles of her marriage.

A Defense Unheard

Eliza's defense, led by barrister Johnathan Hemsley, argued that the evidence was circumstantial and pleaded for mercy, citing her standing in the community and lack of prior malfeasance. Curiously enough, Eliza refused to take the stand in her own defense, citing an unwillingness to embarrass her children. Nevertheless, the jury, swayed by the weight of the evidence before them, delivered a verdict of guilty after mere hours of deliberation.

The Final Act

Eliza Tumblewood's hanging drew a large crowd, a somber testament to the gravity of her actions. Her final words, a plea for forgiveness from the Almighty, were met with silence from the onlookers, a community grappling with the darkness that had lurked within their midst.

A Community Reflects

The aftermath of this tragedy leaves many questions in its wake. How could a woman of such standing commit an act so heinous? What darkness lies in the hearts of those we think we know? As Misty Cove mourns the loss of Charles Tumblewood and contemplates the downfall of Eliza, it is a stark reminder of the complexities of the human soul and the thin veneer that separates the civilized from the savage.

As our town returns to its peaceful slumber, the tale of Eliza Tumblewood will undoubtedly linger, a cautionary reminder of ambition, betrayal, and the ultimate price of vengeance.

H.P.'s heart ached for this poor woman. Whether

she'd murdered her husband, she was certain Eliza Tumblewood's story hadn't been told. "This is horrible. Truly. It isn't just Misty Cove that railroaded women. It happened everywhere. I'm glad you found it, and now you'll have a good source of material for your project!"

"She didn't do it, Mom. I'm sure. Miss Noseinair thinks so too."

"Well, she's not always—"

"She gave us proof."

Chapter Twelve

HISTORY'S MYSTERIES

"Why didn't Gram tell me?"

"Huh? Gram Gram didn't know anything about Eliza Tumblewood."

"Oh...I, uh...only meant that Gram Gram was the Sweetwater family historian. You'd think she would have a scrapbook somewhere containing this information."

"Oh. Well, Miss Bliss said her mom would know. You heard that part of the conversation, right?"

"Her name is Maddysin, son, not Bliss. That's a made-up identity and, just like her identity, her concern is completely fake."

Dex's face tensed, and any openness he'd displayed disappeared like the sunshine on a stormy day. "Wow. That's exactly what Bliss thought you would say. Way to live down to her expectations, Mother."

Her heart sunk with a thud. "Wait! I didn't mean that. Tell me what 'Bliss' knows about Eliza! When I took a Women's History course, I remember that over half of the women convicted of murder in the nineteenth century didn't commit them."

Her son paused, studying her the way she studied him when he swore he'd cleaned the litter box. "Bliss says she heard stories of a woman in their family who lived a secret life. She's pretty sure it's Eliza. Isn't that dope?"

H.P. nodded with vigor. "So dope! What else did she say?"

Dex shrugged and raised an arm over his head, releasing an offensive smell into the air.

"Tildie and I were looking for anything to prove Eliza's innocence, but there's nothing at the library. That's why Bliss was here; she wanted to know what information we had and how she could help. She's really cool, Mom. You always tell me to give people the benefit of the doubt. Maybe you should follow your own rules?"

"You've got me there."

"She said she had lots of family history stuff in her mom's attic at home," Tildie added. "Dexter and I would have asked for your help, but we understand how busy you are, dealing with the diner and the serial killer. Everybody knows you'll catch the killer before law enforcement."

Tildie could butter toast using only her big brown eyes and a head tilt. Abe Bunce and his fancy degrees were no match for his thirteen-year-old daughter.

"What kind of 'help' is Mad—Maddysin willing to offer?"

On cue, Tildie cleared her throat and tilted her head back, jutting out her chin. "Anything you need. I've got endless resources at my disposal, including an attic full of photos."

She paused, waiting for Dex's nod of approval. Her impression of Maddysin was uncanny.

"I'm not ewe-zed to working with children, so for further contact, please text me. My spa is exclusively for powerful women escaping the confines of the traditional family." Tildie's head regained its normal position and she opened her eyes. "Whatever THAT means," she concluded.

Both Dex and H.P. applauded her fine performance. "You've got a future doing impressions. That is, if the whole president thing doesn't pan out," H.P. said.

The shy teen giggled at their praise before all three noticed headlights in the driveway.

"That'll be my dad. It's chicken Florentine night and he wants to get an early start."

"Bye, Dex! Bye, Ms. Sweetwater!" Tildie waved to them. Her father was waiting patiently in the driveway. He never honked, nor did he knock on the door. Abe Bunce wanted his daughter to learn to be responsible for herself, he said. The child was already thirteen-going-on-thirty. Her father had no reason to be concerned.

"Bye, sweetie! Tell your dad hello from me!" H.P.

turned back to her son and smiled. "Probably time for your shower?" She did her level best to speak without gasping for air, and then she used her parenting super-power and breathed through her mouth while she opened her arms for a hug.

"Mom, I can tell you're breathing through your mouth again," Dex spoke into the back of her head. "You really need to take your allergy meds."

H.P. nodded and sniffed as though that were the problem. "Okay, then. Off to the—"

"Just read what Bliss found. Then I'll shower. I promise."

H.P. shook her head, too tired to engage in another argument. "Hand it to me."

Dex held out a paper just as crumpled as the notes he brought home from his teachers, a week late. "It's just a copy, don't worry," he said, as if reading her thoughts. "From a century after she died. Poor Eliza."

Chapter Thirteen

BLISS-LESS

H.P. slid the copied page over to Dexter's side of the table, next to the bowl of oatmeal now grown cold. She put her chin in her hand and tried not to think about the nightmares that kept her awake all night. Nightmares about a terrible miscarriage of justice involving one of her own relatives. They felt so real.

"Did you read it?"

She smelled the entire can of body spray before she saw him. *Do you want him to smell like a forgotten gym bag instead, Sweetwater? Pick your battles.*

"I did. It's just awful. Do you remember when we talked about the mistreatment of women in history?"

Dex nodded as he hunched over his oatmeal. There was still hope that one healthy bite would pass through his lips today. H.P. resisted the urge to tuck his curly hair behind his ear. Oats in his hair was a small price to pay for the kid actually eating a healthy breakfast.

"That's the point they're making in this article."

She pulled it back and re-read, just to make sure she hadn't missed anything last night when she struggled to keep her eyes open.

A Century of Silence Broken: The Innocence of Eliza Tumblewood Unveiled

Misty Cove Chronicle, September 10, 1920

In a revelation that rewrites a dark chapter of Misty Cove's history, new evidence has emerged, casting light on the innocence of Eliza Tumblewood who was wrongfully executed in 1820 for the murder of her husband, Charles Tumblewood. This case, which has haunted the annals of our town's lore, finds itself at the heart of a dramatic turn of events as meticulous examination of historical documents and advancements in forensic science have exonerated the once-condemned woman.

The Shadow of Doubt Lifted

The tale of Eliza Tumblewood has been a specter of injustice, her story a cautionary tale of the peril in presumptive guilt. Known after her death as "Swingin' Sal"—a misnomer that today's investigation corrects—Eliza's life and death were a testament to the tragedies of legal misjudgment. Her trial, characterized by fervent speculation and insubstantial evidence, has now been scrutinized under the lens of modern investigative techniques, revealing a truth long buried.

H.P. looked up and shook her head. "Where's the rest of the article?"

"That's all Bliss found. She said we'd need to visit Noseinair mansion to find more."

H.P. shuddered involuntarily. "No! You can't!"

Dexter looked taken aback. "Why didn't you know about this, Mom? And why don't you want me to visit the Noseinair mansion?"

"I don't have a good answer. When we were kids, Gram Gram showed us her mother's pearls and her father's pocket watch, but nothing about the generation before." H.P. looked up at the ceiling, wondering how many relatives Gram Gram never told her about. She wasn't ready to tell Dexter about her experience at the mansion either. Maybe when he was older he would understand.

"Mom, don't we owe it to Eliza to find out who the real killer was?"

These days, it was rare to find Dex excited about anything outside of Tildie and the newest video game.

"Okay. I suppose it's a harmless endeavor. But if it interferes with your schoolwork or—"

"Thanks, Mom!"

Dex jumped out of his seat and planted a big wet kiss on her cheek. If she'd been better prepared, she would have thrown her arms open first so as to capture her sweet boy for a few precious moments.

"All I ask of you two is to keep me updated. I don't want to walk in on any more...Bliss."

Chapter Fourteen

BALLZ AND BANDZ

"After feedback from our community, I've decided the Misty Cove Ballz and Bandz will proceed as scheduled. I'll be appointing a special group of local citizens to look out for anything out of the ordinary. I would encourage everyone to get involved and help keep this Misty Cove tradition alive. That being said, the band is open to all suggestions to raise funds. Mrs. Delores Tootwhistle would like to say a few words."

Delores jumped up on the stage in one leap, an act that drew admiration from those gathered.

"She works out," someone behind H.P. muttered. "Those types always need to show off."

"Folks, the funds for extracurriculars were cut drastically this year."

Thanks, Noseinairs.

"Even with sponsorship of the football field, we'll need to raise at least ten thousand dollars to cover all our costs."

This time, a dramatic gasp came from the crowd.

"If you come up with an idea, please work out the cost and any other pertinent details before presenting it to myself or my husband. Thank you."

It was the second proclamation by the mayor in a mere two days. He delivered this second address in the same spot as the first, allowing H.P. to supply free coffee and pastries. Those who wanted more could step inside the diner for a full meal.

H.P. handed the last cup of coffee on her tray to Wilbert Whatshisname. "If you bring your cup into the diner when the speech is over, we'll give you twenty percent off your order."

Wilbert glanced at his coffee and back up at H.P., then shrugged. At least she'd tried. Discounts of any kind from restaurants were as foreign as traffic jams in this town. She zigzagged her way through the crowd and back to the diner door, where Sir Stackworth was wagging his tail, eagerly awaiting a friendly hand on his head.

Dex, while haphazardly caring for his cat, was enthusiastic about daily dog walks. Sometimes Tildie came with him and they wound their way through town, giggling and enjoying each other's company. It was more exercise than Dex got in an entire year at Jefferson Starship Elementary School, where breathing exercises passed for P.E.

H.P. bent down and petted his wiggly behind. "Who's a handsome boy? Do you need to go back to your RV?"

Sir Stackworth's lengthy tongue bounced up and down as he pranced excitedly in a circle.

"We need baked goods for the bake sale, volunteers to work the concession stand, volunteers to line up bands for the parade, and much more," Mayor McCloud continued. "Please contact Delores Toot-whistle for more details. Folks, we have two weeks to prepare our town, so let's all get out, clean up the streets, mow your lawns, and prepare for guests!"

Mayor McCloud stepped down from the podium in two clumsy gallops as local members of the press and busybodies shouted questions. "How can we celebrate when our town has lost so many citizens? It doesn't seem right!"

"Mayor! Mayor! You're avoiding us! Tell us about the investigation! Has anyone collected the reward yet?"

H.P. sighed. "The poor man just lost his wife and he's got the happiness of the entire town resting on his shoulders."

She opened the diner door and unexpectedly found herself face-to-nose with Edna. For a moment, she didn't know what to say. Edna's usual scare tactic was a sneak attack from behind.

"Oops! I'm not used to being greeted at the door, Edna. What's on your mind?"

"We're outta eggs, that's what. Your fancy pants new chef uses twice as many as the last chef did. Better up your order!"

"Edna, do you know anything about our waffle

maker? The one we'd been using had an octagon design, but it appears to be missing. There's another one in it's place, strangely enough."

Edna scratched her cheek with one yellowed nail. "Let me see…a missing waffle maker or a breakfast joint running outta eggs right before a post-pep-talk rush? That's a tough one, H.P."

H.P. let loose an even louder sigh than before. "Okay. I guess you're not interested in the fact that somehow a waffle maker like the one used in the murders has made its way into our kitchen."

She turned—no, flounced—her way into the kitchen knowing full well and good that Edna would follow her. Just like leaving a trail of breadcrumbs, or in Edna's case, a trail of white chocolate-covered prunes. Her favorite snack.

"How's that even possible? They don't make those things anymore. Least, that's what I heard in my poker group last night."

"Your poker group is comprised of experts on Wacky Winkie Waffle Makers?"

Frankie looked up from a pot of grits she was stirring. Glancing from Edna's face to H.P.'s, she must've realized there was a problem. She pulled one earbud out of her ear. "Did someone complain about the Polenta Your Poach? I knew I should have left the bacon out!"

Frankie banged a palm on the oven handle. It was uncharacteristic of her to show any emotion other than joy.

"No, it's nothing like that. Any moment now, the crowd will hit. I was just asking Edna about our usual waffle maker. Have you thought more about it? Or how we may have come to be in possession of a potential murder weapon?"

Frankie shook her head. "Sorry. I just keep to my lane. You know why, ma'am."

Edna lifted an eyebrow, clearly upset she was out of the loop.

"Yes, I do, and rest assured, things you told me in confidence will stay that way."

Edna huffed and stomped her orthopedic shoes back to the front of the diner. Far too much stomping from them both for this time of the morning.

"Sir Stackworth is waiting patiently by the front door."

Frankie's face fell. "Shoot. My poor guy. I forgot all about him this morning what with making extra everything for the rush. I can't leave my polenta."

"I'm going to buy more eggs. Do you want me to put him in your RV on the way?"

"Would you?"

Frankie didn't wait for H.P.'s answer. She leaned backward, still stirring the large pot with one hand while digging the keys out of her jacket pocket with the other. It was a true feat of acrobatics to behold.

"Here ya go. And could you make sure there's water in his bowl? He gets awful thirsty after his walks."

"I will."

The diner filled quickly. CeCe tied her apron behind her back and smoothed her hair.

"Thanks for coming in today, CeCe! I'll be back just as soon as I get more eggs."

CeCe gave a thumbs-up as H.P. exited the diner. Sir Stackworth knew the way to his home and yanked so hard on his leash, he almost made her trip.

"You're strong for such a little guy," she mused. He hopped up the wrought iron steps and bounced, barking up and down.

H.P. unlocked the door and went inside. The only RVs she'd been in were the fancy ones at the county fair. Gram Gram made the grandkids go through face and hands inspection before they could get in line.

"Someday, I'm going to have one of these!" each of the cousins said from year-to-year.

Frankie's RV was every bit the fancy setup. There was a couch, a tiny dining table, a king-sized bed, and a full-sized shower. After she filled Sir Stackworth's water bowl, she paused one more moment to look around. Nothing was out of place. Instead of slipping her son cash, Frankie should have been teaching him about picking up after himself.

She stepped backward, dumping the bowl of water all over the beautiful gray-tiled floor.

"Shoot!" She rushed to the sink and retrieved a towel. As she cleaned up her mess, something shiny caught her eye.

Chapter Fifteen

DETECTIVE GWENNIE

"I don't feel great about this. Evidence belongs in the hands of the police chief, not mine."

Gwen adjusted her turquoise sweater and scrunched up her adorable little nose. "I mean, what are you hoping to find? Frankie has a waffle maker in her RV. So what? Lots of people keep them at home."

H.P. turned it over and pointed to the tag on the bottom. "If lost, please return to Honeypie Sweetwater, Honeypie Diner."

"Your grandmother put these on everything?"

H.P. nodded. "She was convinced that everyone was inherently good."

"That doesn't make sense. If she thought everyone was good, why would she need to label her appliances?"

"Because she occasionally loaned things out for fundraisers. A blender for the annual Blend and Bend, the exercise marathon to raise money for the gymnastics team; sheet pans for Sheet Cakes for Sweet Rakes, the fundraiser to purchase new rakes for the staff at the middle school. That sort of thing. Gram thought that if something had her label on it, her property would be returned."

Gwen pulled out a magnifying glass and examined the waffle maker closely. "What recipe do you use in your diner for waffles? Like, what are the ingredients?"

"Huh? I didn't bring this here for a waffle party."

"Please humor me."

Being the owner and not the chef distanced H.P. from recipes of any kind. Dex normally turned up his nose when she attempted to make a dish she'd prepared at various restaurants, so H.P. always kept it simple at home. "Let's see... eggs, flour, sugar..."

"What about yeast?"

A smile spread across her face. "You're good! Yes, Gram's old recipe DOES contain yeast! It's not the common way to make them, but she always got rave reviews."

"I can tell you definitively that this waffle maker was NOT used in the commission of a crime, specifically the murders of Barry D'Live, Pearlie Gates, and Windy McCloud."

"How can you be so confident, Gwennie? Did you see those little bumps on the side? They look like—"

"It's not human tissue, friend. It's yeast that's begun to grow. I sent the waffles to the state crime lab in Seattle. They emailed me an ingredient list that didn't include yeast. Whoever used this last didn't clean it well. But that's not a crime. It IS peculiar she would hide your waffle maker. Unless Frankie was worried YOU were the murderer and she was protecting you!"

"As offended as I am by that idea, I guess it's good she tried protecting me. Isn't it? Now I'm not so sure."

Did Frankie really think she was capable of such a heinous crime? H.P. and Dex had been nothing but kind to her. "Why would she continue working for me if she thinks I'm a killer? Does that make sense, Gwennie?"

Gwen shook her head. "Guess I don't know how to pick friends after all."

"Hey!" H.P. protested, playfully hitting her friend in the arm.

"All kidding aside, friendie, I am curious. She's never questioned you about the murders?"

"Not once. I doubt she knows much about the community, given she spends the day with her earbuds in." H.P. paced back and forth. "Yes, she DOES spend all day with earbuds in... Frankie isn't interested in anyone, but she insists she's being chased around the country. The fact that she's not keeping an eye on anyone or anything is suspicious."

The more she paced, the more things started to come together.

"This silly Breakfast Mafia story never made any

sense. It's the police who are after her, probably for the murder of her parents. There's a Breakfast Mafia, all right, and her name is Frankie the serial killer!"

"There's only one way we're going to get answers."

Gwen picked up her phone and dialed. "Frankie? It's me, Gwen."

Chapter Sixteen

FLAPJACK SCRAMBLE

"It's your turn to bring refreshments to poker night." Gwen turned to H.P. and gave her a thumbs-up. While her forensic skills were second to none, her improvisation needed work.

"Oh, sure! How could I forget anything involving food? You'd probably never forgive me if I brought something from the Zoom Thru Mart, right?"

Frankie chuckled in a deep, husky voice H.P. had come to find comforting.

When Gwen didn't respond, Frankie continued, "I make a mean mini pigs-in-a-blanket."

"Great! That's great. Um... while I have you on the phone, I had a few questions for you. The other morning when I was jogging, I saw Dexter Sweetwater walking your dog."

"Yeah, ain't that a kick? Those two are like toast and jam. If I were the jealous type, I might think he was trying to get my boy to take to him. But I don't do jealousy or juicy burgers. Not my style. So, you saw them out walking?"

It was a feeling of helplessness mixed with a big dose of anxiety that caused H.P. to pace around the tropical-themed office of The Final Fold.

"Yeah, I did," Gwen replied. "But they weren't the only ones on the street."

"Oh?" Frankie's voice wavered. "Somebody you recognized?"

"No, it wasn't anybody local. It was a black SUV with the windows tinted. I jotted down the license plate: GOTBM?"

"No! No, no, no! This is bad, Gwen, real bad. You're positive that's what the plate said?"

Gwen grabbed H.P.'s arm as she rounded the desk. "I just made that up!" she mouthed.

"Is that someone you know? From Colorado?"

"Maybe. This changes everything." Frankie could be heard sighing and alternately smacking her lips. "I thought I was safe, but I was just fooling myself. I'd never forgive myself if they hurt that kid. Let the boss lady know how much I appreciated her hospitality, would you? It's been nice getting to know the folks here in Misty Cove."

"Why do you have to leave, Frankie? And who is it you're running from?"

"The less you know, the better, Gwen. See ya 'round."

Gwen hung up and glanced sheepishly at H.P.

"You've just cost me a chef," H.P. said with solemnity. "And we're no closer to finding the real killer."

"I probably should have mentioned this earlier, but during our weekly poker game, Irma Doubledeck raved about Frankie's volunteerism. She told us that Frankie goes to the nursing home on Wednesday evenings and plays the ukulele for the residents while she sings. She's got a real nice baritone voice." Gwen hit herself in the forehead with her palm. "Dumb Gwen! Dumb Gwen!"

H.P. reached out and intercepted Gwen's arm. "You're not to blame for that, Gwennie. Killers are usually the last people you'd suspect. Don't you remember last year when they caught that prolific killer up near Seattle?"

"I do! I was called in to help examine the forensics before the case was turned over to the F.B.I. I'm not a fan of those know-it-alls!"

"What I read in the paper was that Celia Slashmont was a checker at Grumpy's Market by day and a serial killer by night. She had a weird aversion to Soggy Flakes Cereal and kept track of the unsuspecting people who purchased boxes during her shifts. She snuck into their homes at night and—"

"No, H.P., this isn't the same!" Gwen insisted. "You need to think outside the cereal box. Celia had a podcast called *Soggy Flakes are Satanic* which pretty much gave her away. Our killer hasn't made a misstep yet. Who's been acting strangely in Misty Cove lately?"

They looked at each other and chorused in unison, "The mayor!"

"He's been acting so weird since his wife died. But would he actually whack her?" H.P. asked, immediately sure of the answer. In her time back home in Misty Cove, she found that most everyone was a bit peculiar.

"Not only his wife, but the other victims as well. We need to find a connection between them and fast, before it happens again!" A three-tone bell rang out from the speaker above H.P.'s head. "Shoot! I forgot to turn the sign. Let me get rid of them while you figure out what happens next."

"The first order of business is to hightail it over to the RV and do everything in our power to convince Frankie to stay!"

Chapter Seventeen

BLOWN AWAY

They hopped into Gwen's car and drove three blocks. It would have been a ridiculous waste of gas on any other day, but in addition to their urgency, the weather was atrocious. The wind shoved sand down the street in thick waves. No one was on the sidewalk, nor were there any other cars out and about. During this kind of weather, Covians stayed home if possible.

As soon as they reached the parking lot of Honeypie Diner, where Frankie's RV sat in the most remote corner, H.P. opened the passenger door.

"No! You have to stay here or she'll know we were working together."

Gwen had a point.

"Okay, but if she doesn't agree to stay, give me a wave and I'll come and confess everything to her."

Although Gwen instructed her to slide down in the seat so she wasn't visible, H.P. couldn't help herself. Her curiosity got the better of her.

She watched as Gwen stood on the RV's top step and gestured wildly. The longer she sat, the worse she felt. Frankie was a good person. But why did she insist on making waffles, especially when H.P. specifically told her not to? And how did a suspicious waffle maker find its way onto her shelf?

Feeling helpless, H.P. pulled out her phone. "I can't just sit here and do nothing," she murmured.

"Mayor McCloud? H.P. Sweetwater. I was wondering if I could come over and speak with you about something. If you're busy with city business, I'll—"

"Not at all. Meet me at the station in fifteen minutes."

As Gwen opened the door, a gust of wind jerked it wider, sending her tiny body airborne for a moment. When it stopped, Gwen sat down in the car, calmly smoothed her hair, and closed the door.

"See you soon, Mayor!"

H.P. stared expectantly at Gwen. "Well? Don't keep me in suspense. Do I need to look for a new chef, on top of finding a murderer and planning a fundraiser?"

"Not to worry, best buddy." Gwen patted H.P.'s leg. "Everything is just fine. She'll be at work tomorrow, just like nothing happened."

"How did you manage that?"

Gwen shrugged with indifference. "It's a small town. Weird things happen all the time."

"You'll have to do better than that!" H.P. insisted.

"Tell me what you said, so the next time she decides to confess, I'll have a better idea of what to say."

"I just told her that I was taking a walk after doing an autopsy. The deceased had high levels of Zephyr Zing in his system, and it left me a little loopy. I confused the letters on the automobile, and it actually spelled out, "GALBM.""

"And what does that spell?"

"Gloria Alice Lakeside Buys Milk. You know, the Lakeside Dairy? She's well known in the dairy circles."

H.P. stared at her in disbelief. "And she bought that?"

"Hook, line, and milk carton." Gwen flashed a satisfied smile. "She's coming in a little late tomorrow, since she's now unpacking what she started packing when she thought she had to leave in a hurry."

"Well. That's good news!" H.P. smiled momentarily before frowning. "But it also leaves us back where we started."

"Who were you talking to when I sat down?" Gwen asked.

"Mayor McCloud. Could you drive me over to his office?"

"Sure thing. I'll stop at the grocery store while you're there. I've been needing more greens for my experiment. I'm trying to create an explosive substance for my horror movie miniatures town."

"You'll have to show me when you finish. And warn me if I need to wear an old apron to witness the explosion."

They pulled up in front of the mayor's office. Both women sat in the car until the gust was finished. If they darted in between gusts of wind, they might avoid swallowing half of Misty Cove Beach.

The whining of relentless wind came to a temporary halt. "Ready?" H.P. asked. Gwen nodded.

They threw their doors open at the same time, scampering in opposite directions.

Chapter Eighteen

MCCLOUDY WITH A CHANCE OF MCRAIN

The mayor grinned as he invited H.P. into his office. Not exactly the mood she was expecting, but one he displayed with regularity since his wife's death.

When she was seated, he asked, "What can I do for a lovely lady on a not-so-lovely day?"

"I'm so sorry to disturb you, but Gwen and I are concerned about the waffle killer. We're sure we're not the only ones. What impact do you think this could have on our businesses if the killer isn't caught?"

His expression never changed. "You don't need to worry, H.P. I said I'd keep the community safe, and Mayor Thunder McCloud always keeps his word."

She cleared her throat and directed her gaze behind him, where multiple plaques decorated the wall. The most recent read: "Best Small Town Mayor in Washington State, 2019."

"We've been curious about that too. Why isn't the police department taking the lead? No offense, but don't they have more experience dealing with violent crimes?"

For the first time today, his demeanor changed. A storm was brewing on his pale face, and just the sight of it gave H.P. the chills.

"Now, just what are you implying, H.P.? I've got a college degree in criminal justice, and I've taken several online courses over the years. I can show you my certificates if you'd feel better seeing them." He stared hard as she squirmed in her seat. If he used this tactic to interrogate criminals, those awards made sense.

"That's okay. Just a question we were wondering about." She had to think of a way to diffuse this situation fast. "I can only imagine how difficult it is to conduct an investigation, no matter what your qualifications, when one of the victims is your wife."

He leaned forward and clasped his hands in front of him. "I get the feeling you're going somewhere with this. I've got an appointment with Madcap Motors about a new town vehicle. Thought I'd get my picture on the side. Could you cut to the chase?"

She nodded. What exactly *was* the chase?

"Our... MY concern is that the killer is still out there and we haven't received any updates. You've done a great job keeping the city running, but we have no idea how the investigation is going."

"It just so happens that I drafted a letter that will go out to all business owners tomorrow morning. Would you like to see it?"

She nodded with uncertainty. This wasn't the

reason she came, but one thing Honeypie Chiffon Sweetwater was not was bold.

Mayor McCloud whistled as he dug through a pile of papers on his desk. "You know, Windy adored you. She thought you were as cute as a button. Every time she jogged by your diner, she'd tell me—oh, here we go." He slid a crisp page in front of her.

Dear Concerned Business Owners:

> *The recent deaths in our city are unsettling. I wanted to take a moment to assure you that everything is being done to keep Misty Covians safe.*
> *Below are a few examples:*

1. A local group of knitters, the Knit Wits, have volunteered their services to keep the community safe. The Knit-Wit Watch, a senior citizen neighborhood watch program, will patrol our streets every evening armed with knitting needles to keep an eye out.

2. Whistle While You Work, the local Whistle Band, has donated a whistle for every citizen. They'll offer a training workshop on their use in case of sighting the killer.

3. Grated Expectations, the local culinary school, will offer free knife sharpening on Saturdays. Keep your families safe and your knives sharp!

I firmly believe, with the help of every citizen, we will keep our city safe!
Sincerely,
Your Small Town Mayor of the Year,
Thunder McCloud

H.P. set the page down, searching his face for signs this was a joke.

"Isn't it something, the way everyone comes together in a time like this?" He crossed his arms and leaned back in his leather chair, causing it to groan in protest.

Oh no. Mayor McCloud was dead serious. "Yes, that's a small town for you, Mayor—always ready to help each other." She reached her arm out straight before bringing it in front of her face. It was a masterful performance, if she did say so herself. "I need to get back to the diner." H.P. stood to leave but paused before she opened the door. "Mayor, what was it your wife said about me?"

"Huh?"

"You said she liked me, and..." H.P. felt a little silly asking, but she'd run out of ideas.

"Yes! Windy said you were going to make waves in this town."

Chapter Nineteen

ASKING FOR HANDOUTS

"I'd like to assert my objections to this type of fundraiser."

Delores Tootwhistle pursed her very large lips into a very tight circle. "We do just fine with our bake sale and the t-shirts with band instruments on them."

"I'm not a fan myself," H.P. agreed. "I guess we're outnumbered though."

Of all the suggestions for Ballz and Bandz fundraisers, the only one that included a twenty-page, detailed report denoting exactly how much would need to be donated, how much would be earned, and how much time was needed to set up was the one Tildie and Dex submitted.

Supper and Séance would be a huge event with two levels of tickets. The general ticket holders would spend their evening in a large tent with a variety of entertainment. Those who paid for the more expensive tickets would sit in a smaller, more intimate setting.

Someone would volunteer their services as a psychic medium and someone else would provide the special effects.

They found an equipment rental place that agreed to give them a large tent for the evening, free of charge. Ed's Eats and Meats generously donated fifty pounds of beef and burger buns.

All this was accomplished before they made their parents aware of their plan.

Initially, H.P. had been against a controversial evening where those from the other world would be summoned, whether or not on purpose. When she realized how hard the kids worked, however, it was hard to say no. Even better, it was the perfect opportunity to trap the mayor.

Dex and Tildie, well, mostly Tildie, came up with a cost breakdown for the items that weren't purchased. "How should we raise the money, Ms. Sweetwater?"

"Let me handle that."

The paper products were donated by H.P.'s distributor and the drinks by Gwen. The only thing left was decorations. If she were being honest with herself, H.P. had an ulterior motive for visiting the law firm of Fulla, Bunce and Vinegar.

Abe Bunce, Tildie's not-so-unattractive father, ushered H.P. into his office.

"Haven't seen you in ages, H.P. What's new?"

He moved around his desk and sat with his hands clasped in front of him. A petite man with dark curly hair, he smiled with genuine kindness. His skin was a smooth, light caramel, complementing his striking features and expressive brown eyes. Today, he wore cologne, a mix of cardamom and cedarwood with a luscious burst of citrus. Was this how he softened the blow when he presented his clients with his bill? Well she, for one, would empty her savings account just to drink in his scent a little longer.

"We...um...need a donation for the fundraiser."

Abe raised one stupidly attractive dark brow. "Fundraiser?"

"Oh, didn't Tildie tell you about Supper and Séance?"

It was at this unfortunate moment that H.P. remembered Tildie's admonition: "Don't tell my father, okay, Ms. Sweetwater? He's working on a big case and I don't want to burden him."

"Where's my head?" H.P. slapped her forehead. "What I meant to say is that I'm collecting money for the band day. Mayor McCloud wants to hire extra security and it's not in the budget—"

Abe held up a hand, a sly smile playing on his lips.

"So, you're panhandling for the mayor now?" Abe leaned back in his office chair, a playful twinkle in his eye. H.P. felt her cheeks flush as she scrambled to recover from her slip-up.

"Well, not exactly," she stammered, mentally kicking herself. "I just thought the law firm might want to contribute to keeping the town safe during such a big event."

Abe regarded her with a knowing look then broke

into a wide grin. "You're a terrible liar, H.P., but I'll see what I can do."

Relief flooded through her as she quickly named a reasonable amount for the decorations. Abe reached into his desk drawer and pulled out a wad of cash, counting out the exact sum she asked for.

"Just promise me one thing," he said, gazing at her intently. "Be gentle to this community, with whatever it is you're planning. Misty Cove has seen more than its share of drama lately, and people are quick to anger. Let's make this an uneventful event, if you get my drift."

With the funds secured for the decorations, H.P. threw herself into preparing for the fundraiser. It was easier than thinking about a murderer on the loose and all the children who would be in Misty Cove for the band day.

She visited the walk-in after hours to make sure they were set for the performance.

"You know I'd do anything for the kids," Gram Gram said enthusiastically. She floated back and forth, her image a shimmering silver. "Can I make up my own persona, or do you have a script? If so, I'll need a few hours to memorize it."

H.P. cleared her throat. "Gram Gram, I was hoping you would pretend you were Eliza Tumble-wood for the evening."

She knew that her grandmother would be offended that she was changing the story of someone who'd passed. It was one point on which Gram Gram always stayed firm. *Don't change the past. These people are forever attached to their stories and we don't want to upset them.*

"The kids have been searching the library genealogy section every afternoon in hopes of finding out what really happened to Charles Tumblewood. There's next to nothing written about Eliza that wasn't heavily editorialized. And Mad has given the kids absolutely zero information. No surprise there."

"And you want this information before Maddysin finds it and rubs your nose in it, I presume?"

"You presume right. If she's even actively looking. I can't stand the thought of her throwing this in my face, as petty as that sounds."

Gram Gram floated in thought for a moment, her silver form flickering as if caught in a current. Finally, she nodded decisively. "Very well, darling. I shall become Eliza Tumblewood for the fundraiser. You know, I was quite the thespian in my day. I'll bring the house down. Let us give these children the closure they seek, and perhaps shed some light on the shadows that linger over our town."

"There's one more thing, Gram Gram. It's about catching the person who killed your friend, Pearlie Gates."

"I'm listening."

"Well, I thought... I thought..." H.P. had been an actual adult for two-and-a-half decades, yet she still found it hard to ask her grandmother for favors.

"Spit it out, H.P. There are ice cream festivals to

enjoy and Mr. Beethoven promised he'd breakdance, whatever that means."

"I want to scare the mayor into confessing he's the killer. Do you think... do you think..."

"Spit it out, dear!"

"Well, I'd like you to focus on him and make him squirm."

As Gram Gram laughed, silver sparkles danced from her mouth. "This will be a delight!"

"I have an old photo of Eliza Tumblewood from an article the kids found." She held it up so Gram Gram could see it clearly.

"Don't need my readers up here, but my sight isn't perfect like I thought it would be." Gram Gram sighed. "The afterlife still needs some tweaks. We've got a committee working on it, but you know how unmotivated Hank can be."

"Hank?"

"The eighth. Henry, that is. He begged and begged to be on the committee and, when he was chosen, he tried getting everyone else to do his work." Gram Gram shook her head. "I hate to typecast men, but this one is a lazy bugger."

"Can you pull this off? Her face, her clothing, and everything else that made Eliza the talk of the town?"

"She's about three cups her mother and one cup my grandfather. I'd know her anywhere. She's a relative, Hun Bun. We all carry some of her inside us. It will require some tricks and magic, but I've got help. I do need to warn you, though, it's going to take all the energy I have to appear outside of this walk-in. I won't have the stamina to become two separate beings. Is Eliza your choice?"

H.P. remembered the first time she'd encountered Gram Gram's ghost. It was in Dex's bedroom in San Francisco.

"I know what you're thinking; you've seen me out and about before, right?"

H.P. nodded. "Clear as day, Gram."

"I bet you didn't count the days in between our meetings. This haunting business is a real energy Frankendoodle."

This particular butchering of a popular saying would require a few minutes to ponder. After thinking it through, H.P. grinned. "Do you mean an energy vampire, Gram? And if so, I get it."

"I can probably manage three minutes. That's in costume and voice. Will that be enough?"

"More than enough. I'll make sure I've got all the questions to you ahead of time, so that you can answer quickly." H.P. felt a lump forming in her throat. "This won't hurt you, will it? No fundraiser is worth that. I would be so sad if I didn't get to see you again!"

Tears formed in her eyes, and she was instantly transported back in time, to the fateful day she'd learned of Gram Gram's death. The floor disappeared underneath her, and with that, her legs disappeared too. She was on her knees, sobbing, and she didn't know how she got there.

"You know what? Gwen is a master of tricks. We

don't need you at all, Gram Gram. She's got a real spectacle planned."

The glowing light around Gram turned a dark blue, the same color as the sky before a big storm. "You're as see-through as a glass ornament, child. Of course I'll be there, and I'll be just fine after a few days. It'll take more 'n a garden variety haunting to get rid of your old Gram."

Chapter Twenty

FOOD AND FRIGHTS

As the night of Supper and Séance approached, Misty
Cove buzzed with anticipation. Anyone could buy a
twenty-dollar ticket, which included supper and
Psychic Psarina, who would wander through the room
and stop at the tables where she felt the spirit connection while the audience ate dessert. If the patron
wanted a seat in a more intimate setting, where Guide
Goddess Gwyneth would summon spirits to speak, it
would set them back a hundred dollars.

H.P. could've announced that she'd acquired
enough with one check to fund the entire event.
However, doing so would require she publicly
acknowledge Maddysin as the generous benefactor.
"Then how would the kids learn about working
together for a common goal?" she reasoned.

H.P. was at first doubtful that anyone would buy a
ticket at that exorbitant price. But the amount of
disposable income and the comparable amount of

ghostly curiosity proved her wrong. The tickets sold out in two hours.

"Mad?"

H.P. knocked on an over-sized door and, when there was no response, she let herself in. Each and every time she'd been in this office, which put any palace to shame, she marveled at the detail she observed.

Spacious, with high, gold-accented ceilings, her office featured a grand chandelier dangling over a desk the size of H.P.'s first car. The walls were lined with rich, dark wood paneling, interspersed with plush velvet drapes in deep burgundy, framing tall, arched windows that offered a panoramic view of the lush gardens outside. It was, in a word, ridiculous.

To one side of the room, a cozy fireplace crackled with a welcoming fire, surrounded by a cluster of plush armchairs and a velvet sofa, creating an intimate setting for relaxed discussions or quiet reflection. The area was accented with soft Persian rugs and a delicate tea service set on a low antique table, ready to serve guests.

Personal photographs, awards—most of which Maddysin admitted she'd commissioned herself—and tokens of appreciation were on display.

H.P. hadn't noticed before, but the office also featured a small private balcony adorned with flow-ering plants. H.P. opened the sliding door and stepped outside to admire the view. The ocean, unseen from any other buildings within the city limits, was on grand display. Maddysin had two very expensive-looking lounge chairs placed so this very undeserving woman could gaze at nature's gifts to her heart's content.

It had been forever since H.P. had allowed herself the simple pleasure of relaxing to the sound of ocean waves. She closed her eyes, remembering their monthly picnics as a child.

Gram Gram would assign each grandchild la task for the morning. There was no sleeping in on beach day, not that anyone would have wanted to.

The night before, after everyone had gone to bed, Gram Gram would post the chore chart for the next day. Packing the trunk with towels and toys was the most coveted job, but making a lunch of whatever was left over from the diner made someone like H.P. excited. She could be as creative as she wanted and nobody could complain. If they did, they weren't invited the following month.

Sensing someone behind her, she turned to find a wild-eyed Maddysin holding an expensive desk lamp above her head.

"Sweetwater?" she said in the disappointed tone H.P. had come to expect. Maddysin dropped the lamp and sneered. "How did YOU get out here?"

"You sound disappointed. Were you hoping to clobber someone else?"

"No, it's...someone has been following me. Last night, they tried running me off the road, but I have enough ex-boyfriends to know how to drive defensively."

"Are you admitting to murder?" H.P. couldn't believe her ears.

Maddysin clucked with disapproval. "No, fool. I only meant that when I knew they were with another woman, I followed them until they were out in the country, where I could run them into a ditch."

"Oh. Well that's so much better." H.P.'s voice dripped with sarcasm. "Who do you think is following you?"

"Unfortunately, there were no license plates on the car. Seemed like someone under thirty, as best I could tell. A guy."

Maddysin had been downright cordial for three minutes. Just as H.P. opened her mouth to compliment her high school enemy, Maddysin snapped, "Anyway, you should never have been able to get into my office. Who's losing their job today? Give me names!"

"I've learned all your tricks, Mad. I told your staff you'd set up a meeting with me that none of them knew about. When they asked what it was regarding, I told them—"

Maddysin gasped. "You didn't!"

The moment was too delicious to waste. When she'd watched Maddysin writhe in discomfort long enough, she said, "I didn't say anything about our common ancestor, if that's what's got your knickers twisted." H.P. leaned against the door frame and grinned.

Maddysin's shoulders sagged with relief. "Oh,

good. I can't have my staff thinking I have riff raff in my background. They'd never respect me again!"

They don't respect you now, H.P. thought. "I told them we're meeting about your donations for the band festival."

"I didn't agree to any donations." Maddysin sniffed. "You can see yourself out."

"That's a darn shame, Mad. We're hosting a séance, and the guest of honor, if she shows, will be good old Eliza herself."

Maddysin's permanently surprised expression somehow modified itself to shock. "What? You can't be serious."

"Dead serious. Gwen from the dry cleaners has done quite a bit of studying up on the art of coaxing ghosts into the limelight, and, you know Gwen. She rarely fails."

"So, you're going to make a spectacle, as you always do, of the poor woman who was wrongfully convicted of murder. I'd always pegged you as a do-gooder. This sounds more like you want to exploit her for your own purposes. Pret-ty selfish, if you ask me." Maddysin sat down at her desk and shuffled papers from one neat pile as her face became blotchy.

"This isn't... I'm not..."

"Can't think of the right lie? Poor dear."

She opened her desk drawer and pulled out a gold paperclip, attaching it to her stack of papers. Completely staged, for sure. She'd probably have some poor schmuck come in later and put everything back.

Someone who made minimum wage and had to park in the grade-school parking lot next door, where her car was routinely covered in finger paint.

"You've got me there. The band day is all about benefiting me." H.P. reached into the pocket of her smock and pulled out two tickets. "But if you have a real interest in Eliza and her story, you might consider coming. Keep an open mind, and, well, you never know. Your spa's sponsorship would make great PR, Mad."

Without looking up from her important paperclipping work, Maddysin opened a drawer and pulled out a large checkbook. "Who do I make this out to? And if you say, to you, I will flat-out refuse."

"Boog R. Noseinair Fighting Tissues Band, of course! Geesh, what kind of a criminal do you take me for?"

Her fake outrage went unnoticed.

"Here." Maddysin slid the check across the desk. "And I'm not giving a penny more, so don't ask. I've given to all my usual charitable organizations already this year, and I'm not about to break the bank for a séance."

H.P. picked up the check and slipped it into her purse. "Well, thanks for your generosity, Mad. Really. It's so touching."

Maddysin picked up her phone and pressed a button. "Giselle? I've got an unwelcome guest who needs to leave pronto. Would you mind coming in and escorting her off the property?"

"No need for that, Giselle!" H.P. called out.

She opened the door and walked past Giselle's desk and into the lobby. She didn't stop until she reached her car. Once inside, H.P. pulled the check out of her pocket, bracing for a humiliatingly low sum.

Instead, her jaw almost hit her steering wheel. The check, with nothing in the "to" line, was made out for $25,000!

Chapter Twenty-One

ETERNALLY EERIE

A fitting layer of fog curled around the edges of Misty Cove, adding to the eerie atmosphere.

The pathway leading to the large, green space in front of Honeypie Diner was lined with soft, twinkling lights interspersed with gentle fog machines hidden amongst the foliage. Thanks to Maddysin's generous donation (that H.P. decided was a private matter, done without ceremony), they were able to make the event a real spectacle.

CeCe Scone and her high school art class designed an impressive welcome sign for all those who entered the parking lot. The iconic Honeypie Diner sign, the same red-and-black sign that had been there since Gram Gram bought the diner, was temporarily adorned with vintage-style lettering proclaiming the "Séance and Supper" event, with motifs of musical notes and ghostly silhouettes cleverly blending the themes of music and the supernatural.

Two large tents covered the diner's entire front lawn. Inside the largest tent, a warm glow of candlelit tables, each featuring a centerpiece of antique séance tools—crystal balls, tarot cards, and Ouija boards—stirred the imagination.

The high school jazz band, the Snot Rockets, were seated off to the side. Wearing white dinner jackets, they played all fourteen pieces they'd learned throughout the year. When they reached the end, they turned over their music and started again.

H.P. used the donated meat to create a buffet-style dinner. Spectral Spaghetti, Poltergeist Pancakes, and Mystic Milkshakes were a few of the dishes. The scent of sizzling burgers mixed with incense created a heady blend that made H.P.'s head spin.

A special selection of non-alcoholic "ectoplasmic" drinks was also introduced, featuring swirling colors and served in beakers and flasks, adding a playful nod to the potion-like beverages of a bygone era.

A souvenir booth in the corner sold custom-designed "Séance and Supper" t-shirts, glow-in-the-dark pins featuring musical and mystical motifs, and copies of the evening's menu as a keepsake. It was an impressive evening, pulled together in a mere two weeks' time.

"H.P., I must admit, I had my doubts when I heard you were putting on a say-ants. Don't believe in that kind of thing. But now that I understand what you were getting at, it's darned impressive."

It was hard to believe the mayor was skeptical,

given his enthusiastic embrace of his role as "Master of Scaremonies." He wore a purple velvet cape and dark eyeliner. Someone had loaned him a swami hat, similar in style to a crescent roll worn on the head.

"Thank you, sir. As soon as everyone has eaten, I'll signal you to instruct the premium ticket holders to exit the large tent and join us in the Gold Tent."

"Can't wait, as long as you don't contact my dearly departed wife. She'd be upset to see all these carbs on my plate!" He nudged her and winked, making H.P. extremely uncomfortable.

What an odd reaction to his wife's recent passing, not that it surprised her.

Tables were adorned with flickering candles and black cloths, casting strange shadows across the room.

As guests arrived, H.P. stood off to the side, admiring the work of the kids and their parents. It really was quite stunning.

"Mom, I wish you would've let me and Tildie set up the special effects. You know," he nudged her, "ghosts need a lot of help."

"Ms. Sweetwater," Tildie added kindly. "No offense, but people from our generation know more about electronics than people like you and my dad."

It was the first time Tildie had ever said something that offended her. But she was a sweet girl who probably didn't have any idea that her words cut deep.

"No offense, sweetie, but people my age put computers in watches. I think we're all very capable."

"Oh!" Tildie brought her delicate hand up to her mouth. "I never thought of it that way! I'm so sorry!"

Before H.P. could respond, she felt a tug on her sleeve. "Can I see you somewhere private?" Gwen asked.

They moved to the far corner of the tent, where guests who'd misunderstood the "dress for a spooky séance" recommendation to mean "zombie attire only" waited in line for a Boo Burger and Freakout Fries.

"I think everything is set," Gwen began in a low voice. "I've put the effects on a timer so we can enjoy several at the same time. But I'm still not sure I understand. Are we making a show of pretending to put on a séance, or is this the real deal?"

H.P. glanced around, pleased to see people laughing and enjoying themselves. No one was paying attention to them.

"I want to shock the pants off this town, especially the mayor. I want them hurrying home to tell their neighbors what they missed! If that doesn't make Mr. McCloud confess, nothing will."

Gwen chuckled. "Okay then. I can manage that. Let's ask the guests to migrate over to the other tent in half an hour."

H.P. glanced at her watch. "Seven p.m. on the dot. When we're done, the high school culinary class will bring out three dessert choices: Spectral Sponge Cake, Phantom Phudgecake, or Mystic Macaroons, followed by Creeped Out Coffee."

All ticket holders dined in the same tent. When

they finished their main courses, those in the more affordable main tent were treated to performances by the high school swing choir, The Salty Sinuses, Doby's Dandy Dobermans (a dog act in which Doby asked a question and his dogs found the audience members possessing the correct answer), and a group reading by local psychic, Mistic Mindy.

At the entertainment portion of the evening, the mayor relinquished his Master of Scaremonies position to one of his deputies. It was of utmost importance that H.P. held him to his word.

Patrons with a silver keepsake wristband were allowed into the second tent, where a rectangular table with name cards awaited them. H.P. rented plush, high-backed chairs, like the ones she'd seen in movie séances. What the heck. It was Maddysin's dime, not hers.

The air was thick with the scent of sage and lavender, hinting at the cleansing rituals Gwen performed earlier. She'd also strategically placed mirrors around the tent, angled to catch fleeting glimpses of shadows, enhancing the eerie atmosphere.

To make the séance more convincing, Gwen planned to incorporate a mix of mechanical and technological tricks. Hidden speakers in the tent braces played soft, barely audible whispers and the occasional soft thud, as if someone unseen was moving inside the room. A projector, cleverly concealed behind a curtain, was there for backup in case Gram Gram backed out. It was ready to cast ghostly images onto a thin veil of smoke released discreetly from beneath the table.

Gwen had also prepared a small device that, when triggered, made the table vibrate slightly, simulating the touch of the otherworldly.

"Please find your name cards and await further instructions!" Gwen said solemnly as the guests filed in. Her dedication to her role was admirable. Maybe she, like Gram Gram, had missed her calling.

It was exactly 7:15 when H.P. unlocked the diner and hurried to the walk-in. "We're ready, Gram Gram! Break a leg!"

H.P. didn't wait for a response, instead choosing to take one last pass through the big tent, ensuring those who paid for the extra performance were all in attendance.

"Why did the mayor refuse to play hide and seek with the city council? Because good luck hiding when everyone insists on making a motion!"

There was a polite murmur of claps.

"Mayor McCloud, we're ready for you!" H.P. said in a firm voice. He turned, surprised by her presence. "Oh, is it over? Already?"

Shoving aside feelings of guilt, H.P. was almost giddy about what was about to transpire. Mayor McCloud removed his purple swami hat and handed it to his deputy before following H.P. into the other tent.

Once he was seated, she nodded to Gwen.

"Before we start, I need to remind everyone of the forms you signed when you bought your tickets. No standing, talking, laughing, or recording. If you need to do any of those things, get them out of your system now."

A murmur of giggles subsided quickly. "All righty then! If there's no objection, I'd like to..."

"Miss Folds, you've never spoken of a connection to the afterlife before. How do we know this isn't some elaborate hoax?"

It was Delores Tootwhistle, the one person in the room who should have been happy, hoax or not. "Don't we all need to know how Gwen is competent to lead a séance?"

"Sit down, Delores." A man seated next to her, a stranger who was definitely not Mr. Tootwhistle, yanked on her arm. "You're embarrassing yourself."

Gwen continued, unfazed. "Close your eyes and we'll begin."

She started with a soft, chanting invocation, calling forth any spirits willing to communicate. "We're all here, ready to receive you. If you see someone you love, reach out to them now." Gwen opened one eye and scanned the room. When her gaze reached H.P., she was given a thumbs up.

"I'm feeling something now. Someone... from the distant past who was called upon recently to—"

A cool breeze swept through the tent, one neither Gwen's equipment nor the cool night air produced. It pushed its way to the center of the tables, swirling into a tornado of gold and powder blue glitter.

As the glittery tornado grew, the wind it produced

caused carefully coiffed hair to stand straight up. H.P.'s cheeks shook, something she found terribly amusing. Gram was doing her proud.

In an instant, the wind died down and the glitter dissipated, revealing a ghostly apparition. Everyone in the room simultaneously gasped.

A beautiful vision floated in the middle of the table. A woman with crystal blue eyes and curly brown hair, swept up in the back by a stylish gold comb, appeared before them. A high-necked blue dress with lace around the collar and at the sleeves, gave off the image of a well-to-do, self-confident woman.

H.P. blinked twice. If she didn't know better, she'd think it actually WAS Eliza Tumblewood. But she'd seen poor, uneasy Eliza; this magnificent, self-assured ghost was certainly not she.

The faint aroma of lemon and lavender sifted through the air. It could have been of Gwen's doing, but either way, it was impressive.

Gwen held her chest, temporarily forgetting her role as leader of the séance, until H.P. waved long and hard enough to gain her attention.

"Oh! Right, right. Where was I? Who are you, and why are you here?"

Chapter Twenty-Two

NO AUTOGRAPHS, PLEASE

The lights strung around the inside of the tent flickered. "Who arrrre you, spirit? Tell us your name!" Gwen commanded, lifting her diminutive body as tall as she could. It was as if she'd been training for this role her entire life. "Spirrr-ut! Speak to me now!" She raised her hands, stretching them out wide.

"My name is Eliza Tumblewood. I was hanged for the death of my husband," Gram Gram intoned, her eyes distant as if seeing into the realm of the spirit world. "But I didn't kill him. The true culprit lurked in the shadows, cloaked in deception and malice."

Ooh. Good one, Gram Gram.

Not one sound in the entire tent. They were all captivated by Gram Gram's acting skills. H.P. watched with a mixture of awe and pride, knowing that her grandmother's performance was not just for entertainment but a way to honor their family history.

As Gram Gram continued to recount Eliza's

140

harrowing tale, one originating completely from her creative mind, the room seemed to hum with an otherworldly energy. "Charles Tumblewood wished me dead from our first year of marriage. Forced into matrimony by his overly controlling father, he blamed me for his circumstance and began plotting MY murder."

"Well, I'll be..." the mayor mused.

Just you wait, H.P. thought with satisfaction.

"Spirrrit, tell us more. Why are you here tonight?"

"I've been watching Misty Cove ever since my untimely demise. I've seen good and bad. Now, there is something looming over my hometown more evil than those who framed me for my husband's death. For that reason, I must speak my piece tonight."

"Must be awful for you to disrupt your death to make an announcement!" Gwen was going off-script.

"Yes, indeed. I've seen three wonderful people in my town murdered just this year. Oh, the carnage..." Gram Gram winked at H.P., clearly reveling in her role.

Etta Snackwell gasped, and for a moment, H.P. worried she might faint.

A memory flashed through H.P.'s mind. Gram Gram attended the Holy Mackerel Chapel of Salty Serenity church for five years. Each Sunday, she dressed the grandchildren under her roof in their best clothes and marched them into the chapel. Pastor Praysom Daily was a handsome man with a thick mane of red hair and fiery green eyes. Even H.P., a grade-schooler, found his mere presence exciting.

He had decided to put on a Christmas pageant to raise funds for a new sound system and asked for volunteers to coordinate, perform, and provide food. The single women of the congregation fell over themselves trying to sign up for the most activities and find favor with Pastor Daily.

It just so happened that the entire town of Misty Cove came down with the Flipper Flu on the day of the pageant. Instead of canceling, Pastor Daily had insisted, "The show must go on, ladies!"

That meant that those who were healthy would be required to fill at least thirty minutes. Gram Gram stood before the meager crowd and sang three songs from the hymnal before launching into a soliloquy about a young woman who didn't have any direction for her life.

After becoming lost in Gram Gram's story and her devotion to her character, H.P., along with the healthy residents of Misty Cove, had stood and clapped for five minutes solid.

On the way home, H.P. had asked, "Gram Gram, I never heard you practicing. Did you memorize that all today?"

"Pshht! Of course not, Hun Bun! I made it up as I went!"

The pastor, his new sound system, and the married church organist disappeared a month later. Gram Gram never spoke of him or her performance again.

The mayor appeared to be drifting off, his head bouncing on his chest each time he took a deep breath.

If he was indeed guilty, he certainly wasn't worried about being caught. H.P. cleared her throat, hoping to get Gwen's attention. Fortunately, one throat clear was all it took for Gwen to open one eye, allowing H.P. to mouth, "Keep to the script!"

The aura around Gram Gram turned as dark as a midsummer thunderstorm, and lightning emanated from above her head. "Someone here knows the murderer. Confess now or risk an eternity of pain!"

The flickering lights cast eerie shadows across the room, enhancing the atmosphere of mystery and suspense. Other than an occasional squeak of protest from a folding chair, the guests, and potential killer, remained silent.

"No one? You'll not get off that easily!" Gram Gram swirled around each participant, an ominous cloud enveloping them as she paused. H.P. held her breath when Gram reached her, even though she knew it was all a performance. The woman had missed her calling. When Gram approached the only empty chair in the entire room, she glanced at H.P. "I see there is one guest who didn't have the courage to meet me."

Looking down, she squinted as she read, "Maddysin Noseinair. You are weak of countenance, and you'll regret it."

H.P. nodded, discreetly getting up and moving to the back of the room. She pulled CeCe aside and whispered, "Go to Maddysin Noseinair's home and ring the doorbell until she answers. Tell her there is an emergency here."

H.P. thought back to the day Maddysin wrote the check and practically flung it at her, as though she were far too good to dirty her hands any further. H.P. seethed. "She's going to show up and support these kids if it's the last thing she does!" It came out much louder than she'd expected, and those at her end of the tent frowned.

"Yes, Ms. Sweetwater. I won't let you down."

CeCe shook her head emphatically when H.P. attempted to hand her a rolled-up twenty-dollar bill.

Finally, Gram Gram stopped in front of the mayor, fixing an icy glare on him.

Mayor McCloud cleared his throat and jostled in his seat. "Guess I've ruffled some feathers in the great beyond!" His nervous laugh felt hollow. Gram Gram wasn't the only one putting on a show.

"I can see inside your soul, Mayor. There is a darkness."

Her glare alone would have sent most in the room clamoring for the exit.

The mayor chuckled. "That's probably leftover meatloaf with brown gravy." The mayor chuckled.

"Whether or not you share with this room, the truth will emerge, Mayor."

He smiled and nodded and didn't appear the least bit concerned. His silence frustrated both H.P. and Gwen, who had recorded the evening for potential use in court. H.P. signaled for Gwen to wrap up.

The table shook and a cool breeze swept through the diner as the overhead lights flashed on and off. This was Gram Gram's last cue. With a final dramatic gesture, Gram Gram let out a ghostly wail that sent shivers down the spines of those present. The lights flickered once more before stabilizing, leaving the room in a hushed silence.

After an appropriate wait, one by one, the guests stood and clapped. The clapping changed to cheering, and the mood in the room lifted.

H.P. let out a sigh of relief at the unexpectedly positive outcome of the evening, even though it hadn't elicited the confession she'd hoped for. She felt a tap on her shoulder and turned to find CeCe, as white as a ghost.

"Mad refused to come, didn't she?" H.P. huffed. "I'm not surprised. She's always felt she was too good for—"

"They wouldn't let me go past the police tape."

"What?"

"I couldn't get inside the gate, thanks to all the police, so I asked what was going on. She's gone missing, apparently."

Chapter Twenty-Three

GOSSIP, GOSSIP, GOSSIP

Misty Cove was abuzz with two rather large pieces of news. The first being the séance, and what a marvelous performance H.P., Gwen, and the other volunteers had engineered. "These women need to go into business together. They could make a killing," someone posted on Misty Minds' social media page. There were fifty-six likes, meaning just about everyone who read the post heartily agreed.

The second, and less pleasant topic of conversation, was that of Maddysin Noseinair's disappearance. There was no sign of forced entry, but her cell phone, credit cards, and fancy-schmancy car keys were sitting on the counter. Mayor McCloud, who insisted on being kept up-to-date on any developments, was equally puzzled. Her influential family was no doubt making his life miserable until their princess was located.

According to the social media sleuths, she left work

that day at 4:30, her usual time, and flashed her gold level You-Go-Girl sign-in card at Fit Happens, changed into her stylish workout clothing, and was seen on security cameras turning from side to side, touching her hair, and sucking in her stomach in front of the large mirrors. That was the last time she appeared in public.

H.P. enjoyed working in the middle of Gossip Central, where she heard theories and predictions about everything, from the sunset "It's all the invention of the electric companies. Just started about a hundred years ago to force us to buy their power" to the recent weight loss of the city clerk. "He's had one of them fancy surgeries, so he can change his name and run off to an island somewhere."

More than usual, H.P. was enthusiastic about going to work. Did she feel ashamed that she was feeling joy over the disappearance of Maddysin? Possibly.

"Mom, you have to sign this or I can't go to the college library with Tildie."

After the success of the séance, H.P. was pleased to find that they'd raised enough to sponsor the entire band day. People came up to her as they were leaving that evening and handed her hundred-dollar bills. That, coupled with Maddysin's donation, meant this year's Ballz and Bandz promised to be the biggest, most exciting ever.

"I'm sorry, bud. I've got a million things on my mind. Where is it?"

Dexter reached into his backpack and pulled out an empty bag of chips with a paper stuck to the side. "You can pluck it off, right?"

She stared at him, incredulous. "I'll let you rethink that while I finish my coffee."

H.P. took a brief glance in the mirror, surprisingly pleased by her appearance. She'd been sleeping better these days, thanks to the sleep gummies Frankie gave her.

"I think I got most of the chocolate off," Dex said as he wiped the crumpled paper against his clean jeans before handing it to his mother.

"If you weren't going with Tildie, I would say no. She's going to make sure you're back from the university library by eight, right?"

Dexter ran his hands through the curly mop on his head. H.P. noticed a new acne breakout that she would have to approach carefully. Unless she waited until he was in a good mood, asking him to apply the prescription cream that cost more than H.P.'s first perm would fall on deaf ears.

"Mom, we don't control the bus lines. We'll be home when the bus drops us off."

After walking to the bus station and leaving her son in Tildie's capable hands, she rushed over to the diner to see what news was flowing through the pipeline today.

Edna looked up from pouring Five Meal Gary a cup of coffee. "Late," she muttered. "Again."

"Yeah, I'm sorry, Edna. I had to drop Dex off—"

"Got a visitor in the office. They've waited so long, you might as well take the duster in there and clean 'em off."

H.P. pulled out her phone, blushing at the prospect of mistreating a potential business interest. "I don't see any messages. You should've let me know!"

Edna shrugged with her trademark Edna indifference. "Not your social manager."

H.P. didn't stop to hang up her coat on the hook, glancing wistfully at the walk-in as she rushed by. Although Gram Gram explained that leaving the walk-in and appearing as someone else would require her to use all her energy reserves, H.P. held out hope it was a brief absence.

She didn't recognize the balding man seated in her office. His thick nose, wide hands, and surly demeanor reminded her of the old black-and-white movies she'd seen. A true thug.

"Hello! I'm so sorry I was late. I was tending to some personal business. How can I help you, Mr.—"

He grunted before he said, "Thud. That's all you need to know."

H.P. slid behind her desk and folded her hands in front of her. "All right then, Mr. Thud. What is it you need from me? As I'm sure you saw on your way in, things are very busy and I can't spend much time back here in the office. Just between you and me, Edna has been known to bite the head off an unsuspecting diner."

Nothing. She'd have to try a different tact. "Are

you here about the séance? We're not currently taking bookings. It was a one and—"

"I was hired by the Noseinair family. I'm speaking to everyone who had contact with her this week. Just in case you know something about her disappearance."

That certainly wasn't what she expected. This man looked as though he'd sooner knock her through the wall than meticulously research Maddysin's contacts.

He was decidedly square. The shape of his head, his jaw, and even his shoulders. Compact without an ounce of wasted space. "I don't know how I can help. We knew each other in high school, and since I moved back, we've only been in sporadic contact."

"Saw the camera footage of you coming into her office on Wednesday, at 1:42 p.m. and leaving at 2:12. I can pull up the footage on my phone, if you need convincing."

"No, that won't be necessary."

H.P. sighed. Leave it to Maddysin to have cameras placed everywhere. She probably even had them in the bathrooms. "I did visit her, but only to discuss the high school band fundraiser. Well, that and our common ancestor. You'll be happy to hear that she booted me out after making a hefty donation."

Thud scribbled on the yellow-lined pad he'd retrieved from the pocket of his jacket. He wrote what seemed like twice as many words as she'd uttered.

"Your kid," he continued, without the slightest hint of emotion. "He was on her calendar last week. Why would she wanna spend time with your kid?"

If this were his normal interrogation method, Thud needed a course on killing them with kindness.

"Oh, that. My son and his friend Tildie are doing some genealogy research. As I already mentioned, we have a common ancestor, Eliza Tumblewood."

For the first time in their conversation, Thud showed an interest. At least, that's what she assumed. He took one very large, very square thumb and licked it before turning the page to a clean sheet of yellow paper.

"Tumblewood? Ain't that the broad who killed her husband? Heard about that goofy séance."

"She was falsely accused and convicted. I can assure you, Eliza was very much an innocent victim." H.P. felt her cheeks getting warm as she defended her mysterious great-great grandmother. Was she really so convinced of Eliza's innocence?

"I don't know nothin' about that. When the cops was done, I scoured Ms. Noseinair's office and found this."

Thud slid a worn paper over to her. The paper was aged and delicate, the ink faded but still legible. H.P. picked it up gingerly, revealing a handwritten letter addressed to Eliza Tumblewood. The words jumped out at her, the elegant script looping across the page in a dance of long-forgotten emotions.

My Dearest Eliza,

As I pen these words, my heart

aches with the weight of our situation. Our sweet nothings may remain hidden from the world for the rest of our days, but my love for you remains unwavering. Do not lose hope, my beloved, for I will move mountains to prove your innocence. Use our love as a beacon in the darkest of nights, guiding you towards memories of our shared affections. We will be together there, without fear of danger lurking at every corner. Hold onto our memories, and let them be a shield against the cruel world that tries to separate us at every turn.

I will stop at nothing to exonerate you, my darling.

With all my heart and soul,

B

H.P.'s mouth dropped open. "Eliza had a... lover? This changes everything. How did Mad...dah-son get hold of this?"

"Thought YOU might know. We're taking lots of avenues. This is just one."

He stood and folded the yellowed paper, forcing it into his shirt pocket with a grunt. "My card's out front, with your grandma."

"My what?" she said sharply.

"Your grandma. Ethel somebody. Reminds me of my grandma. Baked me cookies every week."

"Edna. And I will definitely talk to my son this evening when he gets home." It was no secret. Dex and Tildie visited Maddysin to ask if she knew about Eliza. "Oh, could I take a quick picture of that letter?"

Thud shrugged. "Guess so."

"One more thing, Mr. Thud. Do you think Maddysin's disappearance has anything to do with the recent murders? You know, the waffle makers to the head?"

"Cops don't think so. I'm still investigating."

She followed him to the front of the diner. Out of the corner of her eye, she saw the crew taking down the big tent and once more felt a surge of pride at their accomplishment.

Before forgetting, H.P. texted her son:

> See if you can find any info on someone with the first initial B who was involved with Eliza. Enjoy yourself in Seattle but not too much.
>
> Love and butter,
>
> Mom

"What'd that one want?" Edna asked, gesturing

with one elbow and lifting a syrup-covered plate with the other.

"He wanted to know if I had any information on Maddysin's disappearance. He works for her family."

Edna paused to stare out the large picture window, where Thud was maneuvering himself into the seat of his black SUV. "Don't like it. Not one bit. That man smelled of trouble."

"I'll have to agree with you there, Edna."

"Are we talking about the head of Noseinair Enterprises' disappearance?" Five Meal Gary asked. He tapped the rim of his empty coffee cup, his signal to fill it again.

"Yes we are, Gary. What do you know about it?"

Gary leaned back against the vinyl booth and crossed his arms over his stomach—his warm-up to a lengthy story that may or may not have had its roots in truth and could have easily been told in half the time by someone else. "I heard this from her gardener, who heard it from the chef."

"She has a CHEF?"

H.P. was annoyed that her former schoolmate was that pretentious, and, if she were being honest, a little hurt Maddysin hadn't expressed any interest in her culinary skills.

Would I really want to work for her? Of course not! Pure pettiness, Sweetwater.

"Has for years. This gal said she was finishing up some kinda salad and she heard the door open. Instead of the sound of high heels, she heard a 'thump, thump, thump.' Thought it was kinda strange."

"Did she investigate?"

Five Meal Gary shook his head. "Nope. Ms. Noseinair didn't want to be seen until she'd had the chance to apply her night makeup. The chef waited in the kitchen until she heard the footsteps go upstairs and then she set the food on the table. It was still there when she left for the night. Creepy, right?"

H.P. envisioned a large, dark wood dining area with dim lighting. The silverware was top of the line and fresh flowers sat in the middle. And only one place setting. Had she not been fortunate enough to have Dex in her life, that would be Honeypie Chiffon Sweetwater's fate as well.

"So, nobody actually saw her that evening? What about the next day?"

Gary shrugged. "Well, that's just it. Nobody's really seen hide nor hair of her since a trip to the gym on her way home. The gardener mentioned she found some of Ms. Noseinair's personal effects scattered in the backyard, like someone had been looking for something."

H.P. leaned forward, her eyes wide with intrigue. "Personal effects? What kinds of things?"

Gary scratched his head, trying to recall. "Just some jewelry and a few letters, nothing too important looking. But it's all kinda strange, don't you think?"

H.P. nodded slowly, her mind whirling with questions. "Yeah, it definitely sounds odd. Especially with the whole 'thump, thump, thump' business. What else did you hear?"

"Someone took her from the gym and then drove her car home, leaving the keys. Almost like they wanted it to look like she left on her own."

"Given Maddysin's love of recording every aspect of her life, there has to be a camera somewhere that captured that exact scenario."

Chapter Twenty-Four

A SHOCKING VISITOR

Two full pots of coffee weren't enough to keep her eyes open, so H.P. finally resorted to sticking her head in the freezer every few minutes to stay awake. Though she'd never admit it, she hadn't slept since Maddysin's disappearance.

Dexter texted her at seven p.m. to say the bus had broken down and they were waiting indefinitely for another bus.

Even though Abe Bunce probably heard from his daughter long before Dex messaged his mom, she called him anyway.

"Our kids are in a bit of a pickle, aren't they?"

"You could say that," Abe replied in his buttery-smooth deep voice. "Tildie needs her beauty sleep or she'll be cranky for the rest of the week. I'm on the road now to pick them up. I'll have Dexter phone you when we're close."

She was slightly hurt that Abe hadn't invited her to

ride along. Nevertheless, H.P. applied a fresh layer of makeup to her tired face and waited impatiently for them to arrive.

The only hope now was for her to find an old movie that particularly irritated her. After clicking up and down the channels, she found just the annoyance to fit the bill.

"Tulip Sloan, starring in, 'She's Hit the Sauce.'" She chuckled to herself. "That oughtta do it." There was no way she'd fall asleep now.

Although H.P. slept through most of her American History class in high school, she had found the unit on American film particularly interesting. Tulip Sloan grew up in poverty and rose to stardom after landing in Los Angeles and convincing a studio executive to take a chance on her.

To add another layer of protection from unwanted dozing, H.P. donned her summer pajamas and opened all the windows. Nothing like freezing to death in front of an old, sexist movie.

"If I go now, Gram Gram, please make sure Abe Bunce finds me. I don't want these silky bad boys to go to waste."

Ever since the séance, Gram Gram had been absent from the walk-in. She'd explained to H.P. that she would have to wait until she replenished her energy reserves before making her form visible again. H.P. wasn't expecting her grandmother to answer, but a small part of her hoped she would.

"Focus on the movie, Sweetwater," she reminded

herself. Cinnamon Biscuit Maker curled up next to her, and the roar of her purr calmed H.P.

Miranda Delight leaned against the kitchen counter, a look of utter disbelief on her face as she gazed at the bubbling concoction before her. "What's got you so glum, Harvey? Not even my secret sauce has lifted your spirits!"

Harvey Winterkorn leaned in the doorway with a smirk on his face. "A delicate dame can't handle my story."

"Well, I'm no ordinary dame, Harvey."

"Darling, your ambition is as spicy as your sauce. Make me a cup of Joe and I'll tell you."

Harvey sat down at the table and picked up a newspaper, displaying the headline, "Carnage at the Deli!"

When a ruffled-apron-clad Miranda returned with his coffee, she sat across from him and gazed lovingly into his eyes.

"I was doing my thing, working the lunch rush, when a man and woman came in and ordered two grilled ham and cheeses on rye. Next thing I know, there's screams coming from the front of the house. I peeked through the small window where I set plates for pick up. Every lunch order in the place was covered in..."

"No, I can't bear to hear it!" Miranda turned away from Harvey and began fake crying. "You understand why I can't bring myself to make lunch anymore. Now be a good dame and get me something sweet to go with my coffee."

H.P. threw her pillow at the television. "Gahh!" she roared. Cinnie stopped purring abruptly and stood. She stared into the kitchen and then back at H.P. "You already ate, Cinnie." Gently, she coaxed her kitty back onto her lap. "If I have to suffer through this movie, then you do too."

Miranda was dressed in a silky dress and heels and held a baking pan—was she baking a cake? "Perhaps I'll enter my cake in a baking contest, just to make you 'eat your words.' Wouldn't that be a gas, Harvey?"

Harvey chuckled, the affection in his eyes softening his earlier jest. "Miranda, my dear, if anyone can turn the culinary world upside down, it's you. And don't worry your pretty little head; I'll keep you safe from those lecherous villains."

Once again, Cinnamon Biscuit Maker stood, and this time trotted to the kitchen, meowing all the way.

H.P. threw a second pillow at the television. "I can't. I'm sorry, Dex. I tried to stay awake, but I'm done. Even Cinnie's had enough."

She stood and called, "I'll get you a little snack for being such a trooper, girl!"

Just one more thing to keep her awake. Just one more... As she reached the threshold to the kitchen, she had to blink several times to make sure she hadn't entered the hallucination portion of her exhaustion. Cinnie was still meowing, pacing back and forth as the hair on her back rose. She saw it too.

"Whooo are you?" H.P. stuttered. You'd think with all the time she'd spent hanging with Gram Gram, she'd be used to ghosts. This one didn't look familiar, and maybe that was the part that concerned her most.

The ghost wore a dress the color of butter adorned with small blue flowers. Her hair was pulled back tightly in a bun and her gray eyes displayed a desperation that brought a tear to H.P.'s eyes.

"You can help me, miss?"

There was something very familiar about this voice, although figuring that out while she tried to comprehend the scene unfolding in front of her was too much for her brain to handle. "Do I know you?"

The sad-looking ghost seemed taken aback. "You came to my home and you were the first person to hear me in all those lonely years. Do you remember?"

That night in high school, when she was in the abandoned Tumbleood home with Juniper. She pretended it wasn't real..."No, sorry. Doesn't ring a bell."

The apparition was undeterred. "During your séance, you called to me! You want to help!" She smiled slightly, as though she thought it might get her into trouble if she showed too much emotion.

H.P.'s mind swirled with possibilities. "You're... ElizaTumblewood? THE Eliza Tumblewood?"

The ghost nodded. She wasn't as fully formed as Gram Gram, but there was enough of her to make out she was the woman H.P. had seen in that historical photo. "You know I didn't kill my husband and you want to clear my name? I'm grateful for your help!"

Eliza glanced down at her chunky black shoes and, at that moment, H.P. saw her Aunt Gussie's strong jaw line and her cousin Princess's high cheekbones. Good gravy! It was true; Eliza WAS a Sweetwater!

"It was a miscarriage of justice, Mrs. Tumblewood. My son and his friend are hoping to prove your innocence. They've been at the library all day, trying to find out just who wanted to frame you!"

"You won't find that information in a library, I fear." Her voice was soft and soothing, motherly and loving. "My story has been hidden away."

At that moment, a car horn honked, causing H.P. to jump. "That'll be my son. I'm sure he has good news for you, Mrs. Tumblewood. Please stay and speak to him!"

Eliza's eyes widened with fear. She shook her head and backed away, her apparition dissolving with each step. "No! No men! I can't!"

"Please, don't go!" H.P. pleaded as she reached out, as though her human hands could grasp this being from another century. "I have so many questions! Who was B? Was he your real love? Please! My Dex is just a boy! He won't hurt anyone!"

"Mom? Who're you talking to?" H.P. whipped around to find Dexter standing in the doorway. "And why are you dressed like it's Bring a Prostitute Night at the Tipsy Seagull?"

Her hands flew to her hips. "Dexter E. Jenkins!

That's so inappropriate! And what would you know of prostitutes? And the Tipsy Seagull?" Even so, she adjusted her pajamas.

"I'll forgive your hurtful words for two nights of dish duty. But I want to hear all about your day. What did you find out?"

"The genealogist was really cool. She showed us family trees dating back to the Mayflower!"

"Wow! That must've been fascinating!" It was thrilling to hear her son excited about anything that wasn't the result of a video game. "And were you able to find Eliza?"

"Kinda." Dexter threw his coat on the floor and walked over to hug his mother.

Two things hit her immediately: The first was his less-than-pleasing aroma. She'd gotten used to the fact that he was never going to smell like sugar and sunshine again, but spending the day in a stale library brought out a new level of odor she hadn't yet experienced. How did young girls swoon over these smelly beings?

The second thing was that she hadn't been prepared for such a loving gesture. Usually, it was she who sought him out for affection. Instead of yelling at him to pick up his coat as her brain wanted, she asked, "What do you mean by 'kinda?'"

"Well, the Tumblewood family were really rich, so when Eliza was hung for the murder of her husband, they had her erased from their family tree."

"How on earth would anyone do that?"

Dexter cocked his head and gave her his patented "What kind of idiot are you, exactly?" look.

"There were no computers, Mom. They just paid people to get rid of her name. Look." He found his phone and produced a photo he'd taken, enlarging it so she could see it without her readers.

"What am I looking at here?" H.P. knew darn good and well what she was looking at. She also knew her son needed to feel like he was the smartest person in the room.

"It's the family tree. Look—there are her kids August, May, April, and June. But when you run your finger up this way…"

She gasped, not from the photo but from the wicked scent coming full blast from his armpit. How in the heck did Tildie keep a straight face sitting beside him all day?

"Right?" Dexter giggled with excitement. "She's gone. It's like they didn't have a mother at all."

H.P. frowned. "What did this family do to have so much influence in Misty Cove?" All sorts of debauchery crossed her mind.

"Mom, that part's really cool too! They manufactured Tumblewood Tonic, Good for What Ails Ya."

She laughed at his straight delivery. "I can only imagine what the ingredients might have been."

"Mostly booze," Dex replied matter-of-factly. "Eliza refused to give it to her children and even carried a sign in front of the factory with ten other women who were concerned about the bad reaction their children had to the tonic. Charles owned Tumblewood Apothecary, where he sold his tonic."

"Whoa. That's a motive to frame her for murder right there! That tracks with her developing her own healthier tonics. I wonder which one of the Tumblewoods stood to gain the most from having Charles out of the picture and Eliza in jail for his murder."

Although she hated herself for it, she glanced up at the clock. 11:50. "Maybe you can tell me over breakfast? You can pick out whatever you want from the diner menu. Right now, you really need to take your shower and get to bed."

Dexter shook his head. "I'll just take a shower tomorrow," he protested.

"No, son. Tonight. I can sit outside the door, and you can tell me about the Tumblewoods while you're scrubbing up. Would you like that?"

After a moment of contemplation, he nodded.

"Good! I can't wait to hear what you found."

She gave him a gentle push and followed him to the bathroom. These clothes were going to need more than simple detergent. "Oh, and Dex, did you find anyone whose name began with the letter B?"

"Nope. Not one."

Chapter Twenty-Five

RECIPES AND SECRETS

Gram Gram sat perched on the edge of the box of carrots, a look of eager anticipation displayed on her shining face. "Well, my dear H.P., how did it go? Did they believe the tale of Eliza Tumblewood? Was my performance up to snuff?"

H.P. couldn't help but smile at her grandmother's enthusiasm. She was relieved when, three days after the seance, Gram Gram reappeared. "Oh, Gram Gram, you were absolutely magnificent! Everyone was hanging on your every word. Your portrayal of Eliza was so convincing, I think even the spirits themselves would have been moved by your performance."

Gram Gram beamed with pride, her eyes twinkling with satisfaction. "I knew I still had it in me! Now, tell me everything. On the internets, how did they react to my story? Was it Oscar worthy?"

H.P. settled into the armchair opposite Gram Gram, a refurbished, blue, crushed velvet chair she'd found at a swap meet. It was lightweight and easy for her to scoot in and out of the walk-in, undetected by Frankie or Edna.

"We've gotten offers to work birthday parties, bar mitzvahs, even an anniversary party." H.P chuckled. "If I'd known how lucrative the séance business was, I might have skipped culinary school."

Gram Gram frowned. "The only reason this whats-a-ma-diggle was successful was because you had the talent of an actual ghost to help you."

"Of course! I haven't forgotten about your Christmas pageant performance. You had a real talent for acting, Gram Gram."

Her grandmother nodded, seemingly satisfied. "What else has been happening while I recharged the batteries?"

"Dex and Tildie went to Seattle and discovered new information about Eliza."

"Oh?"

"They learned that Eliza had a lover, someone who went by B. Does that ring a bell?"

"Why would I know that? I already told you; Eliza took the train over a hundred years ago. She's not around for me to ask."

Why didn't Gram Gram know that Eliza's ghost was still around?

"Eliza must've needed someone to be her safe place. She found that in B. At least, until she was framed for murder."

"Do you think this B killed Charles in order to

have Eliza all to himself?" Gram asked. "He wouldn't be the first."

"The letter was dated during her incarceration, so he risked being convicted of the same crime, had she turned it over to the authorities. I think B sent this with the knowledge it would either never reach her, or else the warden would read it first."

"Now that's something to ponder, isn't it? Eliza betrayed by her lover? Wish we could ask her about it."

For now, Eliza's ghost would remain a secret. "Dex and Tildie also found out that the Tumblewood family manufactured a tonic that was widely used."

"Ah, yes. Tumblewood Tonic was legendary for its ingredients. We learned about it in grade school, and as a matter of fact, they remade it so we could taste it! Can you imagine?" Gram Gram chuckled. "They claimed the tonic could be used to purify the blood and, in turn, cure a list of other things including rheumatism, pimples, spinal issues, eye sores, ringworm, and dyspepsia."

H.P. opened her mouth to ask a question.

"I know what you'd like to know. Gram Gram, what in the heavens is dyspepsia? It was a catchall for symptoms that included poor digestion and malady of the stomach caused by a poor diet that included a lot of fat and starch. It was one of the most common diseases of the nineteenth century, and many patent medicines claimed they could ease its symptoms, if memory serves."

"What did it... taste like?"

"Like shoes. Don't ask me how I know. You asked for the ingredients? To the best of my recollection: root beer, parsley stems, basil leaves, molasses, bark of a willow tree for laxative purposes, of course," Gram Gram winked at H.P. before continuing, "and twenty-five-proof whiskey."

H.P. scrunched up her face. "And this was deemed acceptable to offer to sick children?"

"Oh, right!" Gram Gram snapped her fingers, a gesture that produced no sound. "I did forget that it also contained cocaine. Our teacher didn't find that a fitting ingredient for her pupils. But the children's formula from the time included blackberry syrup, meant to make it more palatable."

"Yeah," H.P. mused, "that must've really helped."

"It was the most widely used tonic on the West Coast. The bottling factory was the largest employer in Misty Cove, employing a hundred people."

"That family had everything. Why did they need to kill Eliza? Couldn't they just have her slip away quietly if she didn't like their tonic? I mean, to erase her from all the genealogical records seems pretty severe."

"That's where my story ends, I'm afraid. Well, except I neglected to mention that Maddysin is missing."

Gram Gram's eyes widened. "Maddysin? Miss Snootypants is... missing? Oh, my stars, this is dreadful news."

Chapter Twenty-Six

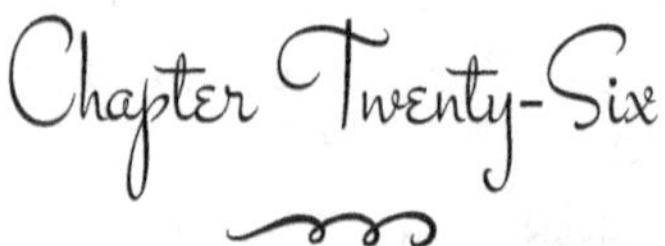

WANTED: A THIEVING WAFFLE WHACKER

"I'm gonna get me that reward money," Five Meal Gary announced to the empty seats around him.

The mayor had just offered a sizable reward for any information that led to the capture of the murderer now known as "The Waffle Whacker."

"And just how you gonna do that? I can barely get you off that stool!"

The corners of Edna's mouth tilted upwards. "Besides, what would you know about a serial killer? You're a plain eggs and bacon." Her attempt at a joke fell flat, but Edna didn't seem to notice. "When you cash that check, I'll expect a big tip."

The mayor scheduled a press conference for that morning. He asked if he could assemble the city council members on the front lawn of the diner, where there was plenty of green space and parking. He wanted them in attendance to show solidarity for his plan, which took money from the public swimming pool fund.

"I'll make some coffee and have Chef Frankie whip up pastries." Never one to miss an opportunity, H.P. added, "I'll open the diner early too. Just in case someone wants a full breakfast."

Her plan paid off. The diner was overflowing with customers, both before and after the announcement that a ten-thousand-dollar reward was being offered by Noseinair Holdings for information leading to the arrest of a suspect.

By the time of Five Meal Gary's arrival, the rush had cleared and the staff could breathe a little. "Thanks for coming in to help us, CeCe," H.P. remarked with a smile. "Though I'm not sure how I feel about being a party to your skipping school. I only hope your folks aren't angry with me."

As CeCe shook her head, her fancy ring, a tiny swirling silver hoop that boasted more curves than a mountain road, bounced against her lip. "My mom has told me crazy stories about her high school years. Skipping Advanced Chemistry and Water Exercise is pretty mild in comparison!"

H.P. leaned her elbow on the counter, smack dab in the middle of a dollop of marionberry jelly, and worse yet, she'd somehow touched her clean apron with her elbow. "Shoot!"

"Here, let me get that." CeCe wiped her elbow and then the spot on the counter before helping H.P. remove her apron. "I'll put this in some cold water and that stain should come right out!" she remarked cheerily.

H.P. shook her head before staring at her newest employee with admiration. "You're too good to be true, CeCe Scone. I hope you'll be around for a long time."

CeCe laughed. "I have enough credits to graduate at semester's end next year. Once that happens, I'm out of Misty Cove and I'm not coming back. My mom said if I helped her... around the house... she'd pay for an apartment in New York for a year."

"Oh? Is that where you're going to college?" H.P. tallied up the hefty price tag of an apartment rental in the Big Apple. She allowed herself a moment to doubt CeCe's too-good-to-be-true story before continuing. "You must be a big help to your mom for her to offer that kind of support. Is she teaching you the marketing business?"

Lately, she'd felt less anger towards the Glitterati. They were a different group in her time. Logan had the right to become someone totally different with the passing years, just as H.P. had.

CeCe nodded. "I've got to get back to school. It's later than I thought." She handed the apron to H.P. "You won't forget to soak this in cold water?"

It was like she thought of herself as H.P.'s parent. *No need to get your feathers ruffled, Sweetwater. She's just trying to help.* "Right away. I'll see you at 2:00?"

"Yes, ma'am!" She placed her own apron in the bin marked "Dirty Aprons" that Edna refused to use on the grounds that she wasn't a five-year-old who needed plastic tubs to remind her to pick up after herself.

"Order up!" Frankie called.

H.P. glanced at the order window, where a steaming plate of waffles topped with whipped cream and marionberries sat. She looked around the diner, where there were plenty of dirty tables but only two customers. Five Meal Gary was already enjoying his omelet, and the mayor sat reading the paper.

"Did you order something?"

The mayor looked up from the paper, surprised by her voice. "Yes, I guess I did. Without my wife fixing those lawn-clipping protein shakes every morning, I'd grown accustomed to skipping breakfast."

H.P. grabbed his plate and set it down in front of him. "Do you want syr—"

She gasped when she noticed the design in the waffle. "This must be a mistake," she mumbled, trying unsuccessfully to take the plate away.

"No mistake." Mayor McCloud grinned. "It's exactly what I ordered. I wouldn't mind some extra syrup, though, if you have some?"

"Of course."

H.P. disappeared into the kitchen, her face as blotchy as her insides felt. "Frankie!"

Chef Frankie wore earbuds while she was cooking, a real pet peeve of H.P.'s. Work was for work, music was for exercise.

"...Boogie, boogie brain, when you hear that train..."

"Frankie!" she yelled, this time poking her finger hard into Frankie's back.

Instantly, Frankie turned around, simultaneously yanking the white objects from her ears. "Sorry, boss lady. It's my favorite song."

"I thought we came to an understanding that waffles were on hold until the killer was caught. And what happened to OUR waffle maker?"

Frankie furrowed her brow. "I just used it, boss. It was working just fine. Why?"

H.P. glanced around the immaculate kitchen, where everything was in its place. The waffle maker she'd taken to Gwen for examination was clean and sitting on the shelf. She grabbed it and shoved it in Frankie's face. "Do you see anything wrong with this?"

"Yes, ma'am. Is this about my vision? I was gonna get it checked, but then me and Sir Stackworth had to leave town so fast that I—"

"Not your vision, Frankie, it's the imprint on the waffle. Ours makes simple octagon-shaped waffles. This one makes a cartoon character."

It was Frankie's turn for an ashen face as she opened the lid, displaying a cheerful design. "Looks like it's maybe a... kanga—"

"It's a wallaby. Winkie Wallaby, to be exact. It's the same design that's been imprinted into the heads of Barry D'Live, Pearlie Gates, Sunnie Daze, and Windy McCloud. The same design that was found on a waffle maker in your RV."

Frankie's expression was blank. "I didn't pay any

attention. I just grabbed it off the shelf this morning like I always do. You said the waffle maker you found wasn't the murder weapon."

H.P. stormed into the office and immediately opened the computer business app. She typed in "waffles" and waited for the page to load.

The mayor ordered them almost every day, ever since his wife's funeral. It was almost as though he was taunting his wife's ghost. When the page loaded, she discovered only the mayor's orders for waffles, every day this week. Given the fact that H.P. just now noticed, had someone snuck in, again, and replaced Gram Gram's waffle maker? Were they trying to frame Frankie or H.P.?

She stomped back into the kitchen and, as she did, Frankie caught her arm. "Look, I'm really sorry, ma'am. I should have been paying attention. My mind has been on other things, I guess."

"I've got some organization to do in the walk-in. You can take off early today if you want. Just turn our sign to *Closed* and we'll let the mayor eat in peace."

"I wouldn't feel right leaving you with all those dirty tables. I'll clean those up and start the dishwasher before I go."

H.P. nodded and placed her hand on the door handle. "Oh, and Frankie?" Her voice took on a softer tone.

"Yes?"

"You did nothing wrong. I'm sure that waffle

maker is as old as the diner. I must've taken it out of storage accidentally."

She paused, giving Frankie a moment to leave the kitchen before entering the walk-in.

"Gram Gram? We've got some serious stuff to talk about."

"Don't we always?"

H.P. jumped, unready for Gram's ethereal image to appear behind her. "I thought we talked about your surprise entrances. Could you make a habit of appearing in front of me instead of behind?"

"Yes, darling. You're absolutely right. What is it that's got your bra strap in a twaggle?"

"I'll let that one go." H.P. sighed. "First, I need to know who's been here after hours. Have you seen Frankie or Edna sneaking around in the dark?"

"You know, your time and mine are completely different. But I can give you an approximate... oh, wait. I know this! Charlie Chaplin and I had a lovely movie night. That man makes a mean tater tot casserole too!"

"That's wonderful, but I'm asking specifically if you've noticed anything unusual happening after hours."

Gram Gram's ghost danced around until it came to rest beside her. That was something she always found so intriguing, that Gram Gram could be sitting shoulder-to-shoulder with her favorite granddaughter without touching.

Gram Gram tilted her chin upward, the way she always did when she was about to lecture a grandchild.

"I have a life here. It's not the same as it was before, but in many ways, it's better. I can visit whomever I want and stay for any length of time."

"What does that have to do with the burglary?" H.P. snapped.

"Hun Bun, how do I say this?" Gram Gram swirled upward again and came to rest on the top shelf of the walk-in. "I worked hard on the living side, giving everything I had to my diner and my community. When I crossed over, I realized it was time to make everything all about me. Honeypie Sweetwater lives her death to the fullest and doesn't come back to the middle unless she dad-gummy feels like it."

H.P. hadn't realized how selfish her actions were, always expecting her grandmother to be at her beck and call. "I'm so sorry, Gram Gram. It makes sense that you wouldn't want to spend your entire afterlife hanging out in the diner."

"Good. Glad you understand. And I love my time with you, my darling. I just need to find some balance in my afterlife. I don't venture out of the walk-in often. It just saps my energy and makes my social events draining. Now that you've brought it to my attention, I'll keep my ear to the door."

H.P. stared at her feet. Even in the afterlife, Gram Gram could put her in her place.

"Now, what was the other thing you wanted to ask me about?"

"You've mentioned that Eliza isn't around," her eyes darted back and forth quickly, "but what about her mother? Or even her husband, Charles? Could you contact them, if they didn't get on the train or whatever?"

Gram Gram swirled around the ceiling of the walk-in, as H.P. imagined she did when she needed the exercise. "I told you how that works, darling. Those who want to pass through this space are welcome to do so. If either of them wanted to find me, they could."

"Gram Gram, I'm asking this as a favor to me. Well, and your great-grandson. Could you seek out either of them and ask for the truth? Dex and Tildie believe Eliza was wrongly convicted of her husband's murder, and I'm beginning to wonder if they aren't on to something."

Gram's head snapped around, the way it did when she'd seen a familiar face in the diner.

"Oh, that'll be Miss Monroe for the poker game. I'll check in with you tomorrow, sweet namesake! Love and squeezes!"

Chapter Twenty-Seven

"You've been real accommodating, Ms. Sweetwater."

The mayor licked his lips, leaving a thin layer of powdered sugar visible. "Mighty fine. Mighty fine. Tell Frankie to keep those lemon thingies on the menu."

H.P. tried to hide her disgust. "They're called beignets. And the lemon custard is what you dipped them in. Usually people order them in place of waffles, not together."

H.P. was more frustrated than usual. "Your three orders of them cleaned us out."

He licked his lips again and closed his eyes, probably reliving his binge. The man came in almost every day, ordering waffles, specifically from the Wacky Winkie Waffle Maker. She had to make a special trip to the grocery store to buy coconut whipping cream, just like the whipped cream on top of the waffle found at his wife's death scene, but two days ago he'd decided he wanted "the good stuff" and she had to make an extra trip to the store.

She stared at him, trying to decide whether she was amazed he hadn't died from a heart attack or disgusted that he chose to honor his wife's memory in such a derogatory way. "Everyone grieves in their own way, Hun Bun," Gram Gram replied when she asked if it sounded unusual.

When he opened his eyes again, he caught her mid-judgment. "Something wrong, Miz Sweetwater?"

"No, nothing at all."

"You'll have Frankie make more of those donuts with the chocolate frosting too? When you brought those out after my press conference, everyone raved about them."

"Yes, I'll mention that."

He glanced around the diner. "Is CeCe around?"

The mayor's sudden interest in a high school girl was the next thing that upset her. She didn't want to make assumptions, but there was definitely something out of whack. "She's probably hanging out with kids her own age."

"Hmm." He stood and flung a twenty-dollar bill on the counter. "Nice kid."

"Mayor? Have you heard anything about Maddysin? It seems so odd, given the wealth of her family, that no one has asked for a ransom."

He moved his mouth back and forth in a swishing motion before answering. "Not odd at all. These types of criminals have their own reasons for kidnapping.

Chances are, they didn't even know her family had money."

Although she couldn't fathom how anyone in Misty Cove or the surrounding communities wouldn't be aware of her wealth, there was no use pressing the mayor further.

H.P. waved as he left, thinking that maybe it was time to have a talk with CeCe about her relationship with the mayor. She could call Logan, but who could say if their old rivalry wouldn't come between H.P.'s concern and Logan's acceptance.

It was laundry day, which jogged H.P.'s memory. CeCe told her to soak her apron to remove the jelly and she'd completely forgotten. She dug through the dirty aprons until she found what she was looking for. As she pulled it from the bin, a folded paper fell to the floor.

She gasped as she read the words.

Chapter Twenty-Eight

MAYOR MCJUNKFOOD

"I'm sorry I didn't tell you."

Frankie stared at the tiled floor as she admitted to ownership of the threatening note H.P. found in the laundry.

"Frankie, this is serious. The BM threatening you means none of us are safe."

"I'll pack my things and be gone by morning," she replied softly, refusing to meet H.P.'s concerned gaze.

"Don't be ridiculous, Frankie. If we know what we're dealing with, we can handle anything."

This was a far cry from the last time they spoke of Frankie's perceived threat. This time, H.P. understood Frankie was worth fighting for. As Gram Gram always said, "Hold onto those precious diamonds you come across. Doesn't matter if they sparkle for someone else or not, as long as they sparkle for you."

Frankie returned to her duties, preparing a new double chocolate waffle recipe. Although it was still a touchy subject (with everyone other than Mayor McCloud), mini waffles with a plethora of toppings made sense for the Ballz and Bandz day. It had been weeks since the last murder, and the mini waffles were easy to freeze ahead of time.

Before reading the letter again, H.P. studied Frankie. Her chef hummed as she listened to her music, oblivious to the dangers ahead. Frankie was in her groove, and Breakfast Mafia notwithstanding, Frankie was a delight. And Dex relished his role as dog walker. Tildie confessed that, on their recent trip to Seattle, he used his dog walking earnings to pay for her lunch at a swanky restaurant.

Turning back to the letter, she read out loud:

> Flapjack,
> We know where you are and, when you least expect it, we'll be there. Your Benedict will curdle when you see what we have planned. Enjoy your last few meals without discomfort.
> Signed,
> The BM

H.P. turned the paper over. It was good quality, heavy weight. It seemed like a huge waste of postage and paper to write so little.

"Do you have the envelope?" she asked before

remembering that Frankie was lost in her daily jam. H.P. poked her on the shoulder repeatedly until she got Frankie's attention.

"Huh?"

"THE ENVELOPE," H.P. mouthed.

"Oh, yeah."

Frankie wiped her hands on her apron and turned around as she reached into her pocket. She pulled out a crumpled envelope and handed it to H.P.

H.P. turned it over, examining every inch. She wasn't even sure what she was looking for, but there had to be some clue.

When her eyes rested on a small circle in the upper left-hand corner, her blood ran cold. She tapped on Frankie's shoulder. "Frankie? What is this?"

Hearing no response, she tapped again, this time much harder. "Frankie! Talk to me!"

Frankie understood the urgency of her boss's voice, even if she didn't hear her words. "What's wrong, boss lady?" She pulled a white earbud out of one ear.

H.P. held the envelope up to Frankie's face. "Do you see this?" She pointed to the symbol.

"Yeah. So? Somebody must like to doodle."

"That's no doodle, Frankie. That's a symbol."

"Okay." Frankie shrugged and returned to her work.

This time, H.P. moved between Frankie and the dark chocolate she was mincing.

Frankie leapt back and yelled, "I could have accidentally cut you!"

H.P. held the envelope up to her face again and tapped it with her index finger. "This is no doodle. It's the mark of the serial killer."

Frankie dropped her knife and grabbed the envelope from H.P.'s hand. "How did I miss this? It's the Wacky Winkie image that's been branded into every victim! The same symbol that's on the waffle maker on the shelf!" Her eyes filled with tears. "This is all my fault! I can't do anything right!"

"Shh. It's okay, Frankie. What do you mean by, 'You can't do anything right?' You're the best chef I've ever had. You ran a successful black market syrup business. Is there something you actually failed at?"

Frankie's face was ashen. "What I meant was, four people would still be alive if I hadn't come to town!" She wiped her eyes on her apron as H.P. patted her back.

"No, Frankie, the murders started before you were hired. I'm sure it's some kind of weird coincidence. I'll ask Gwennie to do some research."

Frankie nodded through her tears. "But they ARE coming. We have proof."

"I know." H.P. swallowed hard. "Why don't you take your break now? I can finish your prep work."

Frankie nodded, wiping her face with the back of her hand.

"And Frankie?"

"Yeah?"

"Thanks for giving my son a job. He's real proud of his dog walking skills and he loves Sir Stackworth."

A smile broke through the clouds of worry on Frankie's face. "That's mutual. If the mafia, you know," she made a slicing motion across her neck, "I know my little guy will go to a good home."

There was no comfortable way to respond, so H.P. began chopping mushrooms for the next batch of waffles, savory Shroom and Salmon.

The diner filled up quickly for a Thursday, and H.P. found herself regretting sending Frankie off. It was too hard to take the orders and cook them, and Edna was extra grumpy, which didn't help.

"Do I need to find my own chicken to make some eggs? Or are you going to scramble them before I die?" She leaned her saggy arms on the window between the kitchen and dining area.

"They're coming, Edna. Just give me five more minutes."

It reminded her of her days in San Francisco. So many unreasonable bosses with no empathy for their employees. H.P. blamed every slight, every uncomfortable encounter, on the "curse." She took whatever they were doling out because, somehow, she deserved it. Meanwhile, she expected her son to stand up for himself and be the person she wasn't.

"You're going home? After fourteen hours? What are you, some kind of lightweight?"

She had nightmares about them even though she and Dex had been in Misty Cove for several months now. It was good to have somewhere to focus her attention today, and scrambling eggs was one of her specialties.

"You're ignoring me, child."

"Huh?" She turned her head so fast that her arm came with it, knocking the bowl of eggs to the floor and shattering it into small pieces.

"Don't worry, boss lady. I'm back now."

"Frankie!"

At that moment, H.P. could have hugged the woman, had they not been in such a dire state. Frankie was already in the walk-in anyway, retrieving more eggs. H.P. leaned back to get a glimpse of the cooler. Sure enough, Gram Gram was seated on the second shelf, next to the chocolate syrup. She waved to H.P. and mouthed "We need to talk!" before Frankie unceremoniously slammed the door shut with her foot while carrying two dozen eggs in her hands.

"I can help you, Frankie! We're really behind and I'm afraid it's all because I've forgotten how to multi-task." She frowned helplessly.

"No, I'm good. I do better as a solo act. The mayor joined me in the alley for a smoke and he'd like a word with you."

"Now?" Her voice rose an octave. When did he start smoking? Was this still part of his rebellion against spending years with a health-conscious wife?

Frankie nodded, placing her earbuds in.

H.P. felt like a kid who'd been sent to the principal's office. What had she done wrong? Why was he here on the only day of the week he typically ate at the café in the grocery store? Just like everyone else, the mayor had the right to go anywhere he wanted to eat. Even though the kitchen at Cheapskate's Choice had been given a frowny face on every single health inspection.

"Mayor!"

He was leaning against the diner's brick wall, humming an upbeat song. She marveled every day at his resilience. Their séance offered no window into his mind, nor did it offer any motive for him to kill his wife.

After losing his spouse in such an abrupt and violent manner, he must've struggled every day to get out of bed. Instead of showing his sorrow, he was always professional in his manner and his words.

"Ms. Sweetwater." He nodded and tipped his wide-brimmed hat, just like she was the madam and bar owner in an old-timey western. H.P. resisted the urge to hike up her dress, placing one leg on a chair while readying her rifle.

"Frankie said you wanted to talk to me?"

He nodded.

"Can we take this conversation inside? I've got two chairs in my office."

Silently, he followed her inside where every patron stopped filling their mouths to stare at them. "We'll be in my office if you need me," H.P. said to Edna, hoping that was enough information for the town gossip mill. "We're working on a menu for the Ballz and Bandz Day security," she added.

"We ALL know what he's going to say already!"

"Good gracious, gal!" Edna tapped an index finger on each ear. "Folks talk. Guess you haven't had your listening ears on." She turned her back and continued pouring a customer a cup of steaming hot coffee.

"She's probably right," Mayor McCloud sighed. The first emotion other than happiness he'd displayed since his wife's death. "And I'd take a coffee and whatever pastry is the freshest today."

H.P. glanced down at the glass case in front of her. "The freshest pastry is the double-chocolate brownie surprise. The surprise being a homemade marshmallow center."

"That'll do." The mayor grinned as though he'd gotten away with something. A quick glance at his bulging waistline confirmed what she already suspected. The man was going to eat himself into oblivion. H.P. removed the brownie from the toaster oven and plated it with a drizzle of chocolate syrup and a pre-cut strawberry. Photo worthy.

She motioned for him to follow her after he'd poured himself a cup of coffee. As they were seated in her office, she placed his pastry in front of him.

"Now, what was it you needed to talk to me about?"

"You know, it's not until people are gone that we see them for who they really were." He took a large bite and groaned with satisfaction. "Tell Frankie these are the best yet."

H.P. was reminded of how many times she didn't

call Gram Gram back because she was tired of her endless optimism. Now, she wished she'd appreciated her every single day of her life. "Yes, that's true. I'm sure it's very painful, you know, losing Windy."

"Huh?" He knitted his brows together. "No, the point I was making was that she had me eating just about every kind of weed in our lawn. Now that she's gone, I haven't gained an ounce. The woman was just trying to torture me because..."

"Because?"

Did Windy have a reason to blackmail her husband? Was that why she was murdered?

"Oh, I... was just gonna say, she liked to get my goat, as all spouses do, I s'pose. What have you heard about the new golf course going in outside of town? My secretary says—"

"Spill it, Mayor. I live with a teenaged boy; I can suss out a stall from a mile away."

He opened his eyes and swallowed hard. "The Noseinair family hired a private detective to search for Maddysin. I tried convincing them to let law enforcement do their work, but they insisted."

"Yes, we've had the displeasure of meeting him. Thud is not the friendly sort." H.P. rolled her eyes, remembering their uncomfortable encounter. It would be a miracle if he actually found Maddysin through interviewing suspects.

"While I appreciate the help with hanging posters and whatnot, I don't need help in my investigation.

We've had enough craziness in Misty Cove that I'm well acquainted with the process."

H.P. glanced at the poster delivered to the diner yesterday by a timid woman, probably one of Maddysin's unlucky spa employees. "Please keep this up, even after my boss is found. She'll need proof of our loyalty."

It was a full-color, glossy poster with a very large, professional portrait of Maddysin. She had both hands on her hips and angled her body forward even though she was looking to the side. Her hair was streaked with highlights, chestnut then blonde, chestnut then blonde, that cascaded down the front of her cream-colored business suit. The picture must've been taken when she was much younger, H.P. noted with satisfaction, because her nose was more of the hook-at-the-end variety than the small, pointed one H.P. noticed when they saw each other for the first time after twenty years apart.

"I agree with you, Mayor. It's not up to them." It was a mystery why it had become HIS investigation instead of the Misty Cove police department's, but it wasn't up to her to decide the hierarchy. "I'm sure you'll find her." H.P. stood up straight, feeling anxious to wait on the tables full of hungry customers.

"That's why this'll be hard."

"Huh?"

"Thud Punchard brought me footage taken at the security gate of the Noseinair mansion." He pulled a phone out of his official mayor jacket pocket and opened it to a video.

"You can see the gate very clearly." The mayor cleared his throat uncomfortably. "And the next thing you see is someone at the gate. When the gates didn't open, presumably because Ms. Noseinair didn't want to see them, they attempted to climb over the gate. Not someone who's as fit as your old mayor, here." He winked as though they were sharing a joke. "Eventually, this gal got up to the door and let herself inside."

H.P. sent CeCe to check on Maddysin the night of the séance. In the grainy video, a woman struggled to hoist her body over the fence. Clearly, it had to be CeCe. At least she had one flaw: she climbed a fence like a forty-year-old woman.

"Kids these days don't get enough exercise," Edna called out as she pulled eggs and toast from the window. "Surprised they don't find more of them dead, with just a sad outline of a body on the couch." That woman had amazing hearing when it suited her.

"What's she talking about?" Mayor McCloud asked.

H.P. got up and closed the door, like she should have done to begin with.

"There's really a simple explanation for—" H.P. caught herself. Did he suspect CeCe was involved in Maddysin's disappearance? Was that the real reason he'd taken such an interest in her? That he thought she was involved with the BM? Maybe he wasn't as much of a bumbling fool as she'd assumed.

Either way, H.P. wouldn't allow this girl to be subjected to an interrogation, probably leaving her in tears and destroying for life, over a case of mistaken identity and poor timing. "It was me, Mayor. After the séance, I was upset that Maddysin didn't attend, so I went to confront her. Do you need me to come with you, down to the station?"

Mayor McCloud shook his head before studying her face. "Wasn't expecting that one today. I was just gonna ask if that person looked like a customer."

Oops.

"I'm sorry, Ms. Sweetwater. It's just procedure. You might want to bring along an attorney if you have one."

She suppressed a smile. This was definitely NOT the time to feel giddy about her attorney. At least she hoped he was her attorney. As they walked through the diner, H.P. suppressed a smile. *Give 'em something to talk about, Sweetwater.*

"Edna," she began with enough clarity that every table understood. "Please call Abe Bunce and have him meet me at the police station. I'm going in for questioning."

Chapter Twenty-Nine

DON'T SAY A WORD!

That morning had been a whirlwind of ups and downs, starting with Frankie's tearful confession to H.P. that she'd received a threatening note from the BM. "I'd hate for you to read it and then fire me," she said mournfully.

H.P. had no intention of letting Frankie go, but right now she had more pressing issues, like proving to the mayor that she wasn't the Waffle Whacker. At the same time, she would have to force herself to focus hard enough that Abe Bunce didn't notice her obvious admiration.

"And you want me to believe you climbed over Ms. Noseinair's security fence because you thought she'd stolen your...cat?"

"Um...yes... Yes, I do, Mayor."

She wasn't good at coming up with excuses on the fly, one reason she only skipped school twice before she got it through her thick head that Gram Gram saw through her hems and haws like a hawk.

"Maddysin expressed an interest in Cinnamon Biscuit Maker when she visited my home. Before I arrived, she'd informed my son and his friend that she appreciated Cinnie's unique brown-and-black striped coat and would pay us one thousand dollars to keep her."

This was easier than she thought. H.P. sat taller, enjoying the opportunity to diss Maddysin without her there to protest. "When I got home and Ms. Noseinair made the same offer to me, I replied that under NO circumstances would I give up our beloved family pet. The day I attempted to scale the fence was the day our cat went missing and I needed to prove to myself she hadn't been cat-napped."

"And was she?"

"Huh?"

"Your cat. Was she stolen?"

"Um...no. I didn't find her as I walked around the property, so I went home and, wouldn't you know it, she was sleeping on the porch."

He nodded as though he didn't believe her but, without more information to contradict her statement, he couldn't disagree. "How exactly did you plan on getting a cat over the fence? You barely made it yourself!"

"I...I guess I didn't think it through. Obviously." H.P. stared at the mint-colored wall, stained with something she didn't want to think about.

"What do you know about Barry D'live? Have you ever heard of Sunnie Daze or Pearlie Gates?"

Mayor McCloud scribbled furiously on a yellow legal pad before H.P. even opened her mouth.

"Don't answer that, H.P."

She gazed at Abe Bunce appreciatively. He smelled slightly spicy, slightly sweet, and one hundred percent irresistible. Abe Bunce wasn't handsome like men in the magazines. He was more the type who sat across from you and drew you in with his smile and confident demeanor. His large, dark eyes were giant pools of compassion.

There was no fighting it—Honeypie Chiffon Sweetwater was crushing hard on Abraham Bunce.

"What was that? I'm sorry."

"This is the third time you've asked for something to be repeated. Should I be drug testing you?" Mayor McCloud's harsh words dragged her out of her fantasy-induced stupor. His face displayed a look of disgust.

"Don't answer that either." Abe placed a manicured hand on her wrist, causing electricity to run up her arm. "Mayor," Abe sighed, "my client has done nothing wrong and, therefore, there is no need for any kind of testing. So far, you've asked for her driver's license, to which she readily complied, and her whereabouts on the night of the seance. I'd wager there are plenty of guests who could vouch for her presence at a fundraiser on her own property."

Abe paused and gave her the side eye. Even that

tiny bit of acknowledgment made her weak in the knees.

"She's distracted because she runs a business and would very much like to get back to work, Mayor."

"I do know that. Frankie's brownie will be in my dreams tonight."

"She'll be pleased to hear you're a fan!"

Abe shook his head and squeezed her wrist again. This time, she was fairly certain it was meant as a warning to keep her mouth shut. "So?" he asked the mayor.

"So, I'd still like to know what she was doing the morning of Mr. D'live's death. Believe that was..." He opened his phone and scrolled through his calendar. "There 'tis. March fifth. Mr. D'Live was found on or abouts 8:15 a.m., apparently while he was out for a jog. Waffle iron to the head, branded with the Wacky Winkie symbol, a chocolate chip waffle with a fluffy whipped cream on his chest." He looked up from his phone. "What can you tell me about that?"

"Huh?"

She'd been fantasizing about their cozy family of four—actually, five (Cinnamon Biscuit Maker was as close to a second child as she would ever come)—and their yearly vacations to a theme park, where they'd buy matching shirts and each display a smile of unbridled joy.

"Ms. Sweetwater, your attitude is doing nothing to prove your innocence. I'm only asking one more time."

The mayor sighed with disgust. "What were you doing the morning of March the fifth?"

"Oh, um...probably the same thing I do every morning. Taking a shower, begging, then demanding, then begging again for my son to get out of bed." She took a moment to glare at Mayor McCloud. His personality turned on a dime and she didn't like it. "I've never heard of that guy. He must've steered clear of the diner because—"

"Is that what's happening here? You're targeting folks, like my wife, who didn't eat at your diner? Some kind of revenge situation?"

"What?"

"Don't answer that. I think we're done here, Mayor." Abe pushed his chair back and took H.P. by the elbow.

"What about Pearlie Gates?" he asked again. "Did you know her?"

"Just what my gram told me." It slipped out as easy as butter off a short stack.

"Your grandmother told you...about Pearlie? Did you two talk about Mrs. Gates often?"

H.P.'s cheeks burned. "They were friends from way back. That's all I meant."

"And now we will be going," Abe said quickly. He tightened his grip on her elbow as she resisted the urge to melt into his body.

"You won't be harassing my client anymore, I hope? You'll need a warrant to compel us to come in again, Mayor McCloud."

This time, Abe escorted H.P. out of the mayor's office. They passed by the police chief's desk and H.P. stared hard. He looked up from his paperwork and shrugged. The poor man had lost his power and he had no way to get it back. Not unless the mayor stepped down from the investigation.

They walked quietly to Abe's car, where he opened the passenger door and motioned for her to enter. The stress of the morning had been more than she realized and, in the moments it took him to round the car and open the driver's side, she'd burst out in tears.

"Hey, hey! There's no need for that!" He slid in beside her, his irresistible scent stronger now. He handed her a pressed handkerchief from his pocket and lightly touched her shoulder while she blew her nose.

"I'm...so...embarrassed," she sniffled. "I've never been accused of murder before, and I guess that gets to a person."

"No need to apologize." There was that disarming smile.

"Abe, I'm going to tell you something and you have to promise not to think I'm crazy."

He didn't even bat an eye before replying. "Last month, I had a client who wanted to leave his entire fortune to his goat. You can't out-crazy that."

She nodded, adding one more amazing quality to his already-lengthy list of perfect qualities: Abe Bunce was compassionate. "Someone is trying to frame me."

He listened intently as she explained the Wacky

Winkie Waffle Makers she'd found on her premises. "…and the more I think about it, the more I'm convinced it wasn't CeCe on the surveillance video trying to climb over the fence."

"Wait—that was CeCe? Why didn't you say something to the mayor?"

"I didn't want to implicate a high school kid, so I said it was me. Can you imagine your own daughter being interrogated?"

In a surprise gesture, he placed a smooth manicured palm on top of her rough, dishpan hand. "Not many people would be that magnanimous, Ms. Sweetwater."

His words made her want to implicate herself in every single crime committed in the last decade. Just to feel the warmth of his hand and the mental boost of his approval.

"Now, I'd like to know who has access to your place after hours."

"Edna Snarlwood, CeCe Scone, Frankie, and me. That is, unless someone who worked for Gram still has a key. I can ask her—"

"No, H.P. I don't think you're crazy, but if you start talking about your dead grandmother like she's alive, this case will take a turn for the worse. I must ask you to hide that waffle maker somewhere that no one else knows about and don't let anyone, and I mean ANYONE, touch it. Understood?"

She nodded like a schoolgirl who'd just been scolded for taking an extra cookie.

"And don't give anyone the idea that you don't trust them, at least until I figure out how to narrow down the list of suspects."

When she arrived back at the diner, it was mid-afternoon and Edna had gone home for the day—something about her mother's favorite group, The Polka-Dot Pineapples and Fred, having a concert in Piney Falls City Park. Edna's mother was ancient, at least that's what H.P. assumed, given Edna's age, and the thought of her grooving to the tunes as Edna looked on in disgust was a picture H.P. kept in her mind.

CeCe Scone was taking the order of the only customers in the diner. She saw H.P. and dropped her pad on the table, running to embrace her boss. "Edna told me everything! I'm so sorry! This is all my fault!" She dissolved into tears as an annoyed customer glared at them.

"Shh. Don't worry about it." H.P. stroked her hair. "This was one hundred percent my fault. I'm the one who asked you to check on Maddysin. I didn't mention anything about staying away from the surveillance camera, so you did what you thought was best."

CeCe pulled away as H.P. smoothed her straw-colored hair. "Do I need to go in and tell the mayor?"

"No! Please don't. Things have already been handled. The best thing for you to do now is go about your business. I promise you, everything is just fine."

CeCe smiled through her tears before picking up her pad.

"Oh, CeCe, there's something I've been meaning to ask you. I heard the other day that your dad has a café in the back of his masonry office."

"Bricks and Scones Café? The menu is limited and entirely heated up in the microwave. The coffee is..." She tilted her hand back and forth, insinuating mediocrity. "I'm going to own my own café by the time I'm thirty, so I needed experience in a serious place."

Those words were the little boost H.P. needed today.

"Do you know if there are people who come in every day? Regulars, like Five Meal Gary?"

CeCe shrugged. "I haven't been there in years. Ever since my folks split up, my mom doesn't like me spending time in the masonry."

"I didn't know."

"It's okay, really. They haven't gotten along most of my life. It was a relief when they split."

H.P. waved to Frankie on her way to the office. She flopped down in her chair, relieved the day was almost done. She leaned her head back and stared at the ceiling, wondering how many times Gram Gram had done the exact same thing.

The more she stared, the more she became aware of the pencil marks in the ceiling. Gram must've thrown pencils upward to relieve her stress. More than half of it caused by her grandchildren, no doubt. She used her feet to move the office chair back and forth and allowed her eyes to close.

"No sleeping, Sweetwater," she whispered.

"Yeah, that's not a good idea."

Her eyes flew open and her body snapped upright so fast the chair rolled out from under her. Luckily, she caught her body before it came crashing to the ground. Where her luck ran out was in the matter of her chin. It caught the edge of her desk, causing her to bite down hard on her tongue. Instantly, she tasted blood.

A tissue appeared in front of her and, when she looked up to see where it came from, she wasn't one bit pleased.

"Tut? Awt are ooh oohing ear?"

He lifted her up with one arm and set her gently in her chair. "Open!" he commanded as he leaned in close to her face. H.P. had a full-on river of blood in her mouth. This wasn't good. She was going to die and Thud Punchard would bury her where he put the rest of the bodies he'd disposed of.

He squinted while he examined her mouth. "Gonna need stitches. Four, I think."

She glared at him. "How ould ew..."

"How would I know? Let's just say I've inflicted my share of injuries as well as been on the receiving end." He stuck his scarred tongue out as proof. "Almost lost mine once. Twenty-nine stitches and a liquid diet for six months. Lost fifty pounds."

She wasn't sure where they went from here. This Thud person was the last person she wanted to see. But who else could take her to the hospital without asking questions? H.P. couldn't even say her name without splattering blood all over the place.

As if reading her mind, Thud grabbed her coat off the hook and guided each arm as she put it on. "My truck's out back."

She stood, motionless, her eyes large with concern.

"Don't worry. I won't hurt you."

When she still didn't move, he pulled a gun from his waistband and placed it in her desk drawer. "There. Is that better?"

Chapter Thirty

SPELLCHECK AND SUCH

"Don't try and speak, bestie!"

Gwen jumped up from H.P.'s recliner, hitting the ground so hard her small feet made a thumping sound. "When you texted me from the emergency room, I scurried over as fast as my little legs would carry me. Twenty-two stitches! Yowzer! You'll have to show me later—you know how much I like to admire the stitching of other professionals!"

H.P. typed furiously on her phone before handing it to Gwen.

> What a day! Thanks for making soor Dex ate somethn in an actual food group and did his homework. You're a lifesuvver!

Gwen giggled as she read. "I AM a lifesuvver! And Dex is a cool dude." She handed H.P.'s phone back to her. "My mom sent over some of her famous Pasta a la

Wilma and your boy ate the entire pan before I could blend it into a liquid mess for you." Gwen shook her head. "I've never seen anything like it. How is that kid so skinny?"

Thanks to the pain medication she'd received in the emergency room, H.P. temporarily forgot she couldn't speak. She opened her mouth to explain that teenage boys had a distinct aroma and the metabolism of a rabbit, but a sharp reminder of her mishap prevented her from doing anything but grabbing her jaw.

"Don't talk. Your boy is in the shower, and I've got something interesting to show you." Gwen motioned for H.P. to follow her to her laptop, which she set up on the unusually clean kitchen table. It wasn't covered with bags of greasy chips or junk mail, and H.P. was the lucky recipient of a very pretty round table. Gram Gram had good taste, she remembered.

"I took the liberty of researching Eliza Tumble-wood. I have secret places to search, thanks to my second job." Gwen winked and, when H.P. didn't respond, she winked with the other eye for emphasis.

H.P. typed quickly and handed her phone to Gwen, who read the screen and shook her head. "No, it isn't a secret closet. Ha ha. As coroner, I have access to lots of things that others don't. Look."

H.P. leaned in close to the screen, grabbing her cheek as her face met gravity. Despite the pain medica-tion, nothing on her head was free from pain, it seemed. She looked down quickly, hoping Gwen wouldn't notice.

"I can't explain why these articles weren't preserved in the obvious places, but someone over a hundred years ago decided this miscarriage of justice was important." She pointed to the screen. "There are two. The first one was written up two weeks before Charles Tumblewood was murdered."

A Glimpse into the Secretive Botanical Endeavors of Mrs. Eliza Tumblewood

Misty Cove Sentinel, 1820
In a quiet corner of our splendid Misty Cove, amidst the elite Tumblewood lineage, resides Eliza Tumblewood, the devoted consort to the esteemed apothecary, Mr. Charles Tumblewood. Notably less acclaimed, yet undeniably well-versed in the herbal arts and natural philosophies, she captivates a select few with her botanical expertise.
It has come to this reporter's attention that Mrs. Tumblewood harbors an enigmatic enterprise of healthful elixirs, heretofore concealed from her revered spouse. In an unanticipated confession, she implored for her craft to be brought to light, seeking to elude the prying eyes of her illustrious kin.
Nestled behind their dignified abode, obscured partly by nature's embrace, a quaint cottage lies where Mrs. Tumblewood enticed this correspondent

to enter. Upon the turn of a key, one is greeted by the zestful fragrance of her potions in the making. The solitary window of the abode frames a verdant display of climbing flora, contributing to an atmosphere of buoyancy despite its curative purpose. Mrs. Tumblewood, a frail woman who speaks in whispers, explained our surroundings with much vigor.

H.P. paused. The ghost she met had a very soft voice. She pictured Eliza, thrilled to have a visitor to her cottage. The poor woman had no idea it would be her undoing.

Gwen gave her hand a shove. "Keep reading until the end, friendie!"

She must've shown Dex this trick. H.P. rolled her eyes before continuing.

The lady of the house revealed the essence of a concoction named Moonlit Mint Mist, a tincture of mint steeped in lunar glow, purported to invigorate the spirit and senses. "While its healing properties are undeniable," the austere Mrs. Tumblewood began, "when combined with Elderberry Echoes, the concoction is lethal. Mixing tinctures isn't for those unschooled in the ways of botanical remedies."

The painkillers were definitely wearing off. Thanks to Thud, she'd obtained an additional three illegal drugs in her pocket. "Don't tell nobody, or I'll have to come back and finish the job you started."

Gwen would insist on examining them, so H.P.

decided to wait to take them for as long as she could stand the pain.

Instead, she typed furiously.

> Someone read this in the paper and set her up! I knew it! We hove to healp her!

Gwen cocked her head as she read H.P.'s words. "There is a way to set up your phone to automatically replace misspelled words. I'll fix it if you want."

H.P. turned away from Gwen, awaiting a sneeze that was sure to be painful. Gwen grabbed her arm. "You haven't read the next article. I was watching your eyes. I know the approximate movement for one line of text. I think you have two-and-a-half paragraphs left."

H.P. rolled her eyes just as the sneeze projected a mixture of blood and spit all over Gwen's face. She grabbed her cheek and breathed deeply until the pain was gone. When she looked for her phone to type her apologies, Gwen, reading her mind said, "Don't worry about it. I've had bodily fluids land in my mouth that were much scarier, friend. See? All cleaned up."

H.P. examined Gwen's face. Nothing left but her smile.

"And now you can finish reading," Gwen insisted.

Relocating from the Tumblewood precincts, I encountered a domestic next door, engaged in her laundering labors. Queried about Mrs. Tumblewood's character, the handmaid expressed, "The mistress favors solitude yet partakes in homely conversations with the help, her interest in meteorological discourse exceeding what might be expected of a lady of her stature."

When inquired about the sequestered garden dwelling, the attendant offered a nonchalant gesture and responded, "Madam is most content in the company of her botanical companions than amongst society, steadfast in her belief that nature proffers remedies for our every affliction."

Such is the portrait of a woman whose passion for nature's bounty challenges the conventions of our time.

H.P. glanced up, her eyes full of tears. Poor Eliza had no one watching out for her, not even the mysterious B.

There was one thing H.P. knew for sure in her drugged haze: they had to find him.

Chapter Thirty-One

THE CURSE

Lately, H.P. had convinced herself she'd overcome her fear of the Glitterati and what they'd represented. Spending time with CeCe gave her the impression that, while Logan wasn't a nice teen, she must be a pretty good mother to have such a sweet daughter. It was time to grow up and move on, and that's just what H.P. intended to do.

When they arrived at the Noseinair mansion, H.P. realized that assumption was wrong.

The sun was dipping below the horizon by the time the four of them—H.P., Gwen, Dex, and Tildie—wound their way outside of town and up a private drive. H.P. thought about the one and only time she'd visited before.

Constructed in the late nineteenth century, the mansion was an exquisite example of Victorian architecture, with a façade that featured intricate brickwork and stone detailing, her history teacher explained. Maddysin had sat in the front row that day, grinning like a Cheshire cat.

H.P. always assumed the teacher was paid to say all those nice things, kind of like a history class sponsorship.

That day they stood, she and Gram Gram, on the ginormous porch together. Gram thumped the back of her head with two fingers when she picked her nose. That was what Honeypie did when she was nervous, learning it from a kid in her class who always dared others to touch his goo-covered pencil.

The big door had opened slowly and dramatically, with a squeaking sound that could have come right out of a horror movie. A dour man appeared in front of them, dressed just as she'd imagined, in a formal black tuxedo and white button-up shirt.

His eyelids hung like heavy drapes over the tired windows of his soul, masking the embers of a once blazing sadness or despair that had since burned down to cold ash. His cheeks, too, seemed to surrender to gravity's relentless pull, sagging with the weight of unseen battles, as if the very contours of his face had conceded defeat.

"You're here to see Mrs. Noseinair," he had said, a statement rather than a question. Without waiting for an answer, he stood aside and motioned for them to enter.

Unlike Gram Gram's place, which always took on the intoxicating scent of whatever leftover she'd brought home for dinner, the air was filled with an old book smell mixed with melted wax. The faint hint of a fireplace suggested the smoky whisper of charred logs, now resting cold in the grate after a night of warmth.

As they followed Mr. Droop, a new smell enveloped them. The clean, crisp aroma of lemon oil. H.P. had recognized it from the spring cleaning she and her cousins did at Gram Gram's church. Each pew was meticulously polished and then polished again. Any kid who dared complain would be sent to clean the bathroom stalls.

The room they were in, probably a backup living room, was a distasteful pale yellow that made everything seem older. Two black-velvet couches with swirling designs supporting high backs sat in the middle of the large, otherwise empty, room.

When Mrs. Noseinair had entered, H.P. felt like curtsying. The woman wore a simple gold skirt and white blouse with a black string of pearls around her neck. Her silver hair was drawn back so tightly it seemed to pull the disdain tighter across her sharp, hawk-like features.

She reminded H.P. of the pictures she'd admired in history books of European serial killers—frightening and intriguing at the same time.

"Seemah," Gram Gram had said, taking care to look sternly at H.P. instead of her formidable counterpart. "My granddaughter has something she wants to tell you."

Without warning, Gram put her hand in the

middle of H.P.'s back and gave her a firm shove. H.P. fell forward and landed squarely in Mrs. Noseinair's chest. When the angry woman pushed her upright, there was a purple stain from Gram Gram's mulberry pie on her lapel. She'd been told to clean her face before they left but forgot. *Served her right*, H.P. thought. *Who gets that dressed up for an apology?*

If Gram Gram had noticed, she kept it to herself. H.P. looked back for reassurance, finding none. "I'm sorry I slit your tires. I didn't—"

Mrs. Noseinair's eyes, a piercing slate gray, contained some kind of dark magic that prevented H.P. from speaking.

"You forgot to mention my daughter's schoolwork and her imported vest that you ruined. Wasn't the tire prank enough for you?"

Had Maddysin been responsible enough to lock the doors, no homework or ugly vest would have been destroyed.

"Do you know how much that cost, young lady?"

Of course not. She didn't even know you could buy clothing in a store until that school year. Until then, she'd exclusively worn her cousins' hand-me-downs.

"I'm so terribly sorry for Honeypie's behavior." Gram's voice was as steady as her grip, although her eyes darted away from Mrs. Noseinair's piercing gaze. "I can assure you, this isn't how I raised her. All of my grands have given me gray hairs. This one," she had reached up and randomly yanked at H.P.'s head, "came from Paisley. Never thought I'd have to explain why you don't bring livestock into the school." She laughed nervously, in the way mothers often did to find common ground with one another. There was, however, nothing about Seemah Noseinair that was remotely similar to Gram Gram.

Listening to Gram Gram's failed attempt to soften Mrs. Noseinair was just as painful as the actual apology. "I never expected that kind of worry from H.P., though. Honeypie has always helped me out in the diner without any fuss."

"I'm sorry, Mrs. Noseinair. Maddysin didn't deserve all my anger. I should have spread it evenly among ALL the Glitterati."

Gram Gram glared at H.P. She'd given strict instructions and H.P. was going off script.

Mrs. Noseinair sniffed, her posture as rigid as an iron rod. "Well, I should think so," she had replied with a tone that could curdle milk. "It's simply unacceptable. In my day…"

Honeypie, whether out of self-preservation or pure boredom, had stopped listening. Her mind drifted to fantasies of an alternate life, where the endless tall trees and lush, green lawn the Noseinairs obviously didn't appreciate belonged to the Sweetwater family. She and her cousins spent hours playing hide-and-seek and kings and queens, staying out until the last few streaks of sunlight lit the sky.

"May I use your powder room?" Gram's words had drawn her back into this uncomfortable scene.

"My butler will escort you."

H.P. felt Gram Gram squeeze her shoulder again. "Mind your manners!" she whispered.

When they were alone in the room, Mrs. Noseinair's lips curled into a sinister smile. "I know all about you, young lady."

H.P. swallowed hard. "What do you—"

"You're no good. Do you think I don't remember how your father stole from us? How my darling husband gave him a job out of pity, and he thanked us by stealing our car and all my mother's jewels?"

H.P. knew very little about her parents. She remembered her father because she was with him until she was nine. He was usually drunk, usually out of a job, and usually sent her to stay with Gram Gram.

"I had my healer put a curse on him, but since he left," she had stuck a long, wrinkled finger into H.P.'s chest and poked hard. "...that curse falls to you. Your life will always be cursed. You will always fail. Nothing in your life will bring you happiness. I'd feel sorry for you if you were the offspring of anyone else, but you deserve this."

H.P. had nightmares for months and was twice as scared of the Glitterati than she'd been before. It was one of the reasons she left her hometown so soon after graduation, planning never to return. Through her failed jobs and nightmarish relationships, Seemah

Noseinair's words echoed in her head. "You'll be cursed for the rest of your days."

Maddysin. CeCe's mother, Logan. They still visited in her dreams, still laughing at the curse on her head.

Chapter Thirty-Two

NIGHTMARE NOSEINAIR

Butler with No Discernible Smile opened the door and ushered them inside.

Gwen set the binoculars down and paused the recording app on her phone. "I wish you would tell me what has you so spooked."

H.P. nodded and looked away, focusing on a gardener pruning tall rose bushes where they were parked. The yard was just as well-manicured as she remembered.

The kids quickly launched into their rehearsed story as H.P. and Gwen listened.

"Sir, we're doing extra credit for a history project and would like to interview someone from the Noseinair family. We're sensitive to the disappearance of Miss Noseinair, but we'll only take a few minutes of their time."

Tildie had a future as an attorney. That, or a

professional con woman. Either way, her future looked bright.

After what felt like an eternity of silence, a gruff voice said, "Follow me."

H.P.'s heart felt like it might run down the street. She was happy to remain silent today.

A series of heavy footsteps on the tile floor followed. H.P. forced her mind to stay in the present and set aside her fear for her son. He was right. He knew how to handle himself.

"Don't ask about Miss Maddysin; you'll upset the lady of the house. And don't touch anything! You can't afford to replace it."

More heavy footsteps.

"Sheesh!" Tildie whispered. "Nothing here worth breaking anyway!"

"She was a closet abolitionist, you know."

The sound of Seemah's voice after all these years still struck a chord of terror in H.P.'s heart.

"It's wonderful to meet you, Mrs. Noseinair. My name is Tildie Bunce and this is my friend—"

"Jeffrey. Jeffrey Jefferson."

Good boy. Don't give her any reason to question your roots. Go over possible aliases with the boy later. What am I thinking? Do I want to encourage deceitful behavior?

"Were you referring to Eliza Tumblewood, Mrs. Noseinair?" Tildie asked.

"Of course I am! She's our most misunderstood relative. Well, my husband's relative. Eliza secretly gave donations to the Women's Freedom Fund. I have the receipts. I'm sure the husband she married wouldn't have approved. When my secretary informed me of your visit, I retrieved those for you, along with the only picture of Eliza that still exists. You can understand why any trace of her was hidden for years."

At least Seemah had one redeeming quality: she saw through that sham of a trial.

There was a rustling sound and then Tildie cleared her throat. "She looks so...sad."

"And that surprises you, young lady?"

H.P. felt anger rising inside. Seemah was just as mean and condescending as she had been when a young, insecure girl and her grandmother visited years earlier.

"Um, can I ask something?"

I'm glad Dex is participating.

Gwen nodded in approval.

"As long as you understand that I don't suffer fools," she warned.

H.P. rolled her eyes. Sweat ran down the back of her neck as her heart raced. Dex was fine. Tildie wouldn't allow any harm to come to him.

"Yeah, um..."

H.P. tensed. He lost track of his words mid-sentence, which meant Seemah would pounce on him like a lioness on a limping deer. It took everything in her to remain seated in Gwen's car.

The sound of Tildie whispering something in Dex's ear made her sigh with relief. That girl was a treasure.

"I was wondering how she got her own money to use, you know, to give to the Woman Flag thingy."

"The Women's Freedom Fund? That's a decent question, which leads me to the next thing I wanted to tell you. Eliza Tumblewood made her own elixir for whatever ails you. It was ten times better than the formula her husband sold." Seemah scoffed. "That concoction was more like driveway cleaner. When my daughter said you'd be visiting, I searched one of the trunks upstairs and found examples of Eliza's tinctures. Would you like to see them?"

"Yes!" both kids replied excitedly.

"Take care, young lady. I don't want to risk this delicate paper tearing. This is priceless."

Tildie cleared her throat and began reading out loud: "Whispering Willow Bark. Harvested only at midnight during a full moon, this bark is said to whisper ancient healing secrets to those who listen closely.

"Giggling Mushroom Spores. These rare mushroom spores are found in the enchanted forests of Misty Cove and are known to induce bouts of uncontrollable laughter, believed to be essential for good health.

"Dancing Dandelion Dust. Collected from dandelions that sway mysteriously without any breeze, this dust is thought to bring lightness to the heart and feet—"

"This isn't a school recitation, child. You can read it quietly and then hand it over to your friend."

"Oh, I've got an eye disease," Dexter replied with the ease of a kid who'd made up more than his fair share of stories. "Yeah, um…Tildie has to read my assignments to me after school."

"It's horrid, Mrs. Noseinair. Dexter's sight comes and goes, and I've had to keep him from walking into walls more than once."

Gwen giggled softly. "They ARE good!"

"Why did you call this young man Dexter?"

"Because she teases me that I look just like the cartoon character, Dexter Do-Wrong. You've heard of him, right?"

"May I continue?" Tildie asked impatiently.

"If you must. Maybe skip to the end though. I need to talk to our tactical team and see if there are any updates on my daughter."

"Yes, ma'am. Let me see what's on the other side… Hmm. It appears someone used this side of the page to write a note."

"Read it to me, please, Tildie. Because, you know, my vision is bad."

Tildie cleared her throat. "It says, 'Combining these three ingredients into a tincture is toxic in humans. Garden and home pest elimination only.'"

"She kept the mixture she used to kill her husband? Doesn't sound very smart to me," Dex said.

"There's more, Dex...er...Jeff. In a different handwriting, 'You must've made a love potion, my darling, because you've taken my heart. I shall refrain from making this tincture. Thank you for your thorough research. With deepest affection, Benjamin.'"

"That can't be right! Give me the paper this instant!"

There was a rustling that, in H.P.'s mind, was Tildie fighting Seemah for control of the illicit letter. A smackdown executed by the young woman she admired most on the woman who ruined her life.

"Paper was hard to come by in Eliza's day," Seemah said in a strangely flustered voice. "I'm sure this was simply a page she picked up, unaware of the writing on the back."

"Mrs. Noseinair, who is Benjamin?" Tildie asked.

"He was the brother of Eliza's husband, Charles."

Chapter Thirty-Three

WITH A THUD

All the way home, the three people in the car with functioning mouths chattered about the new information. H.P., meanwhile, did her best to maintain her composure. Her entire back was drenched in sweat, a by-product of reliving her worst day of childhood. Dex and Tildie did nothing to relieve her stress.

"Eliza was having an affair with her brother-in-law! That was a reason to frame her for Charles' murder," Gwen said excitedly. "I've seen more than a few love triangles end in murder. Or...maybe Charles discovered the affair and, when he confronted Eliza, she killed him."

"I think she didn't mean to kill him," Tildie replied. That child always wanted to believe the best in people, to the point of irritating H.P.

H.P. wiggled her fingers over the back of the seat, hoping someone would understand.

"Here's the picture of Eliza, Ms. Sweetwater," Tildie replied, reading her mind.

H.P. took the photo and studied it. A demure woman, she wore a tight corset, and her dark hair was parted in the middle and pulled back into a bun. Nothing remarkable for the time period. No killer vibes.

She brought it closer to her face, where she recognized the sad eyes Tildie referenced while in the mansion. They were almost...haunting.

"Everything we've read about her makes it sound as though she was a person with morals," Dexter added. "Aren't you always telling me that we shouldn't judge by looks but by morals? And don't answer that, Mother. It was more of a rhetorical question."

H.P. smiled, at least on the inside. Dex hadn't used a word like "rhetorical," well, ever. Tildie's vocabulary was rubbing off on him.

"Maybe Charles thought he was drinking something completely harmless. You know, like when you tell me that drinking your protein drinks is healthy, and that I shouldn't complain that it tastes like the beach?"

Dexter playfully tapped the back of her headrest, causing his mother to snap her fingers over her head in response. "It's so weird that Misty Covians couldn't care less about Miss Bliss's disappearance, especially her mom. If I'm even fifteen minutes late, my mom—"

Gwen glanced over at H.P. before answering quickly, "Not everyone despises her as much as your mother does. But I agree; Mrs. Noseinair sure didn't seem broken up over her daughter's disappearance. I wonder if anyone has tried retracing Maddysin's steps?"

H.P. nodded, realizing that she would have to type everything, and also realizing that Gwen was driving and couldn't read it anyway. After they dropped the kids off, she'd ask Gwen if they could take a quick trip to Punchard Security.

"My dad was wondering if Dex could come over for dinner," Tildie said, as if she were reading H.P.'s mind for the second time today. "He knows you're not feeling well and wanted to help."

H.P. would have squealed and jumped for joy if they hadn't been in the car and she could speak. This small kindness made her insides turn to goo.

So thought!

she typed before handing the phone to Tildie.

"I think you meant to say 'thoughtful.' I'll tell him so!"

After dropping the kids off at the Bunce home, H.P. explained via text what she wanted to do next. Gwen wasn't so sure.

"That big lug? Why would we want to see him? He's always given me the creeps."

Silence was on her side. She didn't have to explain herself and, eventually, Gwen gave in.

They pulled up in front of a colorless brick building. Even the sign over the door, reading "Punchard, We've Got You," was in drab black and white. There were still lights on at this late hour, so the women decided to take a chance.

Just as Gwen raised her hand to knock, the door flew open. "Saw you on the camera. Enter."

Thud moved to allow them inside. The lighting was bright and almost offensive in contrast to the rest of the business. Three men with similar builds sat in cubicles and glanced up in unison as Thud walked them through.

"My brothers—Striker and Mace. We work as a team."

They were already in his darkened office when he made the introductions. The room's only illumination was a small lamp in the corner and Thud's computer screen.

"How's the tongue?" he asked in his flat monotone voice.

H.P. nodded, unsure how exactly he expected her to answer.

"We're here about Maddysin Noseinair, Mr. Punchard," Gwen explained.

He clicked a button on his computer, bringing up a screen that read "M.N. Investigation."

"Go ahead. I'm ready. Tell me everything you know."

"Oh, it's not that, Mr...Sir. We're here to inquire if you've retraced Maddysin's steps on the day she disappeared."

Thud raised one brow, causing the other to follow like a hairy caterpillar. "'Course I did. I look like an amateur to you?"

H.P. typed furiously before handing her phone to Thud.

"Oh, okay... Yeah, you can see her activity log for the day. Just don't tell the Noseinairs about it." He chuckled with a sound like a dry cough. "They think you're the devil or something. But I can read people, and you're not a bad egg."

He pulled up the information. "You two can read it, but no pictures, aww-right?"

Both women nodded. H.P. took the phone and held it, trying to keep a firm grip. Thud's hot breath on her neck made her even more nervous.

As they were reading, Thud's phone buzzed and the theme song for *Wacky Winkie's World* played.

"I gotta take this," he said without explanation as he snatched the phone from her grip. "Back in a minute. You two behave?"

As soon as he was out of earshot, Gwen whispered, "We're NOT going to behave, are we?"

She pulled out her phone and began snapping pictures of Thud's computer screen. H.P. scrolled through the pages of notes regarding the investigation into Maddysin's disappearance.

Just as they finished, Thud appeared behind them. H.P. stood and touched the back of her hair, as though it would somehow cover up their deceit.

Thud crossed his arms, gripping a firm bicep with

each meaty hand. "Does my investigation meet your standards?"

"I don't know what you're—"

Thud pointed up at a black half-circle attached to the ceiling. "Cameras everywhere," he explained. "I've got a job and you two have worn out your welcome."

H.P. was relieved he didn't demand Gwen's phone. Relieved but also perplexed. Why didn't he care that they took photos of his top-secret investigation?

As soon as they were in the car, H.P. showed Gwen her phone, which resulted in one of Gwen's signature nose scrunches. "You think Maddysin ate the market? She has some very quirky characteristics, but—"

H.P. shook her head and re-typed. Slower this time.

"Ohh. I get it! She was meeting with her marketing manager after you met with her?" Gwen scrolled through all her pictures. "That's not on her schedule for the day of her disappearance."

Chapter Thirty-Four

LIKE MAGIC

H.P. had so much to share with Gram Gram, but without a tongue in good working order, she was doubtful they could communicate.

She painstakingly wrote out the events of the past two days on her electronic device. She headed back to the diner, after swallowing as much liquefied food as she could stomach. She messaged Dex on the way, reminding him to finish his genealogy project and take a shower.

"I know, Mom! I'm not an idjit!"

Messaged received.

It still gave her the willies to enter a darkened business, even though, as the proprietor, it was her duty to be the first and last person every day. Her therapist called it "abandonment issues," stemming from her relationship with Dex's father, Eliot, and his leaving her for his second wife. *It's not about a curse, H.P.,* she reminded herself.

As she stepped inside the walk-in, it occurred to her that she lacked the ability to summon Gram Gram's ghost. "Necessity is the mother of inventory," she would repeat, even after her grandchildren corrected the saying time and time again.

H.P. found a soup ladle and brought it back to the cooler. She banged it against the cold metal shelves with the abandon of a three-year-old kid. Feeling free to express herself without a stern reprimand, she went from one to another and then back again, hoping that noise was what it took to summon a ghost.

Just as she was about to give up and go home, she smelled Gram Gram's signature honey pie scent. Turning around, she gasped when she viewed her grandmother's incredible presence.

She was surrounded by a glittery, gold light that lifted her silver hair and splayed it out as though she were posed on a bed. She wore a sleeveless, shimmering, white gown dotted with gold flowers.

"Darling girl, surely you know by now that those utensils are expensive. Denting them will NOT solve your problems."

H.P. waved before pointing to her electronic device and holding it up so Gram Gram could read it.

Gram mentioned before that she still needed readers, even in the afterlife, so H.P. had taken care to make the font extra-large. Despite that, Gram squinted as H.P. scrolled down the page.

"Heavens to blintzes, child. There's an easy way around this. Open your mouth, please."

H.P. closed her eyes and did as instructed, pointing to numerous stitches in her tongue. Instantly, she felt a warmth, like sweet, soothing honey moving around the inside of her mouth. It was both comforting and soothing.

"There. Close up."

H.P. didn't want it to end. It had been many years since she'd felt so completely loved and nurtured. Eliot had brought her new son to her and sat on the hospital bed. "We're a family forever and ever." He'd kissed the top of her head.

"Well?" Gram Gram asked impatiently.

H.P. shrugged, not understanding what she was being asked to do.

"Say something, Hun Bun!"

Maybe Gram Gram hadn't read all that she had painstakingly typed. Maybe she didn't care in the after-life. Whatever the reason, H.P. was going to be forced to demonstrate her current pathetic situation.

"I can't speak," she said, surprising herself with how normal she sounded. It went so well, she decided to continue. "I bit my tongue the other day, and—"

"Does it feel like it's still injured?" Gram Gram placed one hand on her granddaughter's jaw, a gesture that caused a warmth to flow from H.P.'s neck up to her forehead. Magically, her mouth opened without pain. "No, it's healed nicely, thank you."

H.P. stuck a finger in her mouth and gingerly touched her tongue. No stitches. No swelling. It was as if her accident never happened. "How did you do that?"

Gram Gram's ghost swirled around, finding a seat on a crate of eggs. "It's called Houdini's Healers."

"I thought he was a famous illusionist. Didn't that guy wrap himself in chains and escape from a water tank or something?"

Gram Gram nodded. "Yes, and he promised his wife he would return to her via a séance. When he couldn't make that happen, he complained to management. Oh, he put up quite a stink. Finally, they agreed to give him a special power in return for his leaving them alone."

"Oh! Like a superpower!"

"No, not like a superpower." Gram Gram frowned. "You kids and your need to make everything about a movie. Pea Pudding! Houdini gets to hand healers out to those who pass, sort of like a welcome basket. We get nice chocolates too."

There was too much to unpack, and she still had to explain what happened at the mansion to Gram Gram, so she just nodded.

"The only downside is that each ghost gets only seven point five healers."

"Why? And what is the point five about?"

Gram shrugged. "Beats me. Let's get on with it, though. There's a big ball tonight and I don't want to miss the Titanic orchestra. They get the early spot because they're great at breaking the ice."

"I'm feeling bad that you wasted a wish on me. My tongue would have healed eventually."

Gram Gram's ethereal form swirled around her. "This is MY afterlife, sweetheart. Let me decide where and when I make use of the welcome basket." She swirled up to the top shelf and crossed her legs, clasping her hands behind her head. "Now. Tell me everything. What happened when the kids visited the Noseinair mansion? What did they find?"

Although she'd just gotten the power of speech back, H.P. had been thinking about this ever since their visit. "Mrs. Noseinair is still bent out of shape about my incident. Do you remember? You made me go there and apologize for messing up Maddysin's vest." Her words sounded harsh. "Even though she'd been bullying me for years."

Finding she still had Gram Gram's attention, she continued her ruse. "Mrs. Noseinair told Dex his ilk wasn't welcome and, had he not been with Tildie, she would have ordered her butler to slam the door on him."

Gram Gram shook her head. "Isn't that telling? The woman never met a problem she didn't turn into a grudge. I'm surprised there was room in her head, what with all the people she decided had wronged her over the years."

At least her grandmother realized how flawed Mrs. Noseinair was, given Gram's lack of compassion at the mansion. All the way home that day, H.P.'s. body shook. She thought at the time it must be the curse, confirming the old battle axe's words. But Gram never noticed, or if she did, she never said a word.

"What did she know about Eliza?"

H.P. swallowed hard. No apology? After all that?

"She showed the kids Eliza's recipes for tinctures. She didn't mention how she came to be in possession of them, but Tildie read them out loud since we were recording everything. The butler booted them out as soon as Mrs. Noseinair tired of them."

Gram's glow changed from a shimmering gold to a rain cloud dark blue. If H.P. didn't know better, she'd think there was a storm brewing. What she thought was lightning replaced the glittering gold in her aura.

"She's in for a BIG surprise once she reaches this side," Gram Gram sniffed. "Did you find the recipe helpful, Hun Bun?"

"Not the recipe itself, but Eliza noted that it was toxic to humans. Followed by, 'Please be careful, my darling, B. It was written by Charles' brother, Benjamin." She paused for dramatic effect. "It makes her guilt even more likely if her husband discovered the tryst. But I just can't picture Eliza—"

"Purposely poisoning her husband? From what you've told me, Charles was a piece of work. When pushed to our limits, we all do things we never thought ourselves capable of."

H.P. cocked her head. "Like..."

"Like none of your spider's yarn, miss," Gram snapped, uncharacteristically dismissive. "You know, Hun Bun, the way your life works," Gram Gram continued in a softer tone, "everything is connected. What's going on with the murder investigation? Have they found that waffle whacker yet?"

H.P. giggled. "When you say it like that, it sounds like a circus sideshow."

"Well?" Gram Gram asked impatiently. "Did they find the killer?"

"No, not yet, but a waffle maker shaped just like the murder weapon found its way onto my shelf. That's why I asked if you'd seen anyone here after hours. Luckily, the mayor had no idea it was there when he hauled me in for questioning."

"WHAAT??" The cooler shook under the weight of Gram Gram's ethereal power, giving H.P. cause to grab onto a cold metal shelf in order to stay upright. "You buried the leaded pipe?"

"I think you meant to say, 'buried the lead,' Gram."

"That's outrageous! Why would ANYONE think you were a murderer?"

H.P. paused to debate the merits of honesty. If she told Gram she'd sent CeCe to drag Maddysin to her event, her grandmother would ask too many questions. "Wasn't her big check enough? Lies are like flies; the more they buzz, the harder it is to see the truth, Hun Bun."

H.P. pursed her lips as she thought. Once she'd come to grips with the bizarre nature of their meetings, H.P. came to look forward to her time with Gram Gram. They'd become much closer in death than during Gram's lifetime. No, she wasn't about to risk that now.

"Well...Mad's secretary mentioned that I'd been to visit her on the day of her disappearance. The mayor is questioning everyone who was there. All routine. It's so weird he's the one in charge of questioning everyone, but he says it's an old city ordinance. I haven't had the time to—"

"Your grandfather, the scoundrel, was behind that. He was mayor for a year and the power went straight to his noggin." Gram Gram tapped her silver-gray hair. "He and his moonshine-making buddies got caught by the Washington State Police trying to sell their putrid drink, and there wasn't room to house them anywhere but Misty Cove."

The picture forming in her head of her grandfather was a grim one. She'd always imagined him to be a handsome, bearded man with thoughtful eyes and a soft voice.

"And since he was mayor," Gram Gram continued, "he could issue a proclamation, giving him the power to investigate and question suspects. Pretty sneaky."

"That must've been at least fifty years ago. Why is that city ordinance still in effect?"

"Because the city council has always been filled with crooks. They want to make sure that if their illegal business dealings come to light, they can count on the mayor to handle the sham investigation."

Was Mayor McCloud working with members of the city council too?

"This sheds a whole new light on the situation. I'm trying to imagine a city council meeting where they discuss murdering the mayor's wife and Pearlie Gates."

"You're under so much stress, sweetheart. I'm worried about you."

"You know what I just thought of?" H.P. continued, completely ignoring her grandmother's concern. "You probably have a way to see things that aren't here, in the walk-in. You can probably use your superpower vision and find her!"

"Didn't I already tell you that I don't have superpowers?" Gram Gram scoffed. "Take a listen, why don't you!"

"Sorry."

"But yes, now that you mention it, I believe there is a way for me to see beyond my haunting. I'll have to check with management to make sure it doesn't go against protocol first, though."

"Houdini again?" H.P. asked, half-joking.

"Mrs. Roosevelt. She has a no-tolerance policy for rule breakers."

Chapter Thirty-Five

THE CHEWSEUM

"I'm fascinated by your grandmother's ability to completely heal your tongue. If I'd known the dead had those capabilities, I'd be having more conversations than 'What's this in your pocket?' with those that end up on my examining table."

Gwen invited H.P. to go with her to the Chewseum, the local food museum, to do some research. "She only gets a few. It comes in a welcome basket." She stared at her walking partner. "It sounds ludicrous, I know."

Gwen stopped and pulled on her arm. "Not in the least! We've never been lucky enough to see into their world. Think of this as a gift you've received! And your bestie is enjoying it too!"

They continued walking, down Burberry and left on Hurricane. Finally, they turned right on Eatright Way. The bright, yellow roof of the Chewseum was visible from three blocks away.

"What did you tell your son about this miraculous recovery?"

"That tongues are the quickest body part to heal. That the emergency room personnel told me it might be healed in a week or a month, depending on my general health." She laughed. "And it was the perfect opportunity for me to remind my son that I don't eat junk food or red meat."

The large orange sign always turned her off as a kid, but even more cheesy was the Chewseum's exterior. It resembled a giant picnic basket, complete with woven-texture walls and over-sized utensils as decorative elements.

They headed up the cement ramp, through the open picnic basket lid.

Kids at school used to call it the Moldseum, but no one ever explained why.

She pulled on the fork and knife in the shape of an "X" before realizing the "Simmer down. Dishes washed for the day" sign was illuminated.

"Looks like it's closed today. Maybe we'll come back next weekend? At least we got a chance to enjoy the nice weather. We should walk more often." H.P. turned to leave but was halted by a firm grip on her arm. She always forgot how strong Gwen was. The dry-cleaning business must be very physical, she reasoned.

Gwen pushed her glasses up her nose. "I called ahead. Etta agreed to let us in and give us a private tour."

As if on cue, the door opened, revealing a tiny woman, so small she made Gwen look like a giant, with tight gray curls, a round face, and square, wire-rimmed glasses. "There you girls are! I was beginning to wonder if you'd forgotten!"

Etta Snackwell lived above the Chewseum in a bite-sized apartment. She was not only the caretaker of the Chewseum, but also the heart and soul of its existence. Etta rarely ventured beyond the Chewseum doors. She never took a day off and only left for groceries. She was a sweet lady who welcomed each guest as though they were family visiting for a holiday feast.

They followed her through the doors and inside, where the floor resembled a giant checkerboard picnic blanket. Overhead, an assortment of hanging lanterns shaped like fruits and vegetables lit their way. Although H.P. hadn't spent much time there, she always marveled at the exhibits and all Mrs. Snackwell did to maintain the Chewseum.

"Apple red, citrus orange, and berry blue dominate, while the floors are a rich chocolate brown. That's after you leave the welcome picnic cloth area." She'd been there often, so H.P. knew that Etta went through the same welcome each time. It was part of her unique charm.

"Each corridor leads to a different exhibit," Etta continued, oblivious to H.P.'s trip down memory lane. "Follow me, dears."

They struggled to keep up with Etta, who was

chatting excitedly about the events they had coming up, including a farm-to-table dinner complete with local chocolates she and her brother made themselves. "Etta-ble Chocolates." She beamed as she spoke. Evidently, no one had the courage to explain the meaning behind the word "edible" to Etta.

Etta came to an abrupt halt, bringing H.P. and Gwen to an unexpected stop. "Sorry, Gwennie," H.P. whispered. "Didn't mean to run right over the top of you."

"In the middle of our main gallery, we have our Interactive Center, where visitors can engage in food-related activities and games. Currently, we're featuring displays explaining taste buds, flavor chemistry, and sensory experiences. A highlight is the Taste Lab, where visitors can sample unusual flavors, including spices from all over the world."

H.P. nodded toward Gwen, who winked. It was nice being around someone who understood the situation, good or bad. When they lived in San Francisco, she never had time for friends outside of work. Working two jobs most of the time, she was exhausted when she got home and rarely got to see her son, let alone have a social life.

"And, after all of that, Gwen mentioned that you gals are interested in the history of Wacky Winkie the Wallaby and his waffle makers? I was wondering when someone was going to ask."

"The mayor hasn't been here? That surprises me, given his interest in taking over the investigation." It didn't. It was one more reason to believe he wasn't investigating at all.

"NO one." The hurt in her voice was obvious. "I even left a message at his office, but the man never returned my call."

"We are so fortunate you chose to open today, Etta," H.P. continued. "Gwen is the one who realized your valuable information was being overlooked."

"Cover them in syrup and they'll do whatever you want," Gram Gram always said.

"We just have a few—"

"I've taken the liberty of putting together a slideshow. Please follow me."

Chapter Thirty-Six

ETTA SNACKWELL

It was a good thing H.P. had taken most of the day off. Although she intended to enjoy a leisurely lunch with Gwen on her covered and heated deck, the deadline to both make and enjoy a meal together was fast approaching.

"Doodlebug Animation Studios was founded in the picturesque town of Willow Creek, nestled in the heart of an area known for its vibrant art community and lush, inspiring landscapes."

A small mudroom was cluttered with stacks of paper, sketches, several pairs of boots, and a worn winter coat. The homemade sign above the door proudly displayed the name "Doodlebug Animation Studios" in bold, bright letters.

Click.

A thin woman with tight curls, not unlike Etta's, leaned her head on her fist, which rested atop her desk while her long legs stretched out in front of her. Her muscular, bare arms impressed H.P. while her eyes showed a hint of mirth, although in old black-and-white photos, she found it difficult to judge a person's personality.

"The studio was established in 1948 by Dottie Doodlebug, a pioneering animator and storyteller with a passion for bringing whimsical tales to life. Dottie, a graduate of the prestigious Willow Creek School of Arts, was its first female graduate and second to create course material."

Click.

The same woman sat in front of a Christmas tree, holding a curly-haired toddler above her head, while a dark-haired girl dressed in a robe and slippers sat beside her with a doll in her lap.

"Dottie hung up her animator cap when she had children, as most women of the time were forced to do, but the desire to create mirthful images never left. When she struggled to keep the interest of her two small children each night as she read them stories, Dottie came up with a brilliant plan."

Click.

The next slide showed a pig standing on his hind legs, staring lovingly into the eyes of his counterpart. His skin was a deep pink, and he wore a tiny golden crown perched at an angle and a royal blue cloak.

To his right was Princess Puddles of Kingdom Platypus. With her sleek, brown fur, distinctive bill, and long, curled eyelashes, she was a sweet character that H.P. remembered fondly.

Princess Puddles wore a simple tiara made of water lilies and a green robe. The colorful picture brought back memories of Saturday mornings in front of the television, eating cereal straight out of the box. She and her cousins felt like they were getting away with something, even though Gram Gram made them clean the living room every Saturday evening.

"Knowing how beloved her children's stuffed animals were, she used them as the inspiration for her characters," Etta continued. "The first two were Princess Puddles the Platypus and His Royal Pinkness, Prince Paul Pig."

Click.

H.P. marveled at the detail in the early sketches, each animal displaying hair or fur and deep, expressive eyes. All had a distinguishing feature on their robes.

"Soon, she'd expanded to ten main characters. Her husband urged her to contact an animation studio and she did just that." Etta turned to her guests and smirked. "And they promptly turned her away. Was it because she was a woman?"

"Of course it was!" Gwen piped up.

Etta shrugged. "We'll never know for sure. But they did her a great favor. I've always hated that saying, 'Everything happens for a reason.' In Dottie's life, it was her rejection by all the major animation studios that led her to create Doodlebug Animation Studios.

Using all their savings, along with a small loan from her husband's family, Doodlebug Animations was born."

Click.

H.P. glanced at her watch. 11:45. If only there were some way to speed this along without offending Etta. She'd created this impressive program, after all.

"Etta, I see you've got Winkie there on the screen. Can you explain his rise and fall?"

Etta harrumphed but clicked ahead several images. H.P. felt guilty about her obvious wish to leave. H.P. didn't want to burn any bridges, especially since Etta's knowledge was practically endless. "This has been so interesting!"

Gwen stared at her and frowned. Too obvious? She could hear her stomach growling, and desperate times called for desperate measures.

On the screen now were images of Winkie as a stuffed animal. "Dottie's last foray into the world of animation came at the behest of her elderly neighbor. The poor woman suffered from dementia and, frequently, when Dottie went to check on her, the old woman was carrying on conversations with kitchen appliances and utensils.

"Dottie was fearful someone in the woman's family would attempt to have her placed in a care home, even though the neighbors took turns looking after her. That's when she came up with an idea to both keep her neighbor as comfortable as possible as well as entertain her. Dottie quickly created cartoon characters based on her neighbor: Cannie the Can Opener, Millie the Mixer, and—"

"Wacky Winkie the Waffle Maker! Wow! I never knew the story behind it! What a wonderful thing she did!"

"It was," Etta conceded. "But she benefited too. The Kitchen Kavelcade became her most successful cartoons, playing in seventy countries worldwide and finally appearing on the waffle makers used in the murders.

"Dottie didn't want any of that. She had a stroke shortly after her husband died and asked her son to manage her growing empire. Dottie stipulated in her contract with her son that she didn't want Winkie's brand diluted. Her son didn't care. The Saturday morning cartoons, *Winkie's*—"

"*Winkie's Kitchen*! He gave us easy recipes at the end of every episode!" H.P. said excitedly. "I cooked— and burned—my first hot dog using Winkie's Wild Wiener Waggler recipe!"

"Yes, dear. Try and wait until I'm done to editorialize."

"Sorry, Etta. Please continue." H.P. knew her face must be the color of Winkie's Santa Suit stuffed animal.

"*Winkie's Kitchen* was a huge success. For the millionth time, the big animation studios came to Dottie, begging to buy the rights to her characters. She refused. Her sneaky son, Dinkus, met with them behind her back, but Dottie outsmarted them both. She had it written into the contract with Dinkus that the cartoon company stayed in her hands."

Etta cleared her throat and tilted her chin downward. "You know how a sneaky person refuses to give up? Well, Dinkus shopped his ideas around until he found a toymaker who agreed to put Winkie on everything, from gum to waffle makers. He even hosted a waffle recipe contest for kids."

"And who won?" Gwen asked.

"Some girl from Ohio. She had a recipe for Winkie's Wonderfully Wacky Whipped Cream and Walnut Waffles."

"Sounds—"

"They were absolutely disgusting, and one of the reasons the company lost their shirts on the waffle makers. Today, only ten remain in existence."

"How would anyone know there are ten in existence? Couldn't there be some collecting dust on a shelf somewhere?" Gwen didn't bother hiding her disbelief.

"Oh, heavens no. Antique appliance collectors are a serious bunch. When they get them appraised, they have a worldwide database telling them exactly where each waffle maker was sold and if it still exists."

"Are you telling us that Wacky Winkie's Waffle Makers are collectors' items?" Gwen scratched her head. "I've never heard of that!"

It was a rare day when Gwendolyn Folds had no information to contribute to a conversation.

"Yes, they are. The one we have on display here," she pointed to a glass case containing Winkie's Kitchen items, including a shiny waffle maker that looked like it was just out of the box, "was appraised at five thousand dollars."

H.P. grabbed Gwen's sleeve, in part to keep herself upright now that she was faint from hunger as well as in response to Etta's announcement.

"Why would someone want to bonk people over the head with one of these? Something so valuable and so—"

"Heavy!" Gwen said, completing H.P.'s sentence. "The murder weapon has gotta be dented big time by now."

H.P. mulled her words over before her eyes grew as wide as saucers. She turned toward her friend. "Yeah, it HAS to be dented, or even flattened, doesn't it? After thunking three heads, it must look like metal pancake by now!"

"Friendie, you sound...happy? Why would you be happy about a dented waffle maker?"

"No reason, really," she answered quickly. "Any thoughts, Etta?"

"If I were to guess, I'd say they had no idea of the waffle maker's worth. Probably working out some issues from their childhood too, I reckon."

"Is there a way for us to contact any of these collectors?" Gwen asked. "Maybe they can shed some light on exactly which one is missing."

Etta clucked her tongue and gave the women a

sorry look. "I'm afraid they don't like outsiders. I'm not even allowed direct contact. I send a message to a P.O. box and someone contacts me in a week or so. It's all very cloak and dagger."

Gwen and H.P. looked at each other and burst out laughing. "You're kidding, right?" H.P. asked. "This is just as ridiculous sounding as the Breakfast Mafia."

Etta gasped as she reached for H.P.'s arm, pulling her in to her side abruptly. "What do you know about BM?" she whispered.

"Ow! Please let go, Etta!"

When Etta eased her grip, H.P. explained, "A... friend...is being chased across the country by the BM. They burned down her parent's café and—"

Etta reached up and cupped her small hand over H.P.'s mouth. "Don't say anymore, dear. These people have ears everywhere." She leaned in close and whispered, "I've been told they placed a bug in my Chewseum, but I've never found one."

H.P. glanced helplessly at Gwen. Now they'd never make their lunch date because Etta was also under the spell of some tall tale that included underworld breakfast makers.

"Etta, could you elaborate? I promise, we won't tell a soul." Gwen gently removed Etta's hand from H.P.'s mouth.

"Follow me." Etta turned abruptly and marched back to her office, H.P. and Gwen trailing close behind. When they reached a bright, green-and-white-checked door, Etta ushered them inside and looked both ways before closing the door.

"The group of appliance collectors I told you about? They keep watch over other collectors, either by word-of-mouth or online. They don't want anyone selling outside of their group because it will drive prices down. Those who insist upon advertising must pay a fee every month. The muscle that comes to collect is unforgiving.

"I knew a man who collected old toasters. He was planning to make his fortune selling to collectors from other countries and bypassing this group entirely."

"What happened?"

"H.P., he was found in an alley behind his home with four boxes of Snyder's Strawberry Crispy Toasteds stuffed in his mouth." Etta shook her head as she stared at the black-and-white tiles. "That poor man. His entire collection of toasters disappeared, his legacy for his children gone in a poof."

"There are lots of evil people in the world," Gwen sympathized. "How do you know it was one of these collectors?"

"They left their calling card."

Etta opened the top drawer of her desk and pulled out a syrup-stained card, handing it to H.P. "They leave these calling cards as a threat to stay in line."

H.P.'s mind raced. *Where had she seen this card before?*

"This came from those goons." Etta motioned for

both women to come closer. "I believe Dinkus Doodlebug was involved with them."

She turned the card over and pointed to a small, almost invisible symbol in the top corner. H.P. took the card from her and squinted. "A mouth with large teeth. That's the symbol for Doodlebug Studios!"

Etta nodded. "If anyone other than the family used their trademarked symbol, it would be easy to put them out of business. But the fact that these cards have circulated for over forty years leads me to believe it's the one disgruntled family member who would seek out the people he thought had wronged him."

H.P. felt a shiver run up her spine. "I know exactly where I saw this card. It was in Frankie's trailer."

"Etta, you're positive that this comes from the Breakfast Mafia?"

"Yes, I'm afraid so."

"Etta, Dinkus must be getting up there in years. Does he have any children?"

A single drop of sweat rolled down Etta's face, stopping at her chin.

"Do you need to sit down, Etta?"

She clutched her chest and held it tightly until her breathing slowed. "No, I'm fine, dear. I've been afraid to say these words out loud for so long. But, like your dear grandmother used to say, things are most powerful in the shadows. Bring them into the light and they lose their hold."

"Jankies, Etta, you're scaring me!" Gwen said. "Out with it!"

"Dinkus never had children of his own. Instead, he chose to adopt a foster child. Who knows what would have happened to this child in a better situation."

"Who, Etta?" H.P.'s stomach was now in emergency mode, allowing her to snap at whomever she pleased.

"Mayor McCloud, that's who."

Chapter Thirty-Seven

A MESS OF EPIC PROPORTIONS

Although they had to pick up lunch at the Cluck Hut instead of enjoying something on Gwen's patio, H.P. was relieved to have some answers. Frankie played poker with the mayor. Was this "running from the BM" all an act?

She thought back to the day she was doing laundry and found a threatening note. Maybe it wasn't sent to Frankie. Maybe she was planning to send it to someone else.

"Glad you decided to grace us with your presence," Edna snapped. "We had a bus full of snotblowers and none of them knew how to treat a woman with respect." Edna paused for an awkward amount of time while she cleared the entire Pacific Ocean from her lungs. "Told the band director not to bring 'em back when they drive through tomorrow."

"Edna!" H.P. gasped. "You shouldn't ever, EVER turn away business!"

Placing one hand on her hip, Edna's face morphed into her smile/angry look, the one that signaled H.P. that the next thing out of her mouth would be a slight. "You'll want to take a gander in the bathrooms before you get that Mr. Flutist on the horn."

"Why? What's—"

Edna pointed toward the bathrooms and turned away, focusing her attention on a mop in a bucket full of dirty water.

It wasn't that she was squeamish, but H.P. didn't like the kind of surprises contained inside bathrooms. She opened the first door slowly. Instantly, a sweet scent assaulted her nostrils.

Looking around, she noticed red smears all over the walls, the mirrors, and the bathroom stalls. "What in the world?"

"Sour chewies."

H.P. jumped at the unexpected comment. Pivoting, she found her employee standing so close, there wasn't any daylight between them. "Edna!" she snapped. "Don't sneak up on people like that! The next person might have a weapon and hurt you!"

"This noggin's hard enough to withstand a waffle maker!" she exclaimed. "The snotblowers heated them up on the vents of the bus and then poured them out on their hands. They had themselves a good old time. You should see the other bathroom; they threw some chocolate bars into the mix."

Edna exited, her mission complete.

Tears filled H.P.'s eyes as she scoured the room

once more. It would take more than elbow grease to get this cleaned up. The Waffle Whacker, Eliza Tumblewood, the upcoming band day, and, well, just life were flowing down her cheeks as she struggled to prevent what was before her from burying what was left of her spirit.

You'll be cursed for the rest of your days, Honeypie.

"Nobody said this would be easy, Hun Bun."

Gram Gram used that sentence frequently to remind her grandchildren that success wasn't a given. "It's about your attitude. Simple as that. Pick yourself up and keep on a-moving."

H.P. sniffed and wiped her eyes as she allowed the restroom door to close.

"Frankie, it's your lucky day. Actually, tomorrow is your lucky day. I'm closing the diner to clean the bathrooms. Day off with pay."

Frankie glanced up from cleaning the grill and wiped her sweaty forehead on her pancake print sleeve.

"No day off, boss lady. It wouldn't be right after you've kept me on when my life is such a mess. I'll come in and help you, and I won't accept no for an answer."

Tears once again filled H.P.'s eyes. "Thank you, Frankie." She pivoted toward the walk-in. "I need to—"

"I know, I know. Clean the walk-in. This has gotta be the cleanest walk-in known to womankind."

H.P. decided not to reply. She was tired of making up stories. Without time or a valid explanation to retrieve her comfortable chair, she turned over her bucket and sat down. She didn't bother turning on the light.

She'd barely worked up a good cry when she smelled the comforting scent of baking pies and vanilla.

"Oh, my sweet, sweet Hun Bun. I wish I could hold you."

Gram Gram's image was wrapped in a warm, shimmering, golden light. She swirled around H.P.'s body tightly, creating a warmth like one of her famous hugs. It was just what H.P. needed. She closed her eyes, let her body relax, and visualized herself safe in her grandmother's embrace.

"Thank you, Gram Gram," she whispered.

"I tried leaving the walk-in. I wanted to scare those awful brats so badly they'd have nightmares for a month. But ever since the séance, my energy's been out of wonkers."

H.P. hoped Gram couldn't see the blush in her cheeks. "Anyway, we—me and Gwen—had an eye-opening visit to the Chewseum. Etta said there really IS a Breakfast Mafia. They're a violent segment of a group of antique kitchen appliance collectors. Do you know anything about that?"

Gram's eyes widened as her aura became a formidable dark green. "They're still around? I'll be a gorilla's cousin. I thought for sure they'd hurt their last collector when old Fridge Arator was found dead with an entire pickle and pimento loaf in his mouth."

"I don't know how to respond to that…"

Gram Gram snapped her fingers, only since she wasn't a living breathing human, it made more of a whiff-of-air sound. "That makes all the sense in the world!"

"Huh?"

"Your grandfather was a low-ranking BMer."

H.P.'s mouth fell agape. "He was in the Breakfast Mafia? Why didn't you tell me before?"

"I do my best to push every thought of that man from my head. This is MY afterlife, and I'm not going to spend it mushing around in his lumpy oatmeal."

Her grandmother had earned that right, and she felt bad for continuing the conversation. "Never mind, Gram, I can—"

"Under the direction of Dinkus Doodlebug, your grandfather hired a bunch of hoodlums to collect from people who chose to keep unlicensed appliances. Just awful."

It was difficult to imagine her Gram Gram, the most respected woman in the town of Misty Cove, married to such a deviant man.

"They met every Thursday at Number Two, a grubby diner in Seattle," Gram Gram continued. "Six stools reserved for their use. The police in Seattle knew all about their activity but refused to wipe them out."

"Why wouldn't they get rid of them?"

"Because Vinnie the Plunger was the brother of the Seattle police chief. It was a dark time in history. Very dark."

"You say that like nothing is happening today. If Etta was correct, the BM are still throwing their weight around."

"Even Vinnie wasn't safe in the end. It was a cloudy Saturday when Vinnie was found," Gram Gram continued, oblivious to H.P.'s cautionary words. "He was slumped over on the toilet. The official cause of death was a heart attack, but we all knew. He was wiped out by BM for ratting them out to the feds."

"Why didn't the feds raid the BM using Vinnie's info? Were they afraid of the BM too?" H.P. tried hiding her smile. So far, this sounded like a tall tale someone told Gram Gram over their second cup of coffee and a cinnamon roll.

"We assumed there was someone on the inside, but since no one knew for sure, we all waited to see what happened next. When Dinkus died, we went back to business as usual, thanking our lucky stars he and his hoodlums were no more. Clearly that wasn't the case."

"Gram Gram, in our entire time working together, you never once mentioned these people. Weren't you afraid they'd come to collect when you weren't around?"

Gram swirled up overhead, and the color surrounding her turned dark blue. Lightning bolts struck around her head. "You're making fun of me now. Why did I even bother telling you? Might as well get back to the potluck at Julia Child's place. The woman invites us over and then proceeds to critique every dish."

"No, Gram!" She couldn't alienate the one person who understood her. "I'm so sorry, I didn't mean to upset you!"

Gram swirled around the walk-in twice before returning to H.P.'s side. "The reason you never saw them, silly nilly, is because I wasn't one to keep unlicensed antique appliances. I saw no reason to drag myself or my business into that hole."

"You were very wise, Gram Gram."

"I'd heard rumors the BM had a new leader who'd taken them global, but they were just that—stories circulated about a mafioso with a real sweet tooth."

Chapter Thirty-Eight

A MESSY MYSTERY

With the Ballz and Bandz Festival a few days away, there was no time to confront Mayor McCloud about his connection to the Breakfast Mafia. The same went for Eliza Tumblewood and the truth of her involvement in her husband's death. H.P. enlisted the help of Gwen and Frankie for bathroom clean-up. Dex overheard her conversation with Gwen and enthusiastically volunteered himself and Tildie for duty.

"You're always telling me to do charity stuff, Mom," he insisted.

Way to throw my words back at me at the most inopportune moment, kid. "Fine. But I need confirmation from Mr. Bunce before I agree to Tildie's truancy."

Abe Bunce was only too happy to write his daughter a note so she could be of service. "Lessons aren't just learned in the classroom setting," he'd replied, as H.P. daydreamed about the fresh scent of his clean shirt.

Although she had her father's permission, and the school secretary had been notified of her absence, Tildie was crying that morning when she arrived. "I'm so sorry, Ms. Sweetwater," Tildie wept as H.P. rubbed circles around her back, just like she did for her son when he was down. "It's just that I hate to miss out on one minute of my education!"

Dex, on the other hand, couldn't resist the urge to celebrate. "Whoop! Whoop! No algebra quiz for this guy!"

H.P. placed her hands on her hips. "You do realize you'll have to go in early on Monday to make it up?" After everyone enjoyed the pastries and cocoa H.P. provided, Gwen retrieved two large buckets from the trunk of her car. The words "Serene Clean" were written in bold, green letters across the side.

"I'll go mix my concoction and divide it into two buckets, one for the goils and one for the boils." Gwen giggled. She disappeared into the kitchen, humming to herself. The strangest things made her happy, like crime scenes and cleaning up messy bathrooms.

After three choruses of Boog R. Noseinair's theme song, she reappeared carrying two sloshing buckets of something that smelled like oil mixed with salsa. Gwen set the buckets down and adjusted the rubber gloves she wore that extended up to her armpits.

"You all need to remember that this will stain clothing and probably ruin your shoes."

Everyone glanced down at their feet in unison. H.P. was resigned to the fact she would do whatever it took to get her diner back up and running. If that meant placing a group order for new shoes, so be it.

"Gwen said rubber gloves are a must, so I brought enough for everyone." H.P. handed out the ghastly lime-green gloves to everyone. When she got to her son, he scoffed. "I'm not wearing these, Mother. They look stupid."

Tildie nudged his side. "Don't be rude, Dexter!"

"Thank you, Tildie. I appreciate that you know how to respect your elders," H.P. replied approvingly. "And you don't have to wear gloves if you don't want to, son. Your hands SHOULD be healed by next week's one-on-one basketball tournament. If not, I'm sure they'll let you supervise the locker room."

She turned away so that he wouldn't see her grin. Honeypie Chiffon Sweetwater had the upper hand and she needed a moment to relish it.

"Geez! Why do you have to make a big deal of it?" Dex scoffed before gloving up. He and Tildie wasted no time attacking each other with pretend monster hands. They chased each other in and out of the booths as H.P. and Frankie looked on.

"You said you wanted to talk to me, about the BM?" Frankie's voice was high-pitched in a way that made H.P. think she was hiding something.

"Yeah, Gwen and I came across new information."

Frankie sat down on a shiny red stool and cleared her throat. "I'm listening, boss lady."

"I don't think the BM want to hurt you, Frankie. I think that threatening note was meant to tell you to register your Wacky Winkie Waffle Maker with them, or give it back. And don't worry, I'm not mad."

"Okay?"

Her lack of concern was curious. Wasn't this the same woman who insisted she'd leave town once they found her?

"Whoever is chasing you because of your black market syrup, it isn't the BM. They're only interested in appliances."

Frankie looked puzzled. "I don't understand. Waffle makers must be...licensed?"

Frankie tried to stand, but H.P. gently pushed her shoulders back down. "You left the evidence here because they demanded a large sum of money. Either you handed over the antique and pay their fee or suffer the consequences. I get why you were frightened, but lying to me and putting my customers and my diner in danger? That's unforgivable."

"I...know. I was in Idaho when I found a cool waffle maker at a garage sale for only fifty cents. When they asked for my name, I took it and ran. They tracked me down somehow, though, maybe through my license plate." Frankie sighed. "I figured you'd turn it over to the authorities and it would be out of both of our hands!"

"Whatever's going on in here looks too serious for bathroom cleaning." Gwen's head peeked in from the hallway. She knew darn good and well what was happening but, as was always the case with her best friend, Gwen acted like she had no idea what was being discussed. "Would one of you supervise the kids? I'd hate for them to accidentally ingest some of that stuff. It could stunt their growth or put hair on their respective chests before their time."

Before H.P. had a chance to open her mouth, Frankie jumped up. "I'll go," she said. "Thank you for understanding, boss lady."

They both watched Frankie until they heard her voice in the other bathroom. "It sounds like there's a party in here! Can I join?"

"How'd it go?" Gwen whispered.

"Later."

"I see that you're deep in thought, but zonkits!" Gwen's voice returned to its regular high-energy sound. "We've got to stay focused here!"

"Sorry, Gwen. You're right. I have all this good help. Let's get to it!"

Later, over an ice-cold beer, she would ask Gwen for her opinion on where to go next.

"The kids want to make a competition out of this," Frankie said as they reached the bathroom door. She refused to look H.P. in the eye. That was a bad sign.

"What kind of competition? We have to be very thorough in our—"

"The kids' team will have this place shining like the back of Grannie's silver before you ladies roll up your sleeves, Ms. Sweetwater!" Tildie called out enthusiastically.

H.P. squinted as she rolled up one sleeve. "Oh yeah? What's the wager?"

"Pizza twice a week for the next month," Dex's muffled but unmistakable, high-pitched voice replied.

"That's great, son, but what about us? What if we win?"

"We'll make you dinner, Ms. Sweetwater. You and Gwen."

Gwen giggled. "It's on, teenagers!"

Chapter Thirty-Nine

SECURE AND SOUND

"If you'd put some security cameras in the hallway here, we'd have an easier time in the future, ma'am," the police chief remarked. The poor man seemed like a shell of his former self.

"I'll keep that in mind the next time I have spare cash, Officer," she answered sarcastically. "May I ask how the murder investigations are going? Surely you've heard something?"

His pale face turned bright red. "Wasn't my idea to let him take the reins. No, sirree. We've gotta do something about that city ordinance. For now, we have what we have."

He stared at his feet. H.P. had a sudden urge to rub his back in comforting circles.

"Being that YOU are actually trained for this kind of thing, you must have some ideas on the killer. Is there someone you'd want to question, if you could?"

"Now, ma'am, we can't comment on official investigations."

"But you're not involved!" she continued, refusing to back down. "And I'm just asking as a concerned citizen, not as someone who works for local media." It was an open secret in Misty Cove that nothing was, in fact, a secret.

He cupped one hand over his mouth and leaned in close. "The mayor's got himself a girlfriend. Word on the street is he's been courting her since before his wife's death. My mother used to say people who cheat on their spouses have more 'n one secret in the vault."

H.P. was speechless. This was the first she'd heard about a mistress. "What do you think he has in his 'vault?'"

"Well," he whispered, leaning in close again, "and you didn't hear this from me, but the mayor's in some secret society. He AND his lady friend."

"What does the mayor's girlfriend look like? Can you give me a general description?"

He shrugged. "Blonde. Pretty. Younger than my daughter but probably twenty years her senior."

Dexter stuck his head in the door. "Should we save some 'za for you, Mother?" His eyes darted between his mother and the police chief. "And for the cop?"

"That's 'Officer,' son! Show some respect!"

The police chief cleared his throat. "None for me, but 'preciate the offer." He turned to H.P. "You fixin' to open your doors tomorrow?" He scratched his forehead, as though it were his decision to make.

"I don't have any choice, Officer. I have to pay my staff."

Gram Gram left her a nice nest egg, but she understood how replacing one large appliance could quickly empty it. She was proud that she'd only used what was needed to pay the bills she incurred in San Francisco and the spiffing up she'd done in the diner.

"I'll send someone over to install a few cameras 'round your building. Least on the outside."

"Oh, that's kind of you! But I just refinished the floor and bought new booths. I can't afford—"

He shook his head firmly. "No, this one's on the house. All the times your grandmother showed up with end-of-the-day leftovers, heck, she kept my six kids fed." His voice wavered. "Without her...I don't wanna think about it."

That was Gram Gram. Always thinking of others.

They were just finishing the bathrooms when there was a knock at the door. H.P. pushed stray hairs from her eyes, trying in vain to freshen her look when she discovered who it was.

"Abe! Here to pick up Tildie?"

"Yes and no. She hasn't messaged that she's ready to go yet, but I did want to speak with you."

"Oh?"

Shut it down, Sweetwater. He's strictly business.

"Can we speak somewhere privately?"

With the festival just days away, she and Frankie worked on the mini waffles and sandwiches that would be sold in the refreshment booth. She'd only asked to be reimbursed for the food, but since Maddysin gave such a large donation, H.P. took her costs from that money. Delores never asked why H.P. hadn't billed her.

While Frankie hummed to the endless music playing in her ears, she thought about the police chief's words. Who was Mayor McCloud's mistress? Had she come to the diner before without H.P. realizing who she was?

They were just about to finish up for the evening when there was a knock at the back door. H.P. and Frankie glanced at each other, sharing an expression of concern. There was still a murderer on the loose, among other things.

Without saying a word, Frankie grabbed the heavy cast-iron skillet and positioned herself to the right of the door. She motioned for H.P. to open it.

H.P. gulped. She couldn't help but feel a little sorry for the unsuspecting BM that was about to get clobbered.

As the door swung open, the might of Frankie's

muscular arms came down swiftly on the head of
Thud Punchard.

Chapter Forty

WITH A THUD

At the last second, Thud grabbed Frankie's arm and wrestled the heavy pan from her grip. It was an impressive show of strength by both of them. Another minute and Frankie might have clobbered him, despite his made-of-stone appearance.

"Ow! Geez, man!" Frankie dropped the pan, narrowly missing her cowboy boot as she grabbed one wrist with the other. "You didn't need to bend it like that! I'm a chef! These hands are my money makers!"

Although H.P. was concerned that Frankie might have been seriously injured and it was too late to find a suitable replacement before the festival, she was more concerned by Thud's unexpected appearance.

"What are you doing here, Thud? Did the Noseinairs put out a hit on me? The way things are going, I wouldn't be one bit surprised."

He frowned. "Not unless you know something I don't. The police chief sent me over with these security cameras." He pointed to a neat row of black boxes, lined up next to the garbage cans.

"I didn't realize the two of you were acquainted. Do you provide muscle for him, too?" Yes, it was a snarky thing to say. And yes, she meant for it to sound just that way.

"I wish that part of my life paid full-time wages," he mused. "We give law enforcement a big discount so they'll recommend us."

"I'd think with what the Noseinairs are paying you, you could buy a private island somewhere!" Thud's stony face turned stonier, if that were possible. When he didn't reply, she continued, "Well, go ahead. You don't have much daylight left."

He nodded, turned away, and then turned back. "Oh, how's your mouth?"

"Huh?" She'd already forgotten about her tongue and how Gram Gram magically repaired the damage. "Just like new," she replied quickly. "I heal fast! Any closer to finding Mad—I mean, Maddysin?"

"Got a few leads that I can't go into. We'll have her back to her family soon."

"What should I do, boss lady?" Frankie hissed. "Do you want me to stick around until he's done? I don't trust anyone with a face that flat. Looks like he's been on the losing end of his share of fights."

H.P. giggled then covered her mouth. "No, it's fine. He does appear to be a big tough guy, but inside he's all mush. On the way to the hospital, he told me all about his passion."

"And what's that?"

"Painting flowers. Watercolor flowers. He has a greenhouse where he grows flowers just to paint them."

Frankie looked doubtful, but she said nothing.

H.P. walked around the building until she found Thud halfway up a ladder. He was screwing a discreet black box into one corner of the siding.

"Heard you've got yourself a criminal," he said as she approached.

"That's probably a little dramatic. It was a bus full of unruly kids who most likely messed up my bathrooms on a dare."

Thud finished attaching the camera and climbed down. The small ladder groaned under the weight of his muscular body. "When I was thirteen, I started working for Bam Overhead, the local gang leader. I'll never forget his advice. 'Thud,' he said, 'never turn your back to anyone. The minute you show you're vulnerable, anybody has the upper hand.'"

"Bam never met Frankie and her kitchen utensils, though." H.P. cleared her throat. "On that topic, I'd like you to be honest about something." Luckily, she'd grown used to his intense gaze; it no longer gave her the willies.

"I'm not in the habit of lying."

"Are you working for the BM?"

He knitted his bushy eyebrows together. "Who told you about them?"

"It doesn't matter. You said you'd answer my question."

Thud closed the ladder and placed it under one arm. "Look, there's a real dark side to this town." His tone was surprisingly tender, almost as though he were speaking to his favorite grandparent. "You're a nice lady and you shouldn't get yourself caught up in that kind of ugliness. My good buddy, Barry D'live, was as tough as they come. He benched almost twice what I did, and he was still taken down by a waffle maker to the head."

"Thanks, Thud. I don't want to get caught up, but in order to keep myself clear, I need some information."

He sighed. "Yeah, I suppose." He glanced around, a common theme when people spoke of the BM. "What do you want to know?"

"There's a blonde woman currently in charge. Who is she?"

"My dealings have always been with the mayor. The only blonde woman in the organization is Mona the Mole. She's in her seventies and hasn't been active for at least twenty years."

H.P. searched her mind for anyone named Mona. The only person who went by the name of Mona was a little old lady who wore the largest, brightest, flower-print dresses and called everyone "my gal." Even the men she spoke with. "Are you talking about Mona Macaroni?"

"The same. She used to collect for the old mayor. Rumor had it they were an item."

"Mona Macaroni and... my grandfather?" Gram's disdain for her husband was making more and more sense. "Wow. But that still doesn't explain who's doing the dirty work these days."

"Heed my advice," Thud said sharply. "Don't turn your back. And don't ask questions if you're not prepared for the answers that follow."

Chapter Forty-One

THREATZ

The mayor and his Breakfast Mafia were so corrupt, nothing could stop them now. It was becoming crystal clear: if H.P. and Gwen didn't catch the Wacky Waffle Whacker, the murders would continue unchecked.

"I'm glad we're doing this." Gwen sipped her giant latté, leaving a frothy mustache above her lips. "Mmm. This is great. What do you call it?"

"I'm calling it Informant Irish Cream. You can also get it made with a shot of Breakfast Mafia Mistress Mocha."

Gwen wiped her mouth on her sleeve and shook her head. "You're playing with fire, bestie. What if Thud is right? What if they're lurking somewhere, everywhere, just waiting for someone to poke them with a stick?"

"I'm counting on it. Since no one can tell me who the mayor's mistress is, maybe she'll be angry enough to show her face. I've got some questions for her."

Was this more about the previous mayor, her grandfather, and his dalliances? Maybe. Either way, someone needed to get to the bottom of these crimes.

"In the meantime, I've taken the liberty of making a chart." Gwen pulled a large paper from her over-sized bag. At the top, she'd written the names of the victims, including Maddysin.

"Do you think she's dead? I mean…I don't like the woman, but I'd hate to think she was wiped out by the BM."

"It's a possibility. Let's start at the beginning. Barry D'Live was out for a jog the morning he was killed. His car was found parked a mile away, in front of Scone and Stone Masonry. His wallet and money were left inside. No one saw anything odd, and he was discovered by the Misty Moms Who Motor walking club."

When H.P. didn't respond, Gwen continued.

"Next on our list is Pearlie Gates. She was found in her garage, money and personal items still in her car. Same time, 10:30 a.m."

"What was Pearlie's address?"

Gwen looked at her notes. "4110 Sconewood Drive. Why?"

"It's all coming together, Gwennie. That's the street Scone and Stone Masonry is on, and I'm willing to bet the three of them met there for coffee!"

"Huh? You lost me, H.P. And don't you mean four? We're including Sunnie, right?"

"Yes, four. Gram Gram said she attended water aerobics with Pearlie Gates in the mornings. I'm willing to bet they all met up after going to the gym." She snapped her fingers before continuing, "And Maddysin said she usually worked out in the mornings! The day she was kidnapped, she made an unscheduled trip to the gym."

"And now you've lost me. If the afternoon wasn't normally her gym time, how would her kidnappers know she was there?"

"When I visited her office that day, she practically shoved me out the door so she could meet up with her marketing manager."

A loud banging on the door caused them both to jump. "We're closed!" H.P. called without bothering to get up and see who it was.

"What if it's the mafia?" Gwen hissed.

"Relax!" H.P. rose to see what was going on.

Delores Tootwhistle, the wife of the high school band director, was pounding with a fury. She was wearing a Noseinair Fighting Tissues t-shirt, shorts, and a thick orange terrycloth band around her forehead.

H.P. had a decision to make. Either she stood firm that the diner was closed and receive her wrath tomorrow, or she got it over with now. The second choice seemed preferable, given her light sleep these days.

"Delores? What's going on? We're closed. Gwen and I were just going over some paperwork."

Without asking, Delores barged inside. "We need to have a discussion."

She plopped down across from Gwen and stared

up at H.P. "Well? Are you sitting? I'm heading to the gym this evening and it closes at eight!"

Reluctantly, H.P. scooched in next to Gwen.

Delores slid her phone across the table. "I received this text from a dummy number."

H.P. and Gwen exchanged eye rolls.

"Read it!" Delores commanded.

H.P. looked down.

> Delores,
>
> Stop Ballz and Bandz or you're next.
>
> Sincerely,
>
> Wacky Winkie

"You need to take this to the police immediately!" Gwen cried. "Don't mess around with these people, Mrs. Tootwhistle!"

Delores appeared shocked. "I'm sure it's from those unruly children who destroyed your bathrooms. I heard some of the students gossiping about the names of the delinquents, so I reported them. The only reason I disrupted MY nightly routine was to give you their names."

H.P. clasped her hands on the table. "What Gwen means is that these kids weren't afraid to destroy our property, so it's likely they aren't afraid to do the same to the band room, or maybe your home. Right, Gwen?"

Gwen gave her a what-are-you-up-to look before nodding in agreement.

"Well, I'm not concerned about that," Delores replied dismissively. "We use Punchard Security and they timestamp everything, so if they attempt to destroy our property during the festival, we'll know."

H.P.'s eyes grew large. "Wait, they timestamp everything? How long are these videos saved?"

"I don't know. But last week, when I arrived home after a Bandz Parentz meeting, it caught a wolf and I've still got the footage on my phone."

H.P. slid out of the booth and rose quickly. "I'm sorry. I need to check on something." She tossed her keys across the table. "Gwen will see you to the door."

"You're not even a little curious which hooligans damaged your property?" Delores called after her.

"Not right now."

As H.P. walked across the large green space between the diner and her home, she pulled her phone from her pocket and dialed Thud's number.

"'Lo?"

For a moment, she wondered if there were ever an occasion for Thud to show emotion. His house being on fire? A car plowing through the front window of his business?

"Hi, Thud. This is H.P. Sweetwater. Can you tell me the timestamp on the gate to Maddysin's place? Around the time CeCe Scone climbed over?"

There was silence on the other end. "I'm not supposed to—"

"Yeah, yeah. You and I both know there's a whole lot going on behind the scenes here that isn't supposed to happen. Let's cut to the chase. I believe this is important information that might lead to Maddysin."

He sighed as loud as humanly possible. "Okay. Hang on a minute. It's not like I have anything IMPORTANT going on."

"Thanks, Thud. You're a peach."

She tapped her fingers on the dining room table.

"Yeah, it looks like that happened at five-thirty p.m."

Well before H.P. sent CeCe to find Maddysin. "Have you checked out the video at the gym? I know it was the last place Maddysin was spotted. I think the other victims were members there as well. Do you think they had a secret club or—"

"Slow down, Ms. Sweetwater. Are you telling me that the gym is the last place any of these people were seen alive and no one thought to put two and two together? That's outrageous."

His slightly perturbed voice came unexpected. Emotion. Thud-style.

"I have an idea where Maddysin is being held. Care to join me?"

Thud promised to pick her up in five minutes. As she turned around, she almost tripped over Cinnamon Biscuit Maker who was pacing furiously in front of her.

"What's going on, girl? It's not time to eat, is it?"

"Miss, I have urgent news!"

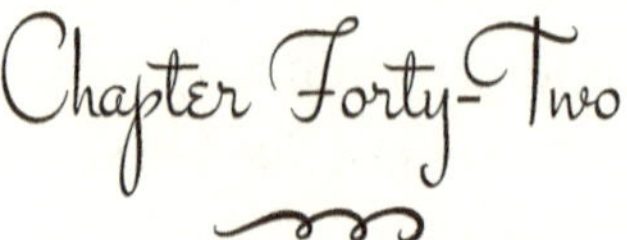

Chapter Forty-Two

NOT SO AUTOMATIC

She jumped up, almost landing on poor Cinnamon Biscuit Maker as she hit the floor. A familiar pair of sad, gray eyes greeted her. A ghost, dressed demurely, stood before her. "Eliza! I would say you're a sight for sore eyes, but I really don't have time to chat right now."

As before, Eliza wore a simple flowered dress. Her gray eyes were just as large and mournful, and this time H.P. could make out a distinct line across her neck. What if she never had another chance to speak to her again? With a sigh, she pulled out her phone and texted, "Give me an extra five. Got to put clothes in the dryer."

"You've been working so hard to find my killer. Thank you, Miss."

"You don't have to thank me, Eliza. But I do need to—"

"We met years ago, ma'am. I thought you'd remembered me on our first meeting. I thought that was why you summoned me and wanted to help."

H.P. searched her mind for any encounter with a ghost before Gram Gram. "Wait—you were in the house, YOUR house, when I was locked in with my friend. We were terrified and didn't think we'd find a way out. Until—"

"Until I opened the door."

"Until you opened the door," she repeated softly. H.P. felt a chill and noticed goosebumps on her arms. "You saved us! Oh, Eliza, how can I repay you?"

"Listen to my story, miss, now that I know I can trust you. My papa sanctioned a union between his eldest daughter and the son of the most prominent family in town. Charles was afforded a mere hour to agree, lest he jeopardize his inheritance of the esteemed Tumblewood Apothecary. It was a union that brought neither of us joy."

Eliza sighed. H.P. wished she could comfort her physically.

"In our sixth year of marriage, Charles' younger brother returned from his time in France. The night we celebrated his return, Benjamin excitedly explained the botanical creations and said he'd learned new ways to heal the body. When he imparted that the cost of healing could be drastically reduced, Charles demanded Benjamin take his leave."

Tears formed in her beautiful gray eyes. "My husband's cruelty knew no bounds; he brought our children to tears so many times at the dinner table, they begged to eat in the nursery with their nurse."

"Kinda how I pictured him, if I'm being honest, Eliza."

"Benjamin pleaded with Charles to examine his formulas for use in the apothecary. He told his brother never to return and forbade myself and my children from speaking to him again. I jumped up from the table, offering to usher him out. As I showed him to the door, I whispered, 'I want to know everything.'

"From that day on, we met secretly in the small cottage behind the estate. He educated me on the herbs that, when combined, could cure any ailment. I found my affections unaccountably entwined with Benjamin Tumblewood. Our first kiss was like a magic only found in the stars."

The best way she could speed this up without offending Eliza (was she really so concerned about offending a ghost? Yes, yes, she was!) would be to stay silent and nod sympathetically.

"During his time overseas," Eliza continued, "Benjamin learned new ways to heal. He imparted to me the lore of botanicals and the manners by which they may render their healing virtues. Not at all akin to the blends proffered by his sibling, concocted as they were with ingredients of scant cost yet abundant gain."

Nod. Nod.

"In concert, Benjamin and I fashioned a thriving enterprise, selling our homemade tinctures to those interested in more healthful remedies. All the while, Charles suspected nothing."

Nod. Nod.

A tremble coursed through her frame as her tears flowed unchecked. "I should have known that a hapless soul such as myself, coming from the poor side of town, wasn't meant for happiness," she murmured with a hint of betrayal.

"None of this was your fault, Eliza. Men leave wonderful women all the time."

Elliot Jenkins, for one. He ran out on his wife and child without a second thought.

"It's much worse than that, miss. Benjamin was determined to gain control of Tumblewood Apothecary. When Charles refused to share in the business with his brother, Benjamin immediately formulated his evil plan. He found in me a simp, an unwitting character in his tragedy."

Eliza trembled. "Everything changed the day my darling daughter, Chiffon, became curious as to the goings on in a hidden cottage. She entered, unnoticed, and watched as Benjamin and I shared amorous words."

H.P. felt horrible for both Eliza and her daughter.

"She went straight to her father and confessed. I thought Benjamin would stand by my side; he'd spoken before of our future together. I never should have trusted him."

"Wait, are you saying that Benjamin killed Charles? And then framed you?"

Eliza nodded as golden tears splashed down the front of her dress. "He used a poison I'd discovered, for use on household pests only. One morning, as I worked in the hidden cottage, he snuck in and filled Charles' coffee with the poison. It was me who found him many hours later. Benjamin taught me how to reverse the effects of this poison, but my efforts were too late. When I returned to the cottage, he was gone, along with everything we'd created together. The police arrived to arrest me soon after, being summoned by none other than Benjamin himself.

"I realized, too late, that it was the perfect way for Benjamin to gain control of Tumblewood Apothecary. He told the police everything I'd relayed in the strictest confidence, only this time it was to support the idea that I had poisoned my husband."

"Benjamin concocted the tincture to kill Charles, didn't he?"

"Yes, miss, that he did."

"That's horrid! I'm so sorry, Eliza. But how can I prove your innocence?"

Once again, she stared at her shoes. "Thank you, ma'am. But there's more you need to hear. His inheritance of Charles' apothecary did not bring Benjamin the wealth he craved. In fact, it was quite the opposite. Without my testing for quality, his tinctures were nothing more than colored water, and Misty Cove soon caught on. He bankrupted the business founded by his grandfather in only six months. That's when he married a widow, an antique dealer. The two of them began dealing in antiques, shorting customers as they went."

H.P. shook her head. Gram Gram's home, H.P.'s home since her childhood, was filled with memories and special antiques. The thought of one of her cousins coming in and stealing all of it made her sick to her stomach.

"Furthermore," Eliza continued, "he assembled a cabal of collectors, a band of greedy souls who agreed to keep the price of antiques inflated and cause harm to those who didn't. At the age of eighty, he took a young man on as apprentice. Dinkus Doodlebug."

H.P.'s mind raced. It was all a big circle of deceit—first Benjamin Tumblewood, then Dinkus Doodlebug, then, finally, Mayor McCloud. This needed to end. Now.

"Benjamin was disappointed in Dinkus. He didn't catch on as quickly as he'd liked, so he formulated a plan to poison Dinkus in the same way he poisoned Charles. Alas, Benjamin's trickery failed."

"What did he do?" H.P. found herself giddy at the prospect of Benjamin's demise.

"After a night at the theatre in the Doodlebug private boxes, Benjamin and his wife arrived home at half-past midnight. Before removing their coats, they were accosted by thugs and hit over the head with antique kitchen appliances. The maid came in late the next morning and found them. She assumed they'd been alone. She was wrong."

For the first time, the corners of Eliza's mouth

lifted. "I summoned all my energy, used my pass, and sat with them as the light drained from their eyes. Benjamin was surprised to see me, and although he couldn't speak, he begged with his eyes for me to end his suffering."

"I certainly hope you didn't. He got what he deserved, Eliza. Especially after framing you. I think I know—"

"Benjamin's legacy endures to this day, his brethren in debauchery lying in wait for innocents wishing to sell their inheritances. And Miss Sweetwater," Eliza said, her chin quivering, "your friend has fallen into their clutches."

"The clutches of...the Breakfast Mafia?"

"Mom? Can we talk?"

Eliza dissolved into thin air.

"Dex? Honey, I'd love to, but I'm in the middle of—"

"This won't take long."

She stared into his beautiful eyes, and she knew there was no way she could say no. "Okay. What's bothering you?"

"No, it's not that. Do you remember the day we left San Francisco? You came to pick me up from saying goodbye to my friends... You drove over the curb."

"I've apologized a hundred times. And I thought you were going to talk to those kids over the internet?"

H.P. couldn't help it, she was feeling antsy. But teenager time always outranked anything else.

"They weren't really my friends. I liked being smart by being with smart kids. But they all were involved in extracurricular activities and we could never afford those. So I walked home from school with five kids every day. They always talked about their expensive toys. One day, I stole one kid's phone. The next day, I stole another kid's portable gamer."

H.P. gasped. "Dexter Jenkins!"

"No, Mom, listen. That day, I decided I wanted a fresh start in Washington, so I returned everything I stole from them. Once we got here, I met Tildie and I could be myself and it felt good. She makes me a better me."

H.P.'s heart melted as she pulled him in close. "Oh, son! That's what I needed to hear!"

A brisk knock at the front door ended their embrace.

"And how is it you came to be in possession of this information?" Thud, in his usual monotone, didn't hide his skepticism about H.P.'s story.

"Does it matter? I know it's true! The Breakfast Mafia has its roots in early Misty Cove, and now they're knocking off everyone who knows that!"

H.P.'s irritation rose steadily, in direct correlation with the speed, or rather lack thereof, of Thud's truck.

"Can't you go any faster? We have to rescue Mad before they get to her!"

Thud placed an arm over the back of the bench seat, as though he were about to enjoy a Sunday drive for ice cream. "If what you're saying is true, then there was no reason for them to keep her alive in the first place."

They were both silent, pondering the validity of his words. Thud pulled into the gravel parking lot of the long-abandoned home of Charles and Eliza Tumblewood.

Now that she'd seen poor Eliza, H.P. felt a deep sadness. The small cottage where Eliza and Benjamin conjured their tinctures had been reclaimed by moss and branches, leaving only one wall with a faded roof sloping to the ground. At the same time, she felt empowered by the knowledge that Eliza saved her and Juniper. Tumblewood Manor was no longer a threat.

"Now what?"

"Why are you asking me?" H.P. asked, incredulous. "You're the guy with all the gadgets. You're the guy her parents hired. You're the guy—"

"Okay, okay." He glanced out of his tinted window. "We'll go in that door." He pointed a thick finger at a small door partially reclaimed by time, covered by vines.

"Why that one?"

"Because it's the only one covered in foliage, so it hasn't been used. No one will expect us."

Thud's logic, hidden beneath a calm exterior,

sparked a nod from H.P. They exited the truck quickly, leaving the doors open to avoid excess noise, and moved towards the vine-covered door with stealth. Thud, a man whose very name suggested the thump of something heavy, carried an impressive lightness that belied his stature.

While H.P. tugged the vines until they dropped to the ground, Thud extracted a set of lock picks from his jacket pocket. Within seconds, the lock clicked open— a testament to Thud's lesser-known, delicate skills. They slipped through the door, entering a dimly lit corridor that reeked of mildew and old newspapers.

"Stay close," Thud murmured, leading the way with a compact flashlight that emitted a powerful beam. H.P. followed, on high alert.

They encountered only cobwebs as they descended a narrow staircase, their breaths loud in the hush. At the bottom, a faint voice floated towards them. It was Maddysin's.

"I can hear you! Since you've made an unexpected mid-day appearance, you'll find I refused to eat your fast-food slop. I'll die of starvation before I clog my pores with that mush!"

Using hand signals, Thud directed H.P. to flank the other side of the door at the end of the passage where Maddysin's voice originated. Thud gave a silent three-count then burst through the door, H.P. swinging in from the side.

The room was sparsely furnished with a small stage on one end. Four wooden folding chairs sat haphazardly around the room. H.P. resisted the urge to explore. Why did the Tumblewoods have a theater in their basement? Instead, she focused on the remaining chair in the middle of the room.

Maddysin Noseinair was blindfolded with her hands and legs bound. H.P. dreamt of just this scene when she was in high school. Now that it was in front of her, she couldn't muster one ounce of enjoyment.

H.P. lowered her blindfold while Thud removed her shackles. As Maddysin squinted, adjusting to the light, she looked like she might faint. Not from hunger but from the sight of Honeypie Chiffon Sweetwater as her rescuer.

"What...? How did you...?"

"Save your accolades for later, Mad. Let's get you out of here first."

As Thud grabbed hold of one of her elbows and H.P. took the other, Maddysin cried, "No! Wait!"

A solitary diminutive figure appeared in the doorway and raised a gun. Thud dropped Maddysin's arm and leapt at the kidnapper with his arms in the air. He brought the perp down in one motion across the arms of the offender, causing the gun to fly across the room.

With the grace of a dancer and the impact of a sledgehammer, Thud incapacitated the kidnapper with a swift blow.

"Let's get out of here before we have anymore visitors!"

Maddysin's eyes were wide, but she nodded vigorously, her relief tangible. Without wasting a moment, Thud scooped up his communication device. "We have her. Extraction, now," he said into the device with a tone that brooked no argument.

Minutes later, they emerged into the cool night air, an unsteady Maddysin between them, just as a sleek black van drove into the gravel driveway. The van's side door slid open, revealing three similarly clothed people. One waved for Thud to join them.

He tossed his keys to H.P. as he hoisted Maddysin over his shoulder. "Take my truck back to town. I'll catch up with you later."

"Huh?"

Maddysin had regained her strength and was pounding her fists on his back. "Put me down, you brute! I'll have your license for this!"

None of this was making sense. "Is that the FBI? Or are you re-kidnapping Mad?"

Thud turned briefly to face her. "You know how to drive a stick shift, right?"

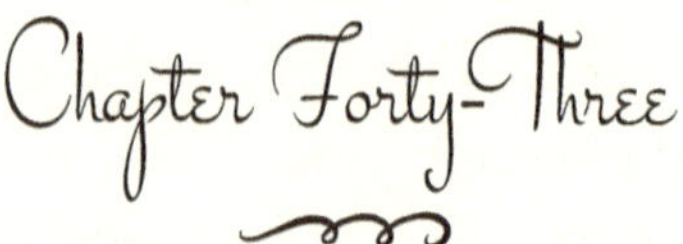

Chapter Forty-Three

BALLZ AND BANDZ DAY

"Welcome, welcome!" a loudspeaker blared. Delores Tootwhistle generously offered to climb up the utility pole herself to affix it outside of Honeypie Diner. Those looking on warned she should hire someone, to which she scoffed, "There's nothing I can't do. Just try me."

"Eighteen bands from up and down the Oregon and Washington coast have joined us, along with thirty-two Ballz teams. Please enjoy yourself today, and practice safety by taking a buddy wherever you go. Report any suspicious activity or unclaimed waffle makers to an adult. No particular reason."

After handing over hundreds of boxed breakfasts, H.P. took a few minutes to wander through the festival before the real breakfast crowd arrived.

As the festival kicked off, the air filled with excitement and anticipation. The main street of Misty Cove buzzed with activity as students wearing bright uniforms huddled in the safety of familiar faces.

The aroma of freshly baked goods wafted from the food stalls, mixing with the echoes of laughter and chatter. The sounds of a random clarinet tooting, a drum banging, and a horn blaring filled the crisp morning air.

After affixing the loudspeakers, Delores Toot-whistle moved to the entrance of the festival grounds wearing an odd expression.

A wide smile gave her face the unusual appearance of a pleasant human as she greeted attendees with infectious enthusiasm. She wore a colorful apron decorated with instruments in blues, greens, and yellows. Her pockets were stuffed with spare screws and nails, Band-aids, a walkie-talkie, and anything else required to tackle last-minute fixes that might be needed.

Ever since they'd rescued Maddysin, she and Thud's whereabouts remained unknown. Not only that, the Noseinair family had gone radio silent. Why? H.P. was tempted to show up on the Noseinair's doorstep and grill Seemah, but common sense prevented that disaster.

She called Punchard Security at least three times a day. Each time, she was greeted with, "Oh, YOU again. Sorry, I can't tell you anything." *Click*. His brothers had the same gift of gab.

H.P. decided to take matters into her own hands. The mayor was crooked, the BM's presence, and whichever one of them liked to kill people with waffle makers were still on the loose. When the note was shoved under her door, it wasn't a surprise.

Ms. Sweetwater:
We know you're meddling where you shouldn't.
Don't be surprised if the last thing you smell is a
chocolate delight waffle.
Always Watching

She tucked the note into her pocket and didn't tell a single soul.

Five Meal Gary was the first to volunteer to guard the Honeypie Diner. Of course. "I won't be needing my second breakfast today," he announced, hiking up the law-enforcement-official green pants he'd ordered from Nine-One-Wear online. He took his role as guardian of his favorite establishment with the authority of a seasoned veteran. "Packed myself two lunches instead, but if things get busy and I'm called on for overtime, I'll be coming in for my usual. You understand, I hope?"

"Perfectly."

"No waffle killer will get by me, I can guaran-darn-tee it."

"I want to tell you one more time that I appreciate your coming to my rescue." She hated the sound of that just as much as she hated needing help.

"Don't you give it anymore thought, Ms. Sweetwater. Not everyone grew up on a tractor like I did. Learned how to drive a stick shift when I was ten."

The Ballz teams were already lined up on Laughing Lobster Lane, waiting for their scheduled fifteen-minute-apiece warm-up. In the midst, H.P. spotted her son practicing his throws and her heart swelled with pride. Her shy kid, unsure of himself and reluctant to leave his room, had blossomed into a confident (albeit smelly and stubborn) teen.

Each team was adorned in their unique jerseys, representing their school colors and their sponsors. The H. Diner Dudes were given a choice of colors since salmon pink didn't seem quite fierce enough. They settled on a stealthy midnight blue and lemon yellow.

The sun shone brightly overhead, casting a warm glow over the festivities. It gave a much-needed boost to the locals after the dark events of the past few months.

As she reveled in the joy of vendors in vibrantly-colored tents, H.P. relaxed. "Nothing is going to happen today. We haven't heard from the Whacker in weeks," she said under her breath.

A loud noise came from out of nowhere, causing her to jump and turn around. A group of students who alternately laughed and blew their horns came galloping down the sidewalk. Wearing identical forest green uniforms with Fighting Flippers emblazoned on the back, the kids had no idea their gaiety was so unsettling. For a moment, H.P. marveled at their confidence.

Maybe Dex should have been in a marching band.

"Those kids come from Tellum, Oregon."

With the nimbleness of a cat, H.P. jumped and turned again. "Edna? Why don't you meet me face-to-face like a normal person? And who is running the diner?"

"All the other schools despise 'em because they win every competition they enter," Edna continued, seemingly oblivious to H.P.'s question. "Personally, I think it's rigged. I heard tell their band director slips the judges a few hundred every time."

H.P. sighed and shook her head. "I'm not engaging in this conversation, Edna. Wait—who's running the diner if we're both here?"

"Oh, CeCe is handling things just fine. She brought along a friend who used to work for your grandma. The two of them are like a well-oiled machine." Did Logan work for Gram Gram?

Despite those assurances, H.P. decided to return to the diner. She paused in front of a tent where a sign read "Grandma Billie's Fortune Telling."

H.P. recognized the woman who attended their séance, dressed in full fortuneteller regalia, from the brown scarf on her head to the jingling bracelets as she motioned for H.P. to join her.

"Sorry. I need to get back to—"

"I'm sensing a darkness surrounding you."

That was dubious, considering Gram Gram told her this woman was a scam artist.

"Umm, yeah. I really have to go. There are teens running my diner and you know how teens can be."

"Someone from your past—maybe a grandparent —wants to give you a message."

Now she KNEW this was a farce. "It was nice seeing you again."

Billie's eyes rolled back in her head as she grabbed H.P.'s arm.

Cool trick. But not exactly original.

"You're the superhero today. Do it for your baby boy, Hun Bun, and look back before you look forward, darling girl." Billie opened her eyes and squinted as they adjusted to the harsh light. "What just happened? Did I black out?"

H.P. hid her shock. "I don't know, Billie. Whatever is going on with you would probably benefit from some good vitamins from the Mighty Vitey Shack. I really need to go now."

H.P. shook her arm free and stomped off. "What do you mean by, 'Look back before you look forward,' Gram? Should I really be solving your riddles now?"

"It's happened! Again!"

In an instant, a cavalcade of terrified faces came sprinting towards her like they were in the streets of Pamplona during the running of the bulls. "What's happened?" H.P. yelled, hoping at least one person would stop. Judging by the looks of terror, it wasn't anything good. Judging by the pit in her stomach, she knew without asking.

Finally, a familiar face came by at a slow gallop. "Gwennie! What in the world is happening?"

"The Waffle Whacker left another victim," she

replied without emotion. "I was trying to find you, but when everyone started running, I had to keep up or they'd trample my sample-sized bod." She shoved her glasses up her nose. "What are you doing here? I thought you'd be at the diner."

"I'm heading there now. Do you have any idea who the victim was?"

"Delores Tootwhistle."

Chapter Forty-Four

THE BLACK VAN CREW

H.P. felt immense relief when she found Delores Tootwhistle very much alive, nursing a head wound.

She fought her way through the growing crowd and bent down beside her. "Delores, who did this?"

Next to Delores sat a gingerbread waffle covered in sliced pears and whipped cream. H.P. swallowed hard. The next waffle would be hers.

She glanced up at H.P. as she pressed a Ballz and Bandz shirt against her scalp. "I didn't see. It was a woman's voice though."

"What did she say?"

"You've been sticking your nose where it doesn't belong, Delores. And now, you get to join the others."

It was all falling into place. "You and the other victims were members of the gym. You didn't go there to work out, though. You were there to save the town from—"

"Ms. Sweetwater, please step aside."

H.P. looked up, unhappy to see the volunteer emergency crew. "I can ride with her to the hospital, can't I?"

"Not enough room, ma'am."

She felt a firm grip on her arm and attempted to shake it off. When she glanced up, she realized it was physically impossible. "Thud! What are you doing here?"

"Come with me, please."

She followed him grudgingly to a large SUV with tinted windows. "I'm not getting in there," she said firmly. "I have a business and a diner to run. I can't just disappear."

"Nothing will happen to you. Get in."

She realized there was very little she could do to dissuade him, so she opened the door.

"Took you long enough, Sweetwater!"

"Mad?"

Maddysin yanked on H.P.'s arm until she was sitting next to her. Thud got in and closed the door as they sped away.

"What is the meaning of this?"

"I've been working with the FBI to bring down the Breakfast Mafia for almost a year. We've had operatives all over the country, but they're always one step ahead of us. Thanks to our undercovers, the frying pan is about to come crashing down on their heads."

"You'd better explain quick." H.P. leaned back and crossed her arms.

"Frankie trucked illegal syrup for years."

"I already know that!"

"You don't know that we caught her. She agreed to make a deal with us to bring this terrorist organization down." Maddysin made a little clucking sound that irritated H.P.

"Quiet, Mad!" she snapped.

"Frankie came here to draw them out. We knew they had a large cell here, run by the mayor. What we didn't realize was that his wife wanted a divorce. She followed him to a BM meeting and discovered everything. That's when she enlisted the help of her gym friends."

H.P. brought a hand to her mouth. "And the BM found out and killed them! I knew there was a connection to that gym." She glanced over at Maddysin, who looked like she was ready to chew through her seat belt. "What? Are you going to tell me why they didn't kill you? And who did you kill at Tumblewood Manor?"

"I need your help first."

Chapter Forty-Five

BM BAGGAGE

H.P. smoothed her Honeypie Diner uniform as she exited the SUV in the alley behind the diner. "Don't screw this up, Sweetwater!" Maddysin hissed. "There's too much riding on it!"

The shock of seeing Mad, Thud, and his brothers wore off quickly as Thud explained his plan. They would lure the killer into the diner, get them to confess to murder, and Thud would swoop in and handcuff the suspect.

"Who's going to lure them in? One of your brothers?"

The only sound in the vehicle was a very loud fan that blew Maddysin's hair into an even higher pile. She'd missed her decade—Maddysin Noseinair had the style of an '80s icon.

"Oh, wait a minute...you think I'M going to be the bait?"

"Wasn't that your plan all along? You made those

drinks to ruffle some feathers."

"Yeah, but..." She hadn't seriously thought the BM would be enticed by a mocha with a little extra chocolate. It was just her way of blowing off oat milk foam.

As they drove around, H.P. became more confident she could do this. She thought about the insecurity she'd fought since high school, that she'd unwittingly passed on to her son. Honeypie Sweetwater needed to show Dex she wasn't afraid any longer.

Today, she wasn't just the owner of a diner; she had the starring role in her own live-action game. H.P. played the role of a mouse in a carefully thought-out game. The cat was, as yet, undetermined. Either way, someone's entire life would change by sundown.

"Is everything in place?" she asked, seemingly talking to herself.

"Like dominoes. Just waiting for the flick," Thud's voice in her ear assured her. Then, with a tone that bordered on casual, he added, "Today, their reign of terror ends."

She nodded, forgetting for a moment the distant nature of their conversation.

H.P.'s heartbeat quickened at the thought of coming face to face with the killer, the head of the Breakfast Mafia. The mayor was going to regret his dismissive treatment of her. What was she thinking? If he didn't regret killing his own wife, he wasn't about to concern himself with H.P.'s discomfort. Her mind inevitably returned to Mrs. Noseinair's cruel words all those years ago: *Your life will always be cursed. You will always fail.*

All the jobs she'd lost, seemingly for no good reason, her ill-fated marriage, and everything else that went wrong, she'd blamed on this curse. Maybe it wasn't a curse at all; maybe it was H.P.'s guilt over what she'd done to Maddysin when it was Logan who'd been the mastermind. She'd allowed herself to be controlled by one woman's vendetta all these years later.

Today, that ended.

As she walked into the diner as casually as possible, a voice blared over the loudspeakers: "There's a special treat waiting for the Breakfast Mafia. Are you sure this is right?"

There was a temporary pause while the announcer consulted with someone, clearly making sure he'd read that correctly. "Okay, folks, yes, it IS the Breakfast Mafia, no typo. They're a couple of hours late to the festival." He chuckled at his joke, referring to the late hour of the day. "And all of you crazy eggs in attendance better ride your buttered toast blankets over to Honeypie Diner."

Frankie, who'd been scraping the grill, knitted her brows together as she looked up. "We're closing in fifteen minutes, boss lady, and we've pretty much used up our supplies."

"Not to worry, Frankie."

H.P. knew about Frankie's secret, that she'd been working with the FBI, trying to bring this group down. But, at the moment, she didn't have time to explain the plan to her. "You can leave and I'll finish cleaning the kitchen. There are some fun booths over at Pep's Coffee Field."

Frankie ran one hand through her short hair. "Ma'am, there are things you don't know about. Things—"

"You've done your job, Frankie. Now let me do mine."

The bell over the door jingled and H.P. grabbed Frankie's arm instinctively. "Go out the back!" she whispered. "It isn't safe for you to stay!"

With as much composure as she could muster, H.P. walked to the front of the diner. There, Mayor McCloud stood with a somber look on his face. "Your grandmother would be ashamed. She wasn't the sort to play these games."

"I'm not either, Mayor, but one of you left your calling card this morning and I didn't have a choice." H.P. reached into her pocket and pulled out the crumpled note, laying it on the counter. "We Sweetwaters don't take well to threats."

The mayor's face turned ashen. "You didn't seem surprised to see me. Why?"

"Ever since your wife died, you've been acting strangely. At first, I thought it was your way of handling grief and I tried keeping my distance. Frankie mentioned that, during your poker game, you always got up to leave at the same time each week. On Thursday, Edna put a tracer on your phone when you went to the bathroom. And guess what she found?"

That was a bluff. Edna and technology weren't friends. In fact, H.P. would go so far as to say they were sworn enemies. Thankfully, Thud informed her that Edna had gone home early with a headache, so she wasn't there to argue.

H.P.'s eyes darted around the diner, looking for CeCe or her friend. Neither were there. How did Frankie run the diner without waitstaff? That woman deserved a raise.

"I won't deny it, I was at the Noseinair place. Seemah and I have been the business end of BM for a number of years. We've kept the price of antique appliances inflated and kept our members in business." He looked up and smiled. Was that pride rolling across his face? "It was going smoothly until Barry decided to break away from the group."

"D'live? Your poor cousin."

"We were never close. He liked talking to the dead more than the living anyway."

"And that's why you killed him? What about the others?"

"After water aerobics class one morning, Barry approached Windy and told her everything. He wanted to break away from the BM and do his own business, and he thought she should know about my involvement. Pearlie overheard and wanted to help, and Maddysin Noseinair came back for her gym bag one morning and got in on the conversation. They met at Scone and Stone every weekday for coffee, trying to figure out how to bring us down."

"Clearly you found out. How?"

"Windy confronted me. I had a listening device placed under the only table and we knew exactly what they were planning."

"Not that I don't believe you, Mr. McCloud, but you have that stupid ordinance that gives you power over the police. You have the backing of the BM. Why would you be afraid of four little gym rats?"

He snorted so loud, H.P. jumped. "I didn't say I was afraid. I was mad that my wife would betray me. She and her gym friends had been following me and documenting my whereabouts. They planned to speak with the governor the following week, so we had to act fast."

He pulled a gun from his holster and pointed it at H.P. "Is that all you wanted to know? If so, I'll make sure everything's cleaned up real nice when we're done. This place will sell quicker 'n sunscreen in July."

"Wait! I know something you don't. You lost a member of the BM today. Wouldn't you like to know who that is?"

He shrugged. "Depends. Are we talking a higher-up, or is it someone who was paid by the hour?"

"CeCe's boyfriend, Timber Logsplit!" H.P. couldn't believe her ears; Mayor McCloud acted as though she were talking about the wrong pizza order, not one of his BM members who'd just lost his life.

"Just a kid who was probably more scared than we were."

"He wasn't an important part of BM," Mayor McCloud scoffed. "Fact is, the only reason I agreed to keep him on after he bungled Maddysin's first kidnapping attempt was because I wanted to keep little CeCe happy." The mayor scratched his forehead and frowned, as though a discarded teen was just an irritant. "Sweet gal. Too bad that blew up in my face."

"Oh, now I get it. His only purpose was to babysit your hostage. Other than that, he was collateral damage. So, by my count, Sunnie Daze, Barry D'live, Pearlie Gates, and Timber Logsplit all lost their lives because of your twisted sense of importance. And, even more atrocious, you planned the murder of your own wife, Windy."

"You left out one. Ms. Sweetwater, it was a pleasure to make your acquaintance, but there's no use in dragging this out." He cocked the gun. "I don't wanna wait too long, otherwise the snack shack will run out of fried dough on a stick."

Chapter Forty-Six

WATCH OUT FOR THAT WAFFLE!

Even though H.P. knew she was safe, and Thud was listening to every word, she felt a chill run down her spine. Having a gun pointed directly at her would do that. Now that Mayor McCloud had confessed, there was no way he'd allow her to leave the diner alive. How could she have been so stupid? Her only hope was to stall him.

"Now that I know WHY they were killed, who was the killer? And why didn't they kill Maddysin too?"

"Complications."

Her mind raced. "Seemah Noseinair wanted her daughter out of the way but she didn't want her dead."

The day Abe Bunce came to pick up Tildie, he pulled H.P. aside. "You're right," he'd whispered in her ear, "someone is trying to set you up." She had trembled at his words as though they were sweet nothings. "You've gotten too close to the truth and they want to take you down. It's the mayor and two influential women. I can't be sure, but..."

"Well..." The mayor rubbed the back of his neck. It was now red and blotchy. H.P. foolishly hoped he'd have a deadly allergic reaction to something in her diner but soon realized he'd eaten everything but the new flooring without so much as a cough. "Shoot. Your hours are numbered anyway, so I might as well tell you. Seemah was more'n ready to eliminate her daughter. Maddysin and her friends knew too much."

H.P. opened her mouth to protest but wisely decided to hear him out. The longer he talked, the more evidence Thud could gather.

"She's the head of a worldwide crime syndicate and Maddysin wasn't going to ruin that for her. But my girlfriend has a working relationship with Maddysin and wanted to give her time to change her mind. She'll be here any—"

"I've been waiting to make my entrance, darling," a voice cooed from the kitchen. It was one H.P. remembered well from the high school bathroom. "Flush again, Maddysin! Keep going until she cries!"

Sashaying like her hips were her weaponry, Logan Berry-Scone slithered out from the kitchen, holding one arm suspiciously behind her back. She sidled up to the mayor and planted a sloppy, disgusting kiss on his lips. For a woman who'd been blonde, caked with makeup, and bathed in perfume all through high school, she looked markedly different. Her trademark teased-blonde hair was replaced by a short brunette bob and her face was, well, manufactured in a lab somewhere.

"If you're going to kill me, please let my stomach settle first," H.P. said with a touch of sarcasm. "And if you were hoping for shock value, I'm sorry to disappoint you. CeCe said her mother was doing marketing now, and Maddysin told me she was meeting with her marketing manager on the day she disappeared. It all fits together now."

The corners of Logan's mouth rose slightly. "Aren't you the clever one? My daughter said you'd developed a spine. At least something worked out for you." She turned to the mayor. "Poor, poor Honeypie. She was the laughingstock of our class. Always dressed in dumpy hand-me-downs and couldn't put a sentence together without stumbling and stuttering."

"You're the hitwoman for the BM? The Logan I remember didn't like getting her hands dirty." *Stall, Sweetwater. Just stall.* "You ordered your simpleton friends to do your dirty work. I never cracked once." H.P. sniffed defiantly. "Just imagine how you'd moan and complain if someone forced your head in the toilet!"

Logan's eye twitched, but she said nothing.

"Actually, I figured it was you I saw trying to climb over Maddysin's security fence. The way you struggled... gotta be embarrassing to be so out of shape."

Logan glared at her. "I've done forty-three hits worldwide and, I can assure you, there isn't an ounce of fat on this body. I spend four hours every day in the gym—"

"Where's CeCe? Did she uncover her mother's dark side, so you hurt her too?"

Logan cocked her head, and H.P. swore it slid over in one chunk. Powerful assassin or not, she'd struck out when she chose THAT doctor.

"I almost forgot. Please excuse my rudeness. Darling?"

"There's no one else here, Logan," H.P. chuckled. "You might be losing what little there was of your mind."

"We've been in the bathroom waiting for you."

H.P. whipped around, shocked to see CeCe's shaky hand holding a gun. It was trained on the most precious person in her life.

"Looking for my daughter, H.P.?" Logan Berry-Scone's voice was syrupy-sweet but laced with venom. "I was just about to tell Ms. Sweetwater about my newest waffle recipe. Please bring those two scrumptious children front and center."

Dex and Tildie clasped each other's hands tightly as CeCe Scone inched them forward, the gun fixed on Dex's temple.

"Mom?" Dex's voice quivered, turning her legs into butter.

"I'm thinking a nice raspberry for this one," she said as she gestured toward Tildie with her gun. "And something savory for this strapping guy. He seems like the cheddar and bacon type, doesn't he, darling?"

CeCe's laugh sounded hollow and, for a moment, H.P. felt sorry for this girl who was placed in an impossible position: do as she was told to gain her mother's affection or do what she wanted and be cast aside.

"My mouth is watering just thinking about it, Mom," CeCe replied with forced enthusiasm. Dex had tried to warn her about this one, but she'd brushed him off.

Doing as instructed, H.P. lured them in and got them to admit to their crimes. But where was the back-up she was promised? Was this part of Seemah's curse too?

Seeing no other option, H.P. summoned all her strength and rushed the mayor as though she were an angry bull charging a matador. Her impulsive move worked. She knocked both Mayor McCloud and Logan to the ground. "My lashes! Thunder, get off them! I just had them done!" Logan cried as she grabbed her face.

H.P. grabbed the mayor's gun which had slid across the floor and ran to CeCe, pointing it directly at her head. Everything inside her screamed to stop, but the Mama Bear voice in her head screamed louder.

"Let them go, CeCe, and you won't get hurt."

CeCe's eyes filled with tears. It was obvious she was petrified, but she still held a gun on Dex.

"Your boyfriend Timber is dead because of your mother and this group of thugs."

"What?" Tears filled her eyes as CeCe dropped her gun arm to her side. She glanced quickly from her mother, who was dusting herself off, to H.P. and back again.

"Just go!" CeCe yelled to Dex and Tildie, giving them a hard shove.

Fortunately, Dex landed in the outstretched arms of his mother and she held tightly to her precious boy. "Baby, I love you more than life. But you and Tildie need to get out of here fast!"

She gave his Ballz uniform a quick nuzzle, far shorter than she would have liked. "Now go!" She gave her son a hard shove.

"No, Mom. I'm not leaving without you."

She felt her son being jerked from her grip at the same time something hard hit her on the head. The last scent to enter H.P.'s nostrils was one of Gram Gram's peanut butter waffles.

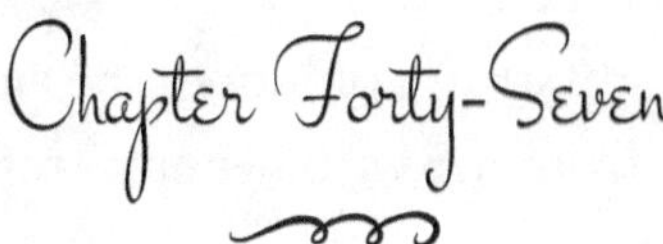

Chapter Forty-Seven

As she fell into a dizzy heap on the tile floor, she thought about her son and how she'd failed him. No curse, just failure as a parent. All the times they shared a bowl of cereal because she couldn't keep a job. Her fractured marriage. Disconnecting from her cousins. She could have done so much better for him.

Her muddled thoughts were of Dex's new and happy life, with Tildie and Abe in their big fancy house. Abe would teach him how to wear suits and speak lawyer. The three of them would become a happy family. That is, as long as Abe didn't remarry some gorgeous young woman...

There was a scuffle going on above her, but H.P. couldn't force her eyes to watch. She heard the words, "Run, kids!"

"Frankie? Is that you?"

Her eyes finally lost out to her curiosity as she opened them just enough to see a shadowy figure detaching from the wall. It was a thick, square silhouette that gave her hope.

She attempted to push herself to a sitting position, but wooziness prevented it. Instead, she lay back down. Through a steady stream of blood, she viewed CeCe directly across from her with her arms restrained behind her back.

The young woman stared at her tearfully. After all the deceit, all the times she seemingly left early for an innocuous event that was really an errand for her mother, H.P. felt compassion. H.P. knew how the teenage mind worked. Defiant and self-serving. At the end of the day, all they wanted was unconditional love.

It all made perfect sense now. CeCe mentioning that her mother would pay her apartment rent for a year. It was small compensation for helping carry out these dirty deeds! And the mayor's friendliness was due to his relationship with Logan.

And the apron... *look back before you look forward*... H.P. assumed the threatening note she pulled out of the dirty clothes hamper came from Frankie, but it must've come from CeCe. She was tasked with leaving it in Frankie's RV.

But why didn't Frankie admit the note wasn't hers? The night Dex came home late and she watched the Tulip Sloan movie, there was something very familiar about the dialogue.

"I was doing my thing, working lunch orders, when a man and woman came in and ordered two grilled ham and cheeses on rye. Next thing I know, there's screams coming from the front of the house. I peeked through the small window where I set plates for pick up. It was carnage, boss lady. Every lunch order in the place was covered in... I just can't talk about it. You understand why I can't bring myself to make lunch orders now."

Word for word from Tulip Sloan's movie.

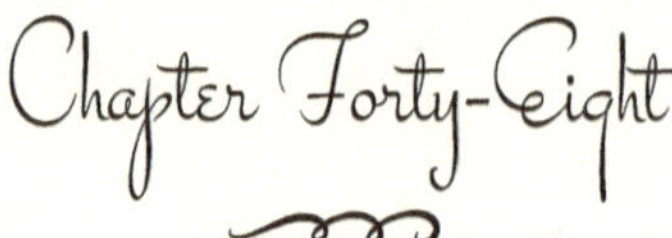

Chapter Forty-Eight

"You think you're tough, lady?" a deep voice growled. "In a minute, you'll be outnumbered!"

"Thud!" H.P. shouted, or maybe she just mumbled. At this point, she couldn't be sure what her face was doing. Maybe Gram Gram's spell had worn off and her tongue was back to being a useless flap of flesh.

Somehow, the petite woman and muscular man were evenly matched, each grunting as they lunged at each other, punching and kicking.

She knew it was wrong, but she couldn't look away. In the midst of round three, H.P. sensed someone standing over her. She rolled onto her back just in time to see the mayor preparing to clobber her over the head with a dented Wacky Winkie Waffle Maker. It was covered in blood—her blood—but there was no time to worry about that now. She rolled one more time to the top of his shoes, where she grabbed hold of his knees, yanking hard until he fell to the ground.

H.P. held tightly as he squirmed, kicking her in the belly. She wondered how long she'd be able to hold on before he hit her again.

"I'll take it from here, bestie!"

Gwen plopped down on the mayor and began trussing him like a turkey. She worked quickly and, despite his attempt to buck her off, Thunder McCloud was no match for the ever-amazing Gwendolyn Folds.

"How did you know I was here? And where did you get that rope?"

Gwen jerked one more time on the impressive combination of knots she'd created, causing the mayor to groan in protest.

"I was judging the three-on-three tournament, and as luck would have it, the Ropin' Rhondas were playing the Bouncing Barbs. As soon as I heard about trouble in the diner, I asked to borrow their prop lassos, and here I am." Gwen's expression became serious. "You've got a nasty knot on your noggin. Go to the medical booth and get that looked at. It's right next to Knotty by Nature, the nautical rope crafting booth. I was in the middle of buying a knot-framed mirror when Dex and Tildie found me."

Gwen stared at her as she held rope in her hand, assuring the mayor wasn't going anywhere. "You need to go now, friendie!"

H.P. didn't want Gwen knowing she couldn't

stand. She took hold of the counter and forced her body upright, feeling okay with the grunt that slipped out. She'd earned it.

She held tightly to the counter and, for once, was pleased that Edna had left a towel out. With no memory of the first aid class she skipped in high school in order to dry her hair, H.P. did her best to wrap the towel around her head. Eventually, the bleeding stopped, giving her the opportunity to glance around her diner.

What she saw shocked her.

Thud continued his wrestling match with Logan, knocking salt and pepper shakers to the floor while they scuffed the recently refurbished black-and-white tiles.

As the mayor fought to rid himself of the pint-sized coroner, she reached over to a shelf for whatever was convenient—a metal napkin holder, a glass coffee pot, and a series of coffee cups—whacking him over the head with each one. No matter what she did, he seemed immune to her blows.

H.P. glanced around her, looking for something, anything, to use as a weapon. A smile crossed her face as she pulled on a cord beside her. She raised the waffle maker above her head and flung it with all her might at Logan.

Immediately, Logan sank to the ground.

Thud was still breathing hard as she held tightly to the counter, making her way to his side. "I know what you're going to—"

"Thanks, H.P.," he whispered.

"Don't move! FBI!"

From out of nowhere, men and women in dark blue jackets with the letters "FBI" written in gold letters across the back swarmed in with guns drawn.

"It's about time!" H.P. snapped. "Thud, didn't you say they were listening? What took them so long?"

He squinted one eye and held onto a suspiciously crooked arm. "They weren't listening, exactly. It was just me. I found out Mrs. Noseinair had double-crossed me and I needed to make sure her daughter was safe before I called in reinforcements. My brother is ex-FBI, so when he called, they came running."

"Hands in the air! Hands in the air!" the agents yelled.

"You'd better get that arm checked out, Thud. It looks like a fracture."

Gwen's small body sat astride the mayor like he was a bucking horse machine at the local bar. Even so, she lifted up her hands in surrender.

Slowly, the agents made their way through the chaos. The first arrest was Logan Berry-Scone. She steadied herself as the cuffs clicked around her delicate wrists, her eyes narrowing. "You think you've won? I have the whole Breakfast Mafia at my disposal," she spat as she was guided past H.P. "You're just one woman."

"Actually, I HAVE won, Logan. I spent my entire high school years in fear of you and Maddysin. Afraid of some stupid curse. Not anymore. You've shown me just how weak and pathetic you, as well as all bullies, are. I hope you're lonely in prison. I won't worry about you ever again." She watched with satisfaction as one of the girls who struck terror in her heart for four, impressionable years was led away.

"I'll expect a plastic surgeon to attend to my injuries," Logan demanded of the agent.

"Doubtful," said the officer holding her arm.

"Sweetwater?"

H.P. was only a little disappointed to see Maddysin Noseinair wearing an FBI jacket. "Mad? We discussed this. You were supposed to show up BEFORE the brawl."

Maddysin rolled her eyes. "I know you're joking, but you're still ticking me off. I suppose I owe you for helping me get away from my kidnappers."

H.P. paused. She could explain to Maddysin that by "kidnappers" she meant one unlucky teen but instead decided to take the high road. "All in a day's work. I'm sorry about your mom. You didn't deserve her betrayal."

"She was everything BUT a mother. I've been tortured since childhood, always told I never measured up. Do you know, right after my tenth birthday, she called in her witch doctor to put a curse on me? Like, I was a mess for the rest of my childhood, always thinking I was cursed. It played head games with me, you know?"

"I do, Mad."

Maddysin took a moment to touch her hair and reapply lipstick. "That's why we're late. I didn't want to give her the opportunity to get away, and there was already chatter from the BMers that something was up. Timber gave me all the details while he spoon fed me lemon pudding." There was a shard of glass on the table that she picked up, hoping to see how her lipstick looked. "I hope that old hag spends the rest of her days wearing scratchy prison clothes."

The back of H.P.'s head throbbed as the adrenaline dissipated. Was it because of feeling the wrath of a Wacky Winkie Waffle Maker? Doubtful. She'd just had an almost pleasant encounter with her high school nemesis. It was enough to stir her brain into a massive headache. "Where are the kids? Are they safe?" She felt her knees buckle, and Thud grabbed her before she hit the ground. "Is it bad?" she whispered. "Am I going to die like the others?"

"Prolly not. I'm guessing five stitches. Less than that mouth of yours that miraculously healed in a few days. Frankie's the real hero. She grabbed the kids and got them to safety."

With a gentle pat, H.P. turned back to Thud. "Ready for the next round?"

Thud's gaze was steely as he cracked his knuckles. "Always am. Just hope it's less... waffle-y."

Chapter Forty-Nine

In a chilling reminder that history often repeats itself, Misty Cove recently found itself ensnared in a web of murder that mirrored the darkest chapter of its past. A series of brutal killings, where victims were found slain by a vicious whack to the head, left our picturesque community afraid to brunch.

Thankfully, the arrest of local marketing maven and con artist, Logan Berry-Scone, her hapless daughter, CeCe Scone, and her accomplices Mayor McCloud and Seemah Noseinair have put an end to this dark time. But the story doesn't end there. Or, rather, it didn't begin with the mayor and his cohorts. A haunting connection to the wrongful execution of Eliza Tumblewood in 1820 has come to light.

Connecting Past and Present

Eliza Tumblewood was a visionary apothecary, far

ahead of her time. Together, with her brother-in-law and secret lover, Benjamin Tumblewood, she crafted tinctures that claimed to cure ailments ranging from the common cold to bubonic plague. Deeply in love with Benjamin, Eliza failed to see that, as a woman and only a Tumblewood by marriage, she was expendable.

Benjamin's motives for both the affair and their shared business vision were suspect, to say the least. He plotted to stage his brother Charles' (Eliza's husband) death as a murder, framing Eliza by using one of her homemade tinctures as the means to kill him. Benjamin hoped that by killing Charles and ridding himself of ties to Eliza that he alone would be heir to the family fortune.

Eliza endured a rigged trial with scant evidence and ultimately faced execution. Historical accounts suggest Benjamin coldly attended her hanging, proclaiming, "Justice for my brother has been dealt!"

Benjamin's inheritance of Charles' apothecary did not bring him the wealth and respect he craved. In fact, it was quite the opposite. Without Eliza's meticulous testing for quality, his fortune dwindled.

Desperate for money, Benjamin searched for a new scheme to line his pockets. He married a wealthy widow and, together, they founded the Breakfast Mafia, a sinister group of investors who controlled the antique appliance market. Dinkus Doodlebug was his successor and, upon his death, our own Mayor Thunder McCloud.

The Path Forward

With the arrest of Mayor McCloud, Logan Berry-Scone, and her daughter, CeCe, Misty Cove stands at a crossroads. The community is called upon not only to seek justice for the victims of the present but also to honor the memory of those wronged in the past by ensuring that truth and fairness are the cornerstones of their justice system.

As Misty Cove confronts this new wave of violence, it must also reckon with the ghosts of its past. The story of Eliza Tumblewood, once a cautionary tale about the miscarriage of justice, has taken on new relevance. Our beloved hamlet will celebrate Eliza in the manner she deserves, and a lesson will be truly learned from history.

Today, we celebrate the first of what is to become an annual event. Be Eliza Day is our slow but deserved tribute to a true pioneer, a woman whose gentle nature and quest for knowledge made her the best Misty Covian.

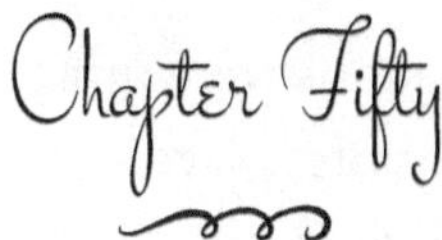

Chapter Fifty

"Hun bun, there's more I need to know."

Gram Gram folded her arms, causing her pale pink sleeves to flutter. She looked resplendent, as always. "First on the list is how in the world you figured out Frankie was working for the good guys."

"She quoted a movie to me while explaining why she was on the run. Luckily, I stayed awake long enough to remember that part. Which reminds me, Gram Gram." H.P. paused, measuring her words carefully. "I know you fibbed too. Remember when you told me you made up the things you said during the séance? Well, I remembered hearing those exact words when you had your theatrical debut."

Gram Gram's aura changed to a deep red. "Sometimes we have to look back to move forward, Hun Bun. I sounded pretty convincing, though, didn't I?"

As the sun dipped below the horizon, painting the sky in shades of peach and lavender, the agents who descended upon the diner disappeared as quickly as they came. She heard them discussing the arrest of Seemah Noseinair and wished she could have been there.

The festival grounds were quiet. H.P. heard the Fighting Tissues got first place and that Delores Toot-whistle donned a Fighting Tissues t-shirt and cap while she spoke with the FBI from her hospital bed. In order to calm her mind, H.P. baked one of her grandmother's signature honey pies and left it cooling in the kitchen.

When she'd relayed all the information, H.P. stifled a yawn. "I'll talk to you tomorrow, right, Gram Gram?"

"Count on it, my darling."

As she stepped out of the cooler, the door to the diner kitchen swung open and her son emerged, his face flushed with the exuberance of youth and the thrill of the day's events. "Mom, you were awesome!" he exclaimed, wrapping her in a hug that smelled distinctly of sweat and maple syrup.

"Thanks, kiddo," H.P. said, ruffling his hair. "Just keeping the town safe for future Ballz and Bandz tournaments. I almost forgot to ask about the basketball tournament. How did you do?"

"My team got disqualified in the first round. Chester tripped the girl on the other team and she got up and decked him. They fought until the referee kicked them out."

"I'm sorry to hear that."

"They're going to the school dance together."

H.P. nodded, sipping her coffee. "Yeah, it's been one heck of a day, hasn't it? I was so proud of you, the way you stayed calm when CeCe held a gun to your head."

"I've got a mom who finds her way out of sticky situations all the time," he said with a grin. "I guess I learned from her."

Chapter Fifty-One

CELEBRATION

Eliza Tumblewood Day was fittingly sunny and warm. Crafters set up booths on the large lawn in front of Honeypie Diner, and the Fighting Tissues played every song they learned this school year over and over again.

With the Breakfast Mafia gone and the waffle maker murders solved, the mood was light and joyous. Picturesque Misty Cove could get back to the business of welcoming tourists and gossiping about things that didn't really matter.

H.P. spent three weeks scheduling events, including a huge science fair, crafters selling their crafts, and a pie eating contest.

She and Frankie were up all night making food for the patrons the night before, but she didn't regret one minute. They laughed and told jokes, making memories as best friends should.

Dex and Tildie created a local history booth. In addition to the history of Misty Cove's founders, they included brochures on the history of the Tumblewood family and how they came to be the most prosperous and deadly family on the Washington coast. Abe Bunce printed the brochures and ordered a banner, made to Tildie's specifications, that read "History Hut."

As the Fighting Tissues began to play the school's theme song, everyone stopped what they were doing to sing along.

In Misty Cove, where fog hugs tight and local stars shine bright, there's a school that stands, both proud and true, Boog R. Noseinair, we sing to you. From the classrooms to the courts, the Tissues triumph without a snort. Our rivals mock, but they'll soon see, the strength of two-ply unity! Sneeze-em out, sneeze-em out. Goooo team!

"Woohoo! Great job, band!" H.P. whistled enthusiastically.

Delores Tootwhistle wove through the mass of students and adults until she reached H.P. "Ms. Sweetwater?"

H.P. tensed. "It's great to see you, Delores! You bounced right back from your injuries!"

"That's because I'm as fit as a fiddle. Which leads me to my point..."

"I added oatmeal and berries to the menu, just for you. I can't change everything because you're the only one who—"

"This community owes you a debt of gratitude, Ms. Sweetwater. You risked your life to rid us of the BM."

She was shocked to hear a compliment coming from disagreeable Delores Tootwhistle. "Thank you for saying that. It's my town too, and I'm glad they're gone."

"I've had the strangest dream six days in a row. Your grandmother whispers in my ear, just as clear as day."

H.P. raised a brow. "Oh?" Gram Gram still had a naughty streak.

"Yes." Delores cleared her throat uncomfortably. "That's why I'd like to offer you free clarinet lessons."

"What?"

"Your grandmother...she says you always wanted to participate in band but she was a stubborn goat and..." Delores paused. "Never mind. This all sounds crazy. I want to offer you lessons and a free clarinet. Not because I'm particularly charitable but because your grandmother said she wouldn't shut up until I did."

"Boss lady? Can we talk?"

H.P. turned away from Delores, relieved to have a moment to think about her kind yet forced offer.

"Sure, Frankie! Are we out of pie slices? I think we've got one more tray of honey pie in the walk-in." She turned back to Delores Tootwhistle. "I'll take you up on your offer, under one condition."

"What?"

"That you try my oatmeal. I think you'll find it's healthy and delicious."

Without waiting for an answer, she took Frankie's arm and began walking away.

"We've got plenty of pie," Frankie continued as they strolled through the crowd. "I've been trying to work out how to tell you this ever since you took down the BM."

"I didn't take them... Wait a minute! Are you leaving me, Frankie?"

H.P. hadn't intended for her voice to sound so needy, but it was too late.

"Now that my debt's been paid to the FBI, Sir Stackworth and I are itching to see the countryside. You know what they say about truckers. You can't boot the tires for long." The day that began as a joyous occasion had suddenly turned sour. "But don't worry, ma'am. I'll stay on until you find my replacement."

"That's where you're wrong, Frankie. There's no replacing you. When you first came to me, I was skeptical about someone who refused to make lunch. I didn't realize how much I missed creating food. Thank you for that gift."

Gwen appeared sporting a headset and a clipboard. "H.P., it's time for your speech."

Gwen insisted on taking charge of the entertainment on the main stage. She was meticulous in her planning, holding all acts to a specified amount of time. Her gravely voice bellowed from behind the stage when the button jugglers went two minutes long. "Buttons out! Buttons out!"

"Okay, thanks, Gwen. You're doing a bang-up job, by the way."

"Boss lady?" Frankie continued. "One more thing —how did you know I was lying to you? I feel terrible about it, just so you know."

"Oh, you quoted a Tulip Sloan movie word for word when you described the hold-up in Idaho. I guess it was lucky for me that I happened to be awake when that part came on."

"H.P.!" Gwen snapped. "You've got exactly twenty seconds to get yourself onto the stage or you'll throw my entire schedule into an off-balance washing machine! Move it! Move it!"

She waved at Frankie before making her way to the stage. Ever since she'd been "cursed," H.P. felt shame. She couldn't make good decisions, she couldn't offer her opinions, she couldn't speak in crowds. Now she wondered if the curse Seemah placed on her wasn't magic at all; it was a small seed of doubt she'd planted into the mind of an impression-able girl.

"As your new mayor, I'd like to thank Ms. Sweet-water for setting up what I hope will be an annual event. I can promise you, from now on, things in Misty Cove will be so normal we'll all be bored to tears." A man wearing an expensive suit and sporting slicked-back brown hair chuckled to himself.

"Here's your mic," Gwen whispered. "I'll be

standing in the back, giving you time cues." She gave H.P. a hard shove.

"And here she is now!" He made a sweeping gesture with his arm as though she were someone of great importance.

She gazed out across the sea of people, some strangers, some that had become friends. Abe Bunce was standing in the second row with his hands on his daughter's shoulders. He gave her a nod of support.

"Thank you, Lon Order. I speak for all of us when I say thank you for getting rid of that ordinance allowing the mayor to run investigations."

He touched his head and pointed his hand towards her.

"Let's pause for a moment to honor those who lost their lives to the Wacky Winkie Waffle Maker Murderer." She closed her eyes and breathed in the fresh sea air, grateful that Gram Gram gave her this gift. She wouldn't have revisited her hometown and exorcised her demons if she hadn't inherited the diner. "Mayor McCloud, his girlfriend, Logan Berry-Scone, and Mrs. Noseinair were just temporary black marks on Misty Cove's storied history."

"Don't forget about the Scone kid!" an anonymous man yelled.

She'd visited CeCe in jail and was saddened to see that, after CeCe followed her mother's orders, no one in the Berry-Scone families had been to visit her. The girl was remorseful and asked if H.P. would help her turn her life around. "I promise, when you've served your sentence, I'll do whatever I can to help you start over."

"Yes, we want to make sure everyone pays for their crimes," she responded to the man in the crowd. "We had very brave citizens who deserve recognition. Delores Tootwhistle, where are you?" H.P. shaded her eyes with one hand.

Delores waved from the area where the Fighting Tissues were seated. "Delores worked with the FBI, giving them information on her exercise friends. Your bravery hasn't gone unnoticed."

Delores sat back down as the crowd applauded, without an acknowledgment.

"My chef, Frankie, had been working with the FBI for months, too. She's taking care of the pie table, so thank her when you get your delicious dessert. Mad...issyn survived a kidnapping through sheer will and wit. She and Mr. Punchard helped apprehend Seemah Noseinair when she attempted to escape." H.P. couldn't believe she was giving kudos to her arch enemy. Maybe it was time to end that feud too. Maybe.

"And finally, my brave son, Dexter Jenkins. He and his friend, Tildie Bunce, have a quest for knowledge that brought us to this point. Dex, I'm proud to be your mom. You make me a better me."

Dex was standing with a group of kids and only glanced at the stage momentarily to nod slightly. It was enough.

She paused to wipe the tears from her eyes. "And now, I'd like you all to visit every booth, especially the

Something Thoughtful booth. Pick a folded paper from the large bowl and perform that act of kindness. Have the paper signed and bring it back to the booth to be entered in one of twenty drawings. All right, everybody, have a great day!"

She stepped off the stage with legs that quivered like Edna's green gelatin. "How did that sound?"

"Amazing, bestie!" Gwen rubbed her back supportively. "What's that?"

"I didn't—"

Gwen placed her finger on H.P.'s lips and used the other hand to push her headphones against one ear. "No, I will NOT make an exception." She rolled her eyes toward H.P. "If the Punked Out Grandpaps wanted to go on before 4:00 p.m., they should have said something when the schedules came out. The nursing home will have to hold their dinners!" She mouthed, "Sorry!" to H.P. as she wandered off, lecturing some poor volunteer as she walked.

It gave H.P. the time she needed to visit Gram Gram. As she wove her way through the throngs of appreciative Covians, her heart warmed.

Finally, she reached her empty diner.

"Gram Gram? Are you here? I don't have long."

The smell of baking pies accompanied a shimmering, golden glitter as Gram appeared. "I was hoping you would have time for me today. How did your speech go?"

"It was...amazing. I felt so much love from everyone, Gram Gram. For the first time in my life, Honeypie Chiffon Sweetwater was...wanted."

It was no exaggeration; this day would stay with her for the rest of her life.

"You've always been wanted, dear heart. But I'm glad you felt it in your bones today!" She swirled around H.P., bringing a warm feeling like a hug to her granddaughter. "Now, I've been wondering something. When I did the séance, you said you knew I was blowing smoke up your tailpipe. How?"

That seemed so long ago. "Oh, I remember now. When you performed at the dinner theater, I was entranced by your words. They were the same words I heard at the séance."

"Oops. Didn't realize it meant so much to you, Hun Bun."

"Gram Gram, I thought all these years that I was cursed. It turns out I took those words and ran with them. There was never a real curse, just a seed of doubt. Seemah used the same method to control her daughter."

"It's amazing how much of our lives we waste hurting ourselves, isn't it?"

There was a knock at the door of the walk-in. "Ms. Sweetwater?"

"It's Thud," H.P. whispered.

"Go! We'll catch up Monday, after the morning rush. You're really impressive, darling. My diner is in good hands."

H.P. nodded happily before exiting the walk-in. "Thud? What do you need?"

Thud ambled up to her with one arm cast and in a sling. He was dressed in a short-sleeved polo shirt and dress pants that groaned under the stress of covering his muscular legs. "I...it sounded like you were talking to someone in there. If that's where you go to work out your problems, I can come back!"

"No, it's fine. You're right, though; it's the perfect place to work out my problems."

"I wanted to thank you for helping me. If it hadn't been for you, I'd still be doing Mrs. Noseinair's dirty work."

"You're welcome. I gave you and Maddysin credit in my speech, but I didn't see her. Surely she wouldn't miss the biggest event of the year!"

"She's on an extended trip to Belize. Said she wouldn't return until she'd sucked the life out of every massage therapist, tarot card reader, and chef on the island."

H.P. smiled. "I don't doubt it."

"So what's next for the best sleuth in Misty Cove?"

Her laughter filled the emptiness of the diner—her diner—with a burst of happiness. "Well, Thud, I'm going to be short one breakfast-loving chef, so I'll be on griddle duty until I find someone new."

He appeared crestfallen by this news. "But you're so good! We'd make a great team!"

Flattered, she replied, "I agree. And who knows?

Misty Cove's next mystery could be right around the corner."

Wacky Winkie's Waffles

<u>**Ingredients**</u>

2¼ cups all-purpose flour (270g)

¼ cup granulated sugar (50g)

Coconut sugar or a 1:1 ratio artificial sweetener can also be used. If you choose to sweeten with maple syrup or other liquid, make sure you reduce the amount of flour in your batter.

1 tablespoon baking powder

¾ teaspoon salt

½ teaspoon cinnamon

2 cups milk of your choice (480ml)

½ cup unsalted butter, melted (113g)

2 large room temperature eggs

3 teaspoons vanilla extract

*optional add-ins: ½ cup mini chocolate chips, dried fruit, nuts, or other ingredient of your choice. If berries or another ingredient with liquid is added, make sure to adjust the amount of flour

<u>Instructions</u>

1. Preheat your Wacky Winkie Waffle Maker (or a boring one of your choosing). If your preference is for darker, crispier waffles, set the heat higher. If you'd like them lighter with a soft consistency, set it lower. You'll need to play around with the settings until you get them just right for you. Unlike the Waffle Whacker, you want your waffles to taste just right when you're done!

2. Melt butter in microwave safe dish.

Protip: Keep your eyes peeled for any waffle whackers sneaking up behind you!

3. Whisk the dry ingredients together. For chefs who aren't of Frankie's caliber, that includes: flour, sugar, baking powder, and salt.

4. In another bowl, combine milk, eggs, and vanilla extract.

5. Pour in the melted butter and whisk the wet ingredients together.

6. Add the wet ingredients to the dry ingredients and stir until just combined.

Protip: Do not overmix unless you're ready to receive the wrath of Gram Gram's ghost!

7. Grease the waffle iron with butter, oil, or cooking spray. By now it should be as hot as the gossip mill after Edna's mother wears her bikini to the beach!

8. Add about 1/3 cup of batter to the waffle maker. That's a guestimate, as each waffle maker is a different size. You'll want to cover the surface, but not so much

that your delicious waffle mixture oozes out the sides.
It may take a little trial and error.

9. Cook 5-8 minutes, depending on your waffle
maker's size and how crispy you like them.

10. After removing waffles from the waffle maker,
place them on a wire rack in an oven preheated to the
"keep warm" setting. Though Gram Gram found the
waffles to shrink slightly in size using this method, it
kept them warm until the entire batch was finished.

Protip: Buy another Wacky Winkie Waffle Maker and
use both at the same time. It speeds up the cooking
process, and if you've got people to whack—I mean,
things to do—you'll appreciate this time saver.

11. Serve with toppings of your choice, which may
include: more chocolate chips, chocolate syrup,
whipped cream (adding a ½ tsp of cinnamon to your
whipped cream brings out the waffle-y goodness!),
fruit, butter, syrup, or whatever wacky idea comes to
mind.

12. Enjoy!

About the Author

Joann Keder is a USA TODAY bestselling author who has won numerous awards. She spent her formative years (over 40) living on the plains of Nebraska. When she and her husband chose to make a move to the Pacific Northwest, she came to an agreement with her soul that it was time to start writing.

Today, she creates stories about strong women, their quirky sidekicks, and the paths they choose. When she's not writing, she and her husband enjoy nature, a good chocolate, and spending time with family. Not necessarily in that order.

Also by Joann Keder

<u>Honeypie Myteries</u>

<u>Slashed Potatoes and Grave-y</u>

<u>Piney Falls Mysteries</u>

Welcome to Piney Falls

Saving Piper Moonlight

Tales of Naybor Manor

Lavender's Tangled Tree

The Twisted Stitch Society

Kinundrum

<u>Charming Mysteries</u>

Oceanberry Blues

Tangerine Troubles

Perilously Pink

A Lime in Time

Violet Vendetta

<u>Emory Bing Bite-Sized Mysteries</u>

<u>Pepperville Stories</u>

The Story of Keilah

Secrets and Sunflowers

Franniebell and Purple Wonder

Be the first to hear about new releases! Sign up for my newsletter here:

http://www.joannkeder.com